THESE WALLS WERE NEVER REALLY THERE

First Edition published 2022 by

2QT Limited (Publishing)
Settle, North Yorkshire BD24 9RH United Kingdom
Copyright © Bryan Blears 2022
The right of Bryan Blears to be identified as the author
of this work has been asserted by him/her in accordance with the
Copyright, Designs and Patents Act 1988

Cover Design by Charlotte Mouncey with imagery from Fabio Hanashiro and
Luke Porter, on Unsplash.com, Ahmet Hezretov on Pexels.com and Chris on
https://www.flickr.com/photos/cr01 under CC BY-SA 2.0

Printed in Great Britain by Ingram Sparks

A CIP catalogue record for this book is available
from the British Library
ISBN 978-1-914083-38-9

THESE WALLS WERE NEVER REALLY THERE

BRYAN BLEARS

ACKNOWLEDGEMENTS

Thank you to Clare, who first took an interest in my manuscript, to Nicholas, Stevie, Hannah, William and Lisa, for their help and input into the writing of my story, and to Neal, Claire, Natasha, Rob, Micky, Sam B. and Sam M. and many others for their encouragement and support. I would also like to thank Catherine and Charlotte, for their excellent editing and design work in turning my manuscript into a proper novel. Finally, I would like to acknowledge Gabriel, without whom there would have been no journey to write about.

PART ONE

1.

I used to hate this place. Not because of the buildings, or the endless roar of traffic, the air full of noxious fumes, or the streets overflowing with everybody's rubbish. It wasn't even because of the rain. It was the way the people walked with their heads down, as though the weather had eroded them over time until they became demented caricatures, like the figures in a Lowry painting.

It was the *dejectedness* of it all, really. I didn't know how anybody could bear it for all of their lives without going crazy and running away.

I was twenty, and everything had come to a head, so I ran. I ran from the wave that had been bearing over me my whole life, threatening to crash down and wash everything away.

It was a quiet Tuesday evening in early June, and as usual my dad (with whom I lived a grim existence at the time) was out at the pub. I didn't know what I was going to do next, to tell you the truth, but what I did know was that the past few weeks had made me sure I was leaving home for good. As I packed some spare clothes, a toothbrush and what little else I had into a small rucksack, preparing to leave my old life behind, I wondered what had changed within me.

Before, I had been hesitant and confused, afraid of every hopeless option laid out before me. But at that moment, for the first time in my life, I felt rock solid.

If you had told me then how it would end, three thousand miles away and almost two years later, would I still have walked out of the door and set off on my journey?

Even now, I don't know the answer to that question.

All I knew was that I had to get away from here. The red-brick estate on which I lived was a never-ending labyrinth, a maze designed purely to keep people from seeing the truth: that nothing any of us did would ever matter. No one here would ever amount to anything. We were a mere footnote in the history of our so-called great nation, stick-figure people without hopes or dreams or futures.

So, with nothing left to cling to, I decided to let go.

I closed the front door behind me, turned out of the garden and hit the road with a confident stride. The sun was beginning to set behind the backs of the houses, and the sky was an orange blaze, with the clouds in the distance sparkling like small islands in an infinite sea.

It was as though a huge storm had passed over me and was gone, the last remnants of thunder rumbling on the distant horizon.

Inside, the people were drawing their curtains, watching TV, having a shower, ironing their clothes for tomorrow, eating their dinners, putting the kids to bed. Off in the distance were the sounds of city life: a dog barking, a shutter slamming, a bus driving past, the sound of glass breaking on the hard pavement.

The first thing you think is that it will never happen to you. The second is: *where am I going to sleep tonight?*

I had walked a good few miles from home by now, but that question, incessantly nagging in my thoughts, was still without a decent answer. I spied a couple of teenagers in tracksuits up the road and quickly changed direction. I didn't have the night to myself, even if I wanted to.

I was still close enough to turn back and save myself, swallow my pride and forget any notions I had about leaving my old life behind, I reminded myself. But deep down, I knew that going home was no longer an option. My fate was fixed, as surely as that of a school shooter who has already fired the first round. I zipped up my fleece tightly against the cold air and put my hands in my pockets to keep warm. The street lights were starting to flicker on in the dusk, and there were very few clouds; it was going to be a cold night.

In the distance I could make out the sound of the motorway, and I was sure, at that moment, that there was no God.

I turned down a quieter street, looking for a dark, hidden place to swallow me up, eyeing up abandoned buildings and alleyways. At the end of the road, I spied a narrow alley behind the back of a church. I looked around, making sure nobody caught me prospecting this lonely piece of real estate, and then I slipped down it and sat with my back against the stone wall of the church. Glad to have found a quiet place of my own, I breathed a great sigh of relief, although the cold concrete was already sapping the warmth out of my legs.

Someone else had been here before, I noticed; probably a group of kids bunking off school, judging by the cigarette ends. Hungry, I opened my backpack and rummaged around inside for a packet of crisps and a drink I had nestled in among the spare clothes. I laid them out on the floor and took out a woolly hat which I pulled down over my ears. Opposite, a ginger cat skulked through the grass. It spotted me, leapt up onto the wall above and disappeared over the other side.

I ate quietly and solemnly, the way ancient Christians must have eaten on their pilgrimages.

I used to walk this way to school in the mornings a long time ago. On summer afternoons, we'd go to play football on Spider Park just around the corner. Everything had been ordinary back then; I'd imagined that one day in the future I would end up buying a house, travelling abroad, getting married and having children. At school, they had asked me what I wanted to be when I grew up. I didn't suppose I would be anything now.

Where had everything gone so badly wrong? In some ways, you might say I was the stereotypical case of a council estate kid from a broken home. On the other hand, you might find my story quite extraordinary. My mother was a schizophrenic who tried to burn the house down when I was fourteen, my dad was a struggling alcoholic; it was fair to say I wasn't given the best of starts in life.

But blaming my upbringing would only be half the picture. I was an angry teenager who struggled talking to girls and wasn't very good at making friends. I listened to the wrong kinds of music and I allowed the wrong types of ideas – ideas that only a depressed, angry teenager can form about life and society– to build up in my head.

Arrogance and a deep-seated hatred towards the state education system did the rest. Once the dreams of college and university had faded away, the realisation hit me that the only life waiting for me was something worse than famine, worse than war. It was long, constant monotony, while the seasons changed and time constantly reminded me of its passing as old age drew ever nearer. It was working long hours at a job that meant nothing to me, and scrounging my way through the week so I could drink a few pints at the weekend and watch my life disappear.

You might think me naïve, or even entitled – and partly, I must admit, that was true. I had no clue what any of those things entailed. But back then I would have swapped places with almost anybody in the world to escape the hopelessness of that future. And so, during my darkest moments, I contemplated committing some heinous crime in order to spend the rest of my days in prison. I stood on motorway bridges, watching the traffic drive by underneath, reflecting on the distance to the ground below and the hardness of the asphalt.

I couldn't do it, I had decided; not even for a day. When I look back now I think I must have been a madman to choose life on the streets, but in my heart it felt like the only option left. Still, that first night was one of the longest I've ever experienced. Already, I felt the slow drag of time, and I had only been stationary for about twenty minutes.

Listening carefully, my ears pricked up at a couple of male voices passing the alleyway, where I was securely hidden from view. I sat still and waited for them to disappear. Then I switched my phone on to check for messages. There weren't any. The voices had faded away, and I rocked backwards and forwards as the temperature dropped. The night seemed to stretch out in front of me like a vacuum, cold and empty.

There was nothing to do except try to sleep, I decided. As I lay there, the cold worked its way through my jacket and down into my lungs with every breath until tiredness came with it, pulling impatiently at my eyelids. I felt myself slipping away into blissful unconsciousness. Then, just as I started to drift off fully, a car door slammed nearby.

It woke me with a start. I half expected to see the police pulling up to move me on, tipped off by some paranoid neighbour, but after a few minutes everything was quiet again, and I was left alone. Time and time again this would happen as I dozed in and out of consciousness: a startling noise, followed by relief, followed by silence. It was probably people coming home from working late shifts, I supposed, but with the adrenaline in my system from the fear of being discovered, it was simply impossible to sleep. I wondered how many nights like this a person could tolerate without passing out or dying from tiredness.

I kept track of the time and of the vague moments which broke up the long, unchanging night. At one o'clock, another group of people walked past. I could smell their takeaway, hot and vinegary, as they passed by on their way home. In half an hour they'd be tucked up in bed at home, warm and cosy with a tray of half-eaten food on the coffee table. At two o'clock I got up to stretch my legs. I walked around the church in an attempt to warm up and unstiffen my muscles, which had locked up from the cold and the way I was sitting on the concrete.

By three, the air was still, and the only thing keeping me company was the silent orange glow of the street lights. The horizon was dark, showing no signs of changing soon, and the cold, thorough and unforgiving, was less of an anaesthetic than I'd anticipated. I slept a while, woke up and moved around for warmth, sat and fell asleep again. When I checked my watch again, it was almost four. I noticed the drops of dew glistening on the grass as I fantasised about a hot cup of coffee and a comfortable place to sit indoors. At last there was a faint, promising glow of light on the edge of the horizon.

I held out for what felt like an eternity, waiting for the sun to rise above the rooftops.

Before the morning broke, the first lights went on in the houses. The people inside were getting ready for work; I watched them stumble out to the cars with their flasks and packed lunches and start up their engines. Steam billowed up in the early morning air. The last part of me clung desperately to the idea of walking home and climbing into bed. My neck was sore from sitting uncomfortably, and the cold had penetrated deep into my muscles – it took some effort to straighten my legs, and last night's cold sweat was still clinging uncomfortably to my skin.

The sky grew lighter as morning drew close, and the first proper activity of the day was the bin lorry. It drove up the street and stopped as men in high-vis jackets hopped on and off and dragged the bins around with a rumbling, thudding sound. After ten minutes that noise, too, was gone. In the distance I could hear the steady flow of traffic building up as the city came to life.

A flurry of thoughts flew through my head: where to go, what to eat, what to do? But weren't those the same questions I had before, anyway? Was I going to waste my days away working in some corner shop for minimum wage or even less, my nights spent hanging around with so-called mates until the early hours of the morning, while the rest of the people – the ones who came from the rich, leafy parts of the country, the people who mattered – went on holidays and published books and ran for parliament?

I pictured myself growing old in the same place I'd grown up, the only difference being fading eyesight and missing teeth, wondering what it was that I'd achieved during my life on this earth, and I knew I could no longer stay still. These streets were all dead ends, a ratway of brick walls and alleyways and broken dreams. I stood up, ready to commence my journey.

The first few rays of sun broke over the rooftops and flooded the pale sky as I waited by the side of the church until, finally, the sunlight fell over me. The light was warm and forgiving, breathing life into the cold, wet grass and the stonework and into every cell of my body. It shone over the rooftops and onto the red brick walls of the houses and the metallic surfaces of the cars, and the warmth dissipated through my body until it reached my heart, and the dull, empty feeling of last night was washed away.

The first children were being dragged out of the houses in their school uniforms, arms huddled together because of the cold. As I walked by I saw them bundled into the backs of cars by their parents and hurried off to school. What I felt was no longer fear or sadness or uncertainty; it was hope at the day ahead, a world that was mine to see, and a warmth that came from knowing the night was far away again.

I started to walk in the direction of the city.

It was before I met Jacob. I don't know what he was doing back then, but I imagine his life at that point was in some ways similar to mine, given the way our paths were to cross in the future.

2.

Tony's story was this: every Wednesday night he ended up in the bookies. It started as a way of winding down after a long day at work, then very soon it became twice a week, three times a week, until going to the bookies became a necessity of life. He used to make (and lose) most of his money on the football; twenty quid on a team like Leicester to beat Manchester United, 10/1, and when he was really down on his luck he would put his last pound on a team like Newcastle or Stoke, in the hope of recouping what he'd spent from last week's wages.

The first time he got into trouble with his gambling, he'd borrowed from a mate to get by. The second time, he borrowed from a stranger who later came around to Tony's house and took the TV and everything else he owned because Tony hadn't paid him back on time. He punched Tony to the floor and knocked out two of his teeth, but Tony never went to the police. After that, Tony signed up to a counselling service to deal with his gambling addiction. But the waiting list to be seen was over six months long. Tony defaulted on just two rent payments before his landlord changed the locks, and by the time he was able to get some money together to set things straight, the place had already been leased out to new tenants.

That's how he had ended up like me, sleeping on the streets.

Tony and I shared a spot down by the canal. He was about forty years old, give or take, and from what he told me, at least twenty of them had been utterly miserable. He held his previous life at a distance from himself, glancing at it only occasionally as if through a rear-view mirror, and although he only talked about it once in a while, you could see there were all kinds of traumas lurking in the shadows.

No matter who you spoke to, everybody's story was more or less the same. There were always the addictions, because usually you'd have to be really, *clinically* addicted to something to ignore the warning signs telling you that if you carried on along your current path, things would take a turn for the worse. Then there were the failures of the system to help, as spiralling debts and mental health problems took their toll, the long waiting lists for help and support, the stress and strain of dealing with public services, the helplessness which followed. And in the end there was always some bastard who owned property or ran a credit card company who dealt the final, fatal blow.

'What was I going to do, go to a solicitor? I can't afford cigs, let alone an effing lawyer,' Tony told me. 'That prick threw my things out into the middle of the street and all. What's someone like me supposed to do about it, eh? Let me tell you, Cam, the whole thing's set up for those with money: if you haven't got it, you've not got a chance, and there's not a thing you can do about it.'

I was scribbling in a notebook with the worn-down end of an old pencil. 'Did you try to get back in touch with your wife after that?' I asked.

'Once or twice, aye.' Tony rubbed his hands together and breathed into them. 'Not that it made much bloody difference. What's your story, anyway? Did your parents throw you out, or what?'

'No,' I said. 'They didn't throw me out. My parents . . . split up a couple of years ago. I just left, in the end.'

'Why?' Tony said.

'I don't know. It's hard to explain, really. I just saw a dead end in front of me.'

'What do you mean?'

'I'm not sure, Tony,' I said, looking down at my dirt-covered shoes. I knew it must have been crazy, offensive even, to someone like Tony that a young boy would leave his home for some vague . . . what? Sense of meaning? No. The truth was that I was clinically depressed. Come to think of it, in the six months since I'd left, I had almost forgotten how desperate things had seemed back where I grew up. 'I just couldn't stand another day of it. That's all.'

'I see. Look, don't worry. You'll get yourself sorted out soon enough,' he said. 'Give it time. You're young, after all. Look at me, five years on the street. Five years. Nobody's going to help people like me. They've all been taken up by this . . . this idea, of a brand new pair of trainers and an iPhone. You see 'em walk past every single day. They don't care, mate. Not about someone like me.'

I'd spent the first couple of desperate weeks in the city centre, cold, wet, half-starved, and terrified of everybody around me, until Tony had taken me under his wing. Appearances aside, he was one of the nicest people I had ever met. He let me share his shelter down beside the canal, and whenever the nights got too cold and it felt like nobody in the world knew I even existed, I was glad to have him for company.

Sometimes Tony was gone for two or three days at a time. He came over whenever he saw me down by the canal, and he would always have some little thing he'd saved for me – a bar of chocolate, or a sachet of coffee, or half of a leftover sandwich. Tony's kids were growing up without a dad because he liked to bet on football matches, but Tony had a heart of gold out here on the streets. I think he was trying to make up for it somehow, in the hope that God would look down on him one day and decide to pluck him out and put him back in a house with his family and make everything good again.

'Here, got something for you, lad,' Tony said. He took out a paper bag carefully from his pocket and unpacked a bacon roll, the smell of brown sauce wafting up around our alcove under the concrete bridge. He held it out to me. I tore half of it off and handed the rest back. I took a bite and savoured it for a moment, carefully putting my notepad away in the dry.

'Did you buy that?' I asked.

Tony bit down greedily. I could see his teeth had gone brown, and there were a few missing at the front. 'Why's he always ask where the food comes from? Just eat up, will you?' he said.

I tore off a piece of the sandwich and threw it into the shadows. There was a rustling movement, a flash of black fur, and then squeaking, as the rats fought over it in the darkness.

'Hey, what are you doing? You can't do that!' Tony picked up a stone to hurl at the squirming creatures, but I laid my hand on his arm to stop him.

'Leave them,' I said. 'They're just trying to get a bite to eat.'

He frowned at me in disgust. 'I don't know', he said, 'bring him some food and he throws it to the rats. Talk about gratitude. By the way, forgot to tell you. Sam's after me. Says I owe him a fiver.'

'What for?' I asked. As far as I knew, Tony had never borrowed from anyone, ever, since he'd wound up sleeping rough.

'Don't remember. If you go down to the market, think you could save a couple of quid for me?'

'Of course, Tony.'

'I'll pay you back.'

'Don't worry about it.'

Tony said nothing. It was something he knew I would do to help him, no questions asked. After all, it was Tony who had given me so much advice when I first came into town, Tony who told me who to avoid and what not to get caught up in, and you couldn't really put a price on that. I reckoned he would make an excellent dad, if he ever got his life back on track. No amount of missing teeth could ever make him an ugly person – to me, at least.

Somewhere in the dark, the rats swallowed down the bacon sandwich and ran off into the night. A rat was just the same as a dolphin, or a snow leopard, or any other animal; it was only humans who deemed them pests that didn't deserve to live. They were just like us, really: hungry, desperate and dirty. That same mentality could apply to a person, too – declare them unfit for society, and let them starve to death or freeze in the snow in the middle of a city that had plenty of warm shelter and food to spare, if only people thought they were genuinely in need of it.

You could clean a rat up, I thought. People had pet rats. It was the city that made them dirty – them and us, covered in dirt from the traffic, forced to live in other people's rubbish, and treated so badly we grew rough around the edges and started to bite at each other until we became the thing everyone had believed us to be all along.

It was almost six months since the night I'd left home and started off on what was supposed to be a great journey, but actually, I'd only moved five miles. The city centre seemed to suck everybody into it like a black hole, and at the bottom everything was all squashed together like compacted rubbish. On the plus side, there were plenty of places to sleep and plenty of food left behind at restaurants or thrown in the bins. All you had to put up with in exchange were the exhaust fumes from the cars, the occasional bother from the police, and the constant noise and movement of the people around you.

I left Tony by the canal and turned left, up the steps and across the bridge towards town. The traffic had ground to a standstill, with the people walking past it in an ever-increasing crowd which grew bigger as you got towards the centre of town. A taxi pulled out in front of the queue, and the car behind it started beeping aggressively. The taxi driver leant out of his window and swore. I walked over to Piccadilly Gardens, where I sat down in the light of the sun and watched the people for a while. I didn't talk to all the other homeless people. I knew who they were, saw them showing up in their usual spots across the city, but so many of them were drunk or on drugs that you couldn't approach somebody first. You had to wait for them to approach you, but when that happened, it usually meant trouble.

On the whole, I kept myself to myself. Wherever I stopped to sit, I would place a cup or a hat on the floor with a couple of coins in for the passers-by. Tony said I should beg more. He said I would do well because of my young looks, but I hated sitting there, looking up pitifully at the shoppers and trying to make them feel guilty enough to dig out their purse or wallet.

The first time I could, I got hold of a small notebook and started writing poems for people who passed by. I learned fairly quickly that it was much better to have something to offer people, rather than just relying on their moral conscience. At first I wrote poems about myself and what it was like to be homeless, but eventually I found it a lot more successful to write about the people who stopped instead. In the end, I had a couple of go-to templates; I could alter a few words of one or the other, and the person would think I had invented the whole thing on the spot.

By now the magnitude of what I had done to myself was starting to hit home. I was living hand to mouth in a city full of people – dangerous people, sometimes – and I had absolutely no plan to get myself on track towards anything. I needed money to find somewhere to live. I needed a job to get money. I needed so many things to get a job: clean clothes, an address, a haircut, and luck – so much luck that it seemed completely impossible to think about escaping my current situation.

I thought about what Tony had said to me next to the canal: *Five years, mate. Nobody's going to help a person like me.* Had I really thrown everything away?

While I sat and thought about it, an assortment of people passed me by, all busy in their own little worlds. They usually came into town in the morning, dipping in and out of the shops and squandering their money through the day, eating their lunches over in the food court or by the fountains in the centre of Piccadilly Gardens, and as the afternoons drew late they left via the trains and the buses and the trams and went home. The same thing happened every day, and no matter how long I spent in the city, I couldn't figure any of it out. I didn't know why I was so different, what I had done wrong, what I needed to do to become a part of what everyone else seemed to be a part of.

I didn't blame people for walking past with their heads down. They just assumed that someone else, the state maybe, would sort something out for us. Or they thought we were scroungers pumped full of drugs. To be fair, in many cases that wasn't far from the truth.

As I sat lost in my thoughts, another passer-by tossed a coin into the hat at my feet. Normally, I didn't give any more than a grateful nod, or a mumbled 'Thankyouverymuch', but this was different. An eerie feeling of familiarity brushed across me for a second. The person had walked a few yards but now stopped, hesitated, then turned her head to look back at me. She took a few steps back over towards where I was sitting, and stooped to see me more clearly.

'Thank you,' I said, hoping to break the tension. Embarrassed, she looked as though she was about to walk away again, but something was holding her back. Suddenly I realised who she was, and in that moment she must have recognised me, too, because she brushed her hair behind her ears and smiled. 'Oh my God,' she said. 'Cameron? It is you, isn't it?'

We both paused. *You should have just walked away,* I thought. *Better to have saved us both the embarrassment.* But it was too late now. 'How are you doing?'

'I'm . . . I'm good, I suppose,' she said, awkwardly holding her handbag with one arm and glancing off to the side every once in a while.

I didn't have any idea what to say. The girl in front of me was Jenny Tarrant. We'd dated once, back at the beginning of high school. But the woman in front of me barely resembled the girl I'd once known. She had let her hair grow longer, and she was dressed in a proper-looking shirt and jacket, with a black skirt and tights, a designer handbag in one hand and a cup of Costa coffee clutched in the other. I dreaded to think what I must have looked like.

'What happened?' she asked. There was no other way to say it, really.

'Good question,' I said. The sun was beating down, and all around us streams of people were walking past, chatting and giving us barely more than a moment's thought. I shrugged, trying to speed the conversation along. 'Life, I suppose.'

'I don't think I've seen you for two, three years? What about your parents?' she asked.

'It's a bit of a long story,' I said. 'Thank you for the, you know.' I gestured at the money in the hat. It took Jenny a minute to register that she had just given me some of her spare change, a social transaction that must have made her uncomfortable. She held her coffee in front of her face like a boxer's guard.

'Oh, God, not at all!' She checked the time. 'Listen, are you going to be here all day?'

I looked around. There *were* other things I could be doing. The urge to run away came over me again; I had no desire to let an old memory back into my already troubled life. 'Well, probably,' I said.

'I finish work at about half-five,' she said. 'Will you wait here for me then?'

'I can. But listen, Jen . . .'

'No, you don't have to say anything. Listen, you will be here? You promise you're not going to disappear off somewhere, right?'

'Sure, OK,' I said. But that was exactly what I had in mind. The fact she had plucked it straight out of my head was excruciating.

'Great. I'll see you later, then. I have to go.' She smiled and gave a tiny wave. 'Boss is waiting. It's good to see you, Cam.'

'See you,' I said.

With that, Jenny turned and walked away from me down the high street towards wherever she worked, off to finish her latte in a meeting somewhere. She carried herself differently now than when we were schoolchildren, and I was nervous watching her. She must have felt it, too, because her shoulders were still tensed up when I lost her in the crowd. I could imagine the conversations at work later. She'd probably tell her colleagues that she'd bumped into an old friend from school, and you'd never guess what he was doing, out on the street dressed like a tramp. Still, I couldn't really blame anyone. At the very least, I should have got a bus ticket to another city where nobody I knew would be able to find me begging on an ordinary Thursday afternoon.

'Who was that?' a man growled over my shoulder. It was Sam. Sam was somebody you never wanted to bump into, let alone catch you doing anything out of the ordinary. He must have been watching me the whole time from the other side of Piccadilly Gardens.

'No one. Just an old friend from school.'

'Yeah? Well, if you see her again, ask her if she's got any money. Tony owes me, you know. Send you down here to clear his debts, did he?'

'I didn't know he owed you anything,' I lied.

'Well, now you do, don't you?' Sam laughed. 'Don't think I don't know where you two bunk down. I know everything that happens around here.'

'Don't worry – I'm sure we can sort things out.'

'Better had do,' he said, patting me on the shoulder. 'Right, well, best be off. Things to do. You have a good day, yeah?' He left, not looking back, in the direction of the Northern Quarter.

I could have cursed Tony for bringing us trouble in the form of Sam. But trouble found you sooner or later; it was how you dealt with it that counted. I hoped that giving Sam a few quid by the end of the day would keep him off our backs for a while. But not the fiver he'd asked Tony for; if you complied too easily, he knew he could keep upping the demands, and before long you'd find yourself in further trouble with him.

Sam got arrested regularly – for shoplifting, assault, possession of drugs and knives and, of course, for violent assault. The police didn't know what to do with people like him, so they placed him back out on the streets to keep the rest of us on our toes. There was a philosophy out in the world which said – whether consciously or subconsciously, or because of some misguided sense of justice against scroungers and free-loaders – that life out here should be hard and short, that people who didn't pay their taxes shouldn't expect to have luxuries like personal safety. It was worse for the women who sold themselves underneath the bridges on the other side of town. The police would see them covered in bruises and wouldn't do a damned thing. But the point was that people like Sam were allowed to exist because they kept the rest of us down. And that, in many people's eyes, was a Good Thing.

As the rest of the afternoon went by, I counted the change in my hat, and took some out every once in a while so that I didn't appear too successful. The secret was to have a small bit of change – not nothing, because that made it look like there was something wrong with you – but just enough to trigger something in people's minds to make them want to make your little pile much bigger. It was peer pressure with a bunch of egotism thrown into the mix.

Everybody on the street became an expert in behavioural psychology, because playing the crowd was how you earned a living. I'd often see somebody sitting out in the rain on a rotten piece of cardboard when there was a perfectly good shelter just around the corner. Begging outside a coffee shop or a fancy restaurant was a mug's game. Those people had just had their egos rubbed; they weren't interested in the slight endorphin boost that came from giving money to a stranger. You had to target people when *they* were at their lowest, when they could do some small act of kindness, preferably in front of other people, and walk away with that warm, fuzzy feeling they call the 'helper's high'.

The chance encounter with Jenny kept sticking in my mind. I replayed the moment she'd leant down to put some change in my hat and then walked away before stopping to look at me over and over again. One of the traits people said I had was a tendency to dwell on the past. Some unfortunate thing would happen which an ordinary person would quickly plaster over in their memory, but I would become fixated with it for years. What could I have done differently, or what should I have said instead of whatever had blurted out of my mouth in a panic?

Even before I finished school, I knew my life was going to fall apart. In fact, I was quite confident I wouldn't live to see my twentieth birthday. I don't know where that feeling came from, but it didn't seem like a feeling at all to me; it was just the way things always had been. To me, everything that had led up to me becoming an actual, real-life bum was some sort of cosmic joke at my expense. Including Jenny turning up like that.

Ever since my mum got taken into care, my philosophy had been that anything good was fleeting and temporary and that something bad was always waiting just around the corner. Sam, for example. He could turn up any time he wanted, out of his mind, ranting about some ten or twenty pounds I owed him, and stick a knife in my chest. Some might say I deserved nothing less.

3.

The truth was that I wasn't a good person. Nobody was who ended up on the streets; just ask Tony. Sure, it would be a nice story if we'd all been trampled on by the system – just poor schmoes without two pennies to rub together, but deep down at the bottom of it nice, virtuous, law-abiding people. That would be a story you could tell to your grandkids. The reality was more complicated than that. I didn't have the energy to figure it all out, but it was something about how the poor were sometimes worse people, in truth, but that you had to help them out in spite of their worseness, and that it was much easier to be virtuous when you didn't have to worry about making ends meet. I thought Jesus might understand what I meant, because he was always talking about being kinder to your enemies than to your friends. Treating your friends kindly was what the Romans did.

I kicked the kerb with my trainers. There were scuff marks on the sides, and the soles were close to splitting apart. I remembered the couple of hundred pounds I had in the bank, and wondered whether it might be worth getting a new pair from Primark, for a measly fiver out of my life savings.

Since ending up on the street, I hadn't told anybody about the little money I had. I hadn't touched it at all, either, mostly out of pure conviction. My belief was that anything which happened out here was hand to mouth; you started with zero, and you ended with zero. It wasn't only that I wanted to keep the money for whatever exit strategy I was hoping would emerge at some point, when I was ready for it. It was that I considered using money from the bank a form of cheating.

After a while I saw her approaching: Jenny, minus the coffee cup. She walked towards the benches, decisively picked me out from the crowd, and strolled over, the uncertainty of the morning all gone now, her face flushing full of confidence.

'Hey. There you are,' she said, her eyes looking directly into mine. She didn't appear to care about the crowd, not like that morning. Somebody whistled from the concrete step over to the left. I could have punched their face in, knowing what it meant, the last jealous kick of someone who was a lost cause and wanted you to be one too, who would do anything to spoil the conversation. But instead I tried to keep my cool and not make things any more awkward than they already were.

'Hello. I didn't think you'd come.' I didn't say it to put her on the spot, but I genuinely didn't think there was a chance in hell Jenny would ever risk another encounter with me on the street. I had half expected her to start walking some other route home in case she bumped into me again.

Instead of being put off, the Jenny of this evening seemed more confident than ever. She nodded in the direction of the Printworks. I picked my stuff up and walked slightly behind her, trying not to stray too close in case I stank. If I did, she pretended not to notice.

We waited for the traffic to pass on Fountain Street, and then we crossed together. Outside Jessops, I recognised a couple of homeless blokes in sleeping bags and the woman who was with them. More and more women were sleeping rough nowadays, but I tried to stayed away from them; homeless women attracted all sorts of trouble. They looked up at me momentarily as I passed, but nobody could really tell I was with Jenny, given the way I walked behind her.

We carried on for a while, me unsure of what to say, already dreading the idea of somebody like Jenny taking pity on somebody like me, or even being seen with me.

'I've got a good parking spot down here, just past the Crowne Plaza,' she said as we left the shops behind and began to walk side by side. 'It's two pounds for a full day.'

'Wow, even I can afford that!' My joke lingered slightly too long.

We finally turned onto a smaller road behind the backs of the apartments. 'Come on, that's my car,' she said. The lights flashed on a white Audi in the corner.

'What do you do?'

'I work for an estate agent,' she said, then motioned at my backpack. 'You can put that in the back.'

Dumbly, I took my worn, dirty backpack and placed it in the boot of the car, which was spotless inside and out. Jenny got in the driver's seat and I lingered for as long as possible outside while she swapped her high heels for flatter shoes. She beckoned me to get in the passenger side. I opened the door and shuffled in uncomfortably, opening the electric window as quickly as I could.

'It's OK. Do you mind?' Jenny asked, waving a small bottle of perfume at me. I shrugged, and she sprayed a few bursts in my direction. The sweetness stuck at the back of my throat for a second, and although it should have been the least of my worries, I thought about whether I'd smell like a girl later, when I got back to Tony's spot underneath the bridge. But I was glad Jen had done it in such a quick and direct way.

We pulled out and headed back under the railway bridge, towards the dual carriageway. I kept my eyes fixed firmly ahead.

'I live down by the Quays at the moment,' she said. 'It's not a big place, but you can sleep on the settee.'

'It's up to you. I'm fine, honestly,' I said.

Jenny raised her eyebrow at me as if to say *I dare you to say that again.* And of course, I wouldn't.

'It's no problem,' she said, 'but I don't have much in to eat. I'll need to stop off at the Co-op on the way.' When we pulled in at the shop, Jenny went inside and left me in the car. A group of students walked past as I waited for her to come back. I noticed she had taken the keys with her. After a few minutes she emerged with a laden bag of shopping, a bottle of wine sticking out of the top. She placed it on the back seat and smiled. 'I hope you like lamb.'

The day before, I would have been over the moon to be given a cup of tea. I nodded.

'I managed to get you some spare clothes to change into, too,' she said, 'courtesy of the Co-op.' She turned the radio on and pulled out of the car park. I felt strangely uncomfortable sitting on the firm leather. A few minutes later, we turned into a gated car park next to some apartment blocks. Jenny reached out of the window and placed a plastic fob against the receiver. The gate opened slowly, and she drove to the end and reversed carefully into a parking space.

I got out of the car, suddenly aware that at any moment a

security guard could see me on the CCTV cameras and come along to ask Jenny if she was alright. Then I would be calmly escorted out of the place with my backpack without much of a protest from her. All the goodwill in the world was powerless against social standards, those unwritten rules of who can be seen with whom and who can set foot in where! Quickly, I followed her into the building.

The ground floor was set up like a hotel lobby. The receptionist had his head down, filling in some documents. There were potted plants in each corner, and the carpets were freshly vacuumed. I wondered if Jenny would crack now, but she showed no signs of it as she took me through the doors and onto the corridor. The receptionist didn't look up, or say anything, but I suspected I saw him glance at us from the corner of his eye as we passed through the lobby.

Then we were walking down the corridor, up the stairs to the third floor – we didn't use the lift – and left until we reached Jenny's apartment. She passed me her handbag, then reached into it for her keys and unlocked the door. As we stepped inside I breathed in the earthy smell of her clean and tidy place; the apartment was new, by the looks of it.

I looked down at the wooden floor to discover I had already muddied it with my trainers. Frantically, I apologised and bent down to take them off.

'Don't worry about it, the place gets cleaned twice a week,' Jenny said, but I was still mortified at the mark my presence had left. I took my shoes off and stood waiting in the living room while she went to put away the food in the kitchen. Jenny went into another room and came back with a towel and some toiletries. 'Here's some clean clothes for you,' she said. 'Put your old stuff in the washing basket and I'll put it on to wash for you. Have you got a toothbrush?'

'Of course. Thank you.'

'Great. Give me a shout if you need anything.'

As she walked back to the kitchen, I could hear the sound of pans clattering and the opening and closing of the fridge door. The bathroom was pristine and sparkling, smelling of citrus air freshener. I stood for a moment, lost in thought, and then took the dirty clothes out of my rucksack and placed them in the washing basket.

I started to undress and looked at myself in the mirror. I'd never had any facial hair when I was a teenager, but now there was some awful stubble clinging to the edges of my neck, and I used a small pair of scissors to trim the worst of it away. My body had changed, too, it seemed: where I'd previously been a bit firmer and fatter, some of the muscles had wasted away, and I could see the outlines of my ribs. I wasn't starving, by any means, but walking around the city had worked off any excess weight.

The shower was warm, and I let the water run over my hair, which was sticky with the greasiness of the traffic fumes and the grime of the city. You found ways to wash, of course, but generally it was in a sink with a bar of soap, or even using the cold water from the toilet bowl when you managed to secure yourself a cubicle. From the other room I could hear the sizzle of something frying as Jenny cooked. I worked a thick lather onto my body and scrubbed myself up as decent as I could. Then I brushed my teeth in the shower; I checked each and every one of them was still rigid, scared they would start to fall out just by virtue of my being of no fixed abode, despite the fact that I hadn't touched any booze.

Underneath the bathroom door came the aroma of onions and spices and cooked meat. It reminded me of the curry shops down on Oxford Road, near Rusholme, where I'd found myself a while ago looking to see if I could find work at any of the takeaways. There was a nice park down there, but of course the students would never give you a penny.

It didn't take me long to work out that I would never find a job in this most diverse part of Manchester. The restaurants were run by an assortment of Pakistanis, Syrians, Lebanese and Afghans, and as a general rule they only employed Eastern Europeans. An English male represented everything they were afraid of down there: the taxman, the immigration officer.

People on television were always going on about how easy life was for white men, but the truth I had seen was that we were one of the loneliest groups in Britain, with no support network or community whatsoever; at least, that was the case for those of us at the bottom of the ladder. I had little in common with people like Tony except that we were both poor and unwanted, and we clung to the underside of society like barnacles. It was amazing how people fell into certain circles whether they wanted to or not.

By the time I had fully changed, Jenny was serving the food on a little dining table next to the balcony. She'd made the lamb with some chickpeas and rice, by the look of things, and the steam coming off it was infinitely appetising. She pulled up a chair and invited me to eat. I sat down and eyed the food eagerly while she brought over a bottle of wine and a couple of glasses.

'Would you like a drink?' she asked.

I shook my head. I had no interest in drinking at the moment.

Jenny seemed glad. She brought me a glass of lemonade instead, then poured the wine for herself. It was quiet as we ate, and she turned the radio on quietly in the background. She kept looking over at me, inspecting my face and thinking some unspoken thing. It reminded me of the way a scientist might look at a rat with a tumour.

After I'd finished the dinner, Jenny offered me seconds, which I declined. My stomach must have shrunk, I realised, because I was full after a single plateful.

'So,' she said, taking a sip from her second glass of wine after some time had passed, 'why don't you tell me what you're doing?'

'What do you mean?'

'Oh, come on. Don't act coy like that,' she said. 'What are you doing playing homeless out on the street?'

'Well, it's a long story, really.' I said, slightly taken aback. 'My dad was drinking a lot. Ever since . . . you know. I couldn't afford a place of my own, so what was I supposed to do? I couldn't stay at home any more.'

Jenny laughed. 'You expect me to believe that? That's a nice story to tell your new mates, but you never tried to contact anyone for help, did you? Is there something heroic about what you're doing? Stop me if I'm speaking out of place, Cameron.'

'No, you're not. I don't know, Jen. This is very nice,' I said, gesturing at her apartment, 'but it's not for me. I don't know what is.'

She took a deep intake of breath. 'Cam, let me tell you something you already know. Those old blokes sitting outside the shops – you're not like them. You're just wasting yourself at the moment. You need to get a grip, because before you know it you'll have spent a year, two years, five years, doing absolutely nothing. And then when you want to start, you won't even know how to any more.'

'It's easy for you to say,' I said, but I could instantly picture what she meant. A permanent beard which never got cut; watching the seasons unfold under an archway in the middle of town, spring turning into summer, summer into autumn, autumn into winter; slowly turning into one of those guys who had been out here so long they didn't have a hope left in the world. I knew the life expectancy for someone sleeping rough was somewhere in the forties. I knew they died shivering in sleeping bags and lay there unnoticed until someone arrived to move them along in the morning.

But I also knew that the people I had seen living out in Manchester were real people, not some statistic on the nine o'clock news. Eventually, as I grew older and more dishevelled, Jenny would move me from the category of 'friends she once knew' to 'nonentity' like the rest of the homeless people out there. She would justify it to herself because I hadn't managed to pull myself up by my bootstraps.

Whose fault was it, anyway, if you didn't have the will or the drive or the determination to get yourself out of the pit you found yourself in? Your own? Or the people who dug it in the first place?

'Look, forget what I said. I'm just trying to help, you know,' she said, smiling at me and letting her shoulders down. 'It's your life, at the end of the day.'

'No, don't worry about it,' I said. 'And thank you, honestly. You've been really kind.'

'I'm going to shower,' Jenny said. 'Let me know if you need anything else, OK?' She drew the curtains to the balcony, locked the front door and laid out a blanket on the settee. She placed her car keys in a little dish on the table, next to her purse.

I sat down, plugged in my phone to charge, and watched her out of the corner of my eye as she entered the bathroom, leaving the door ajar. I could hear her humming amidst the sound of the running shower. There was a gap of about an inch at the side of the sliding door; if I'd got up and walked over to the other side of the room, I would have been able to see her, but whether she'd simply forgotten to close it, I didn't know. Hot steam lingered around the edges.

I wondered what an existence it was, living here on your own in the middle of the city. Did she bring somebody new home every Friday and Saturday night for company, or was she used to sleeping alone? It was hard to say. In the corner was a framed picture of Jenny in her graduation robe and cap, smiling, presumably to her parents behind the camera. I heard the hairdryer starting up in the bathroom.

I was lying down when she emerged. There was a pause for a moment, and then she went into her room. Pretending to be asleep, I listened to her rummage around for a while; I guessed she was getting her things ready for work. About half an hour later, she closed the bedroom door to. The light was off. If there was a cue for me in there somewhere, I must have missed it.

In the comfort of Jenny's apartment, it didn't take me long to drift off to sleep. A few hours later I woke up and tiptoed to the kitchen to pour myself a glass of water. The apartment was silent. I wondered if Jenny was asleep or listening to me walk across the wooden floor, but nothing stirred and so I got back in between the sheets.

It was an unusual feeling, being in a warm bed. I thought about Tony sleeping down by the canal, about my mum looking up at the whitewashed ceiling of a psychiatric ward, about my dad, drunk and snoring, about a baby orangutan in its mother's arms hoping the logging trucks didn't come back tomorrow.

When I woke up, it was around five and the sun wasn't yet up. I took my clothes out of the dryer quietly and folded them away in my bag, nicked a couple of bags of crisps from the kitchen counter, slipped my shoes on, and filled up a bottle of water from the sink. The door to Jenny's bedroom was still closed. I did want to thank her, but it was too early to knock and besides, I didn't want her to start preaching at me again. This was something I had to sort out on my own.

I stood up to leave and went over to the table, where Jenny's car keys still sat next to her purse. There was a ten-pound note poking out of the top, almost as though she'd left it there for me intentionally. I debated it for a moment . . . and then I pocketed it anyway and slipped out of the door. The receptionist wasn't there this time, but my heart was still pounding as I went down the stairs and let myself out of the gate.

Morning hadn't broken yet, and the horizon bore an orange glow against the backdrop of the city. I found the train tracks a few streets down from the apartment building and followed them back towards town, parallel to the main road. I passed a drunk-looking man at a bus stop waiting for the first bus home. The stream of cars started up quickly, and a couple of Lycra-clad cyclists passed me on their way to work. When I found my way back to town, I stopped to pick up a cup of coffee which somebody had left half-empty on a bench. It was still warm, and somewhat welcoming. I thought about what Jenny had said to me about getting used to the feeling of being on my own, about not knowing what it felt like to be normal any more, and I shivered.

4.

When I got back into town I made my way up to Albert Square, in front of the town hall, to watch the sun rise. I sat on a bench, coffee in hand, as the sun eventually cast its rays over the monument to the soldiers who had died in both World Wars. As the sunlight lit up the white stone and the bronze faces of the men, I took out my notepad and made a couple of comments about the night before.

I was hoping for something different today. Maybe it was Jenny's talk last night about getting complacent, or maybe it was just that a hot meal and a decent night's sleep had finally opened up some breathing space in my head for me to think.

Being out here had taught me more in six months than I had ever learned during my years at school. They were harsh lessons, but they'd already changed the way I viewed the world. What could somebody like Jenny know about it all?

I wondered what would happen to her in the end. I already assumed the worst for myself, but all the expectation in a life like hers made the inevitable fall from grace so much harder. After seeing the life she lived – cooking meals for herself every evening in her one-bedroom flat and falling asleep while scrolling through Facebook late at night – I realised the reason she had probably invited me round was because she needed the company.

It must have been nearly seven o'clock when the first buses pulled into town and the people starting walking across the square to work. A young man wearing a suit sat across from me for a while, looking down at his phone, waiting for whatever job interview or meeting he had. He glanced over at me, checked his watch, and left on some adventure of his own. I doubted I'd ever see Jenny again. But at least I'd managed to wash my clothes and have something decent to eat. My pocket was ten pounds heavier, and I reminded myself I had to help Tony with his debt later on today.

I thought about the money I had tucked away in the bank: enough to get me a decent phone, at least, and with that I could get access to public Wi-Fi networks and start applying for jobs. Or I could get in touch with some of my old friends, like Jenny had suggested. There was surely somebody who'd be able to give me a place to stay for a while, or who could put me in touch with somebody who was hiring.

The phrase *job opportunity* had a bitter irony when I said it out loud. Starting my life over again would surely mean grovelling to people who didn't respect me in the slightest and working long hours in order to watch all my money disappear on bills. I'd have direct debits and end up in an endless spiral of buying things I needed like shoes and coats, and fixing things when they broke down, and buying new things, and throwing old things away until, finally, I became the old thing and somebody decided to throw *me* away, as well.

If there was some satisfaction in mowing the lawn or watching *Eastenders* or having a barbecue on a Sunday, I couldn't grasp it. There was some fundamental barrier there, sticking in the way, and I couldn't explain it to myself, let alone to Jenny or anyone else.

I got up, stretched my legs and headed off, not in my usual direction towards the shops on Market Street but away from there, towards Oxford Road and the university. I passed the Manchester Aquatics Centre and the music school, cut around the back of the apartment blocks which housed the richer students who came here, usually from abroad, and across the rest of the campus. A group of girls walked past, chatting and laughing to themselves about whatever had happened at the weekend. They looked me up and down as I passed, then started giggling once they thought I was out of earshot. The campus was a pleasant area, though, and I enjoyed the stroll across the university plaza, past the trees that were lined up outside the new, modern buildings of the student union and the old, parliamentary-looking shell of the Manchester Museum.

After the student union building, all covered in flyers and posters for some political party or cause or whatever it was the students were interested in these days, I came to the edge of the park. It was a clear morning, and there were a few people sitting on benches reading through their textbooks, or walking across the park towards the university buildings. A group of pigeons pecked the ground where someone had left half a pasty behind. They fought and squabbled over it as I walked up to the top of the hill.

I sat down where I could see the park below me, a big expanse of grass dotted with trees and encircled by steel railings. Beyond that there was a road lined with terraced houses whose red-brick walls ran along the far edge of the park. The people who lived there must have had a really nice view, but you could tell they were poor; the curtains were ripped and dirty, and the bins were overflowing, and the houses didn't really have any gardens except for a small square of block paving, littered with broken toys.

It was a street of immigrants, I realised. A group of young Muslim boys appeared from round the corner and made their way to the park, carrying cricket bats. I watched them fashion a stump out of a couple of bottles and start to play. They were wearing traditional Islamic dress, but underneath you could see they had ordinary trainers on. I didn't understand why everybody had so much hatred towards them.

At school we had a single Muslim boy in our class, Jamal; we used to call him Jazz. He was no different from any of us except that he was dark-skinned, and it was only after he had grown a bit older and started going out that anybody started to give him any trouble. I remembered how shocked we all were the first time something like that happened. We'd have been about sixteen, sitting in the back of the pub, when some pissed-up middle-aged man had walked up and asked what a 'fucking P***' was doing in there, and before I knew it punches were being thrown. One of our biggest mates, Alex, had gone straight for the man, and it was a good job the bartender had pulled him away before he got the shit kicked out of him. I remembered it well, because it was one of those experiences that shook you out of childhood and threw you head-first into the real world, showing you there was a dark side to England around every corner.

'Oi, you there,' came a gruff voice from over my shoulder. I turned around in time to see two men marching towards me across the grass. They were homeless – I could tell straight away from the look of them – and one of them was pulling a black Staffie dog along on a lead. The dog had a white patch over one eye, and its mouth was hanging slightly open; I could see drool running down its exposed bottom lip, and the fierce canines above. Before I had time to assess the situation, the men had paced right up to me, and the dog was looking at me as if to determine whether its next assignment was to maul me or not.

They bore a look I'd seen before – nearly always on people who took spice. You never knew where you stood with people like that.

'Alright,' I said.

'You know Terry?' asked the taller of the two, the owner of the voice I had heard behind me. He was thin with wild hair, and one of his eyes was lazy. The man next to him was slightly shorter and somewhat stupid looking – as though he followed the taller one around all the time and did his bidding. I knew I had my work cut out with the two of them.

'Nah, mate,' I replied in the thickest Manc accent I could manage. It was the tall, wiry one I was most worried about. He seemed to be the decision maker, and I knew if he started anything his friend was sure to follow. They lingered uncomfortably, the shorter one looking straight at me, the taller one glancing down the hill at the Muslim boys and their cricket game.

'For fuck's sake,' he said, finally, to no one in particular.

'What do you reckon?' asked his friend.

'I don't know,' he said. 'But I ain't walking around all day trying to find one of his lot. What a piss-take.' I tried to make myself invisible, hoping for some quick distraction, anything to rid myself of these two who clearly had nothing better to do but to harass strangers in the middle of the morning.

'He won't even remember, Johnny. Let's just leave it,' said the shorter one.

'Could try up near Piccadilly,' Johnny said.

'Doubt anyone will know him up there.'

'What a joke. As if we've got nothing better to do,' he said. 'I'm tempted to throw it in the fucking canal, you know.' He tugged the lead, and I realised they were talking about the dog. It seemed like the two of them had forgotten about me completely, but I wasn't naïve enough to be unaware of the possible start of a scam, either. I held back from asking anything but took on a quiet, pondering look.

Finally, they turned back to me and the one called Johnny ran his hand through his dirty hair. 'Do you want a dog, mate?'

'What?' I said.

He nodded down at the dog, which was standing stationary, waiting for the end of whatever it was the humans were talking about. Actually, it might have been watching the boys playing cricket. Either way, I was sure it found itself in this position over and over again, moving from owner to owner and being grateful for whatever food it was given.

'Terry's dog,' said the shorter one. 'He won't be needing him any more. Johnny's going to throw him in the canal, if not.'

'What do I want a dog for?' I asked.

'Don't get cocky,' said Johnny, glaring at me for a moment. I held as firmly as I could. 'Right. Forget it, then.' He gave a weary sigh, then yanked the lead and started off down the hill. The shorter fellow looked at me with disgust and then ran off down the hill after him.

'Wait!'

Johnny turned and caught my glance; it took a second for it to register that it was me who had shouted after them. He walked back up the hill, and in the couple of seconds it took I went through the sinking feeling of having opened my mouth and now needing to follow it up with something.

'Well?' he said.

'Alright, I'll take it off you,' I said.

He scratched his head, looked at his mate, then took a step forward and narrowed his eyes. 'How much?'

'What do you mean, how much?' I said. A minute ago, the man had seemingly been ready to leave the dog he was lumbered with any place he could think of. But now he'd seen the want in my eyes – and wherever there was want, there was an opportunity to make a profit.

'Do you want it or not? How much have you got on you?' he said.

I was cursing myself inside, not just for opening my mouth, but because I only had a ten-pound note on me, which I didn't intend to spend. Even worse, there was no way of asking for change off people like that. 'Nothing,' I lied.

The pissed-off Johnny came towards me with a wild look in his eyes, and next to him his mate must have picked up the mood, because he came at me, too. Everything was a moment away from kicking off, and I didn't fancy my chances. 'I've got a fiver owed off a mate, though, if you'll still be about in half an hour,' I added quickly.

'A fiver?' said the second one.

I shrugged as if to say *take it or leave it*.

'Half an hour,' Johnny muttered to himself. 'Alright, but I'm not staying longer than that. You hear me?'

'Yeah, no worries,' I said. 'I'll be back soon.'

'Good. Make sure you are.'

I picked up my bag, left them there and jogged down the hill, following the path along the railings, then turned right out of the park and onto the street. I walked for a while, making a few turns to make sure I wasn't being followed, and then dived into a corner shop. I bought a packet of ham with the ten-pound note and put it away in my bag for later.

As I wandered back up the street, I wondered what on earth I was getting myself into. A dog? I could barely look after myself. And who knew whether this was all just some elaborate scam? They'd probably just nicked somebody's dog and were trying to get a couple of quid for it, I thought, and all the stuff about throwing it in the canal was probably just to scare me into taking it off their hands. But on the other hand, if they *had* stolen it, there was still no reason why they wouldn't throw it in the canal after all. I remembered the look in Johnny's eyes, that strange mix of laziness and electricity that looked like it could fire off at any minute.

There was no way of saying for certain what the situation was, and I felt a certain fatalism as I headed back to the park. In the end, the better part of my nature had decided the creature stood a better chance with me than it did with a couple of spice-heads.

When I got back to the park, however, there was no sign of the two men. I made my way back up the hill and looked around. The boys had disappeared now as well, even though I'd only been gone about ten or fifteen minutes, and I was starting to feel as though the morning's events had been a hallucination when I spotted the pair walking up past the railings, near the side of the shops, leash in hand. I headed in their direction; when the taller one spotted me, he made a beeline straight for me.

It was busier here near the street, with people walking past, so I hoped it would be a quicker encounter than the previous one.

It was.

'You got the money?' the twitchy man asked. The dog looked at me curiously.

'Yeah – here you go.' I handed him the five-pound note and he passed it to his friend, who made some sniggering comment about checking for forgery. I ignored them both as he tucked it away in his pocket.

'Right then,' I said. The man stepped in front of me, blocking the pavement.

'You got any more on you? I know you have. Dogs aren't cheap, you know,' he said.

For fuck's sake, Cameron, I thought. I considered the possibility of walking away a fiver down and calling it a lesson learned, but the thought of what might happen to the dog, and my own sense of fair trade, held me to the spot. I reached into my pocket and pulled out as little change as I thought I could get away with. Fortunately, it was only a pound coin and a fifty-pence piece.

'Alright.' The man sniggered. 'A pleasure doing business with you.'

I held out my hand stiffly for the lead, and he paused for a second before handing it over. Finally, they left me standing there. I watched the pair of them walk around the corner, talking and laughing, until they disappeared from sight. The dog watched them leave, too, and then the two of us were left alone.

I looked down at it; its unkempt, matted fur was patchy in parts, almost burnt looking. Its head was down as if in prayer; its skull possessed a quiet strength, like the hull of a battleship. I crouched down. Its ears twitched, then it glanced up at me.

'Well, I can't just call you 'it'. Let's see if you're a boy or a girl.' I had a look. 'A boy, then. I'm going to call you . . . Tatum. That OK?'

He made a quiet, inquisitive noise, and when his tail started to wag instinctively, he stopped it as though he didn't yet know me well enough to let his guard down.

'I know. This doesn't mean we're bound for life,' I said, flicking his ear. 'I don't know if I can keep you. But at least you aren't with those two any more.' I had become an instant cliché, talking to him like that, but you would be surprised at how little I got to speak during the day. Even the conversations with Tony were brief and usually about food or begging.

So that was how I ended up with Tatum. I named him after the Mike Tyson-like boxer in *The Simpsons*, which I used to watch as a kid. He had a staunch set of shoulders on him, and even though he looked a bit too skinny for a dog of his breed, I thought his previous owner must have been feeding him well. He seemed quiet and reserved, but also attentive.

I didn't know quite what to do next. 'Well, come on, I guess,' I said, tugging his leash lightly. I walked through the park and back up past the university.

By now there was a steady stream of students milling around the university buildings. As I walked past, they gave me a wider berth than usual, but Tatum kept his eyes fixed ahead of him and even waited for me to tell him when we could cross the road. He was a good, clever dog who seemed to know the streets well.

As we walked past a set of bins, Tatum pulled his head towards them and sniffed the ground. Somebody had thrown a packet of chips on the floor; they lay in the ripped paper, smeared with ketchup, and he went for them almost immediately. Somebody walking past looked at both him and me with disgust.

I dragged Tatum away with all my strength. 'That's bad food,' I warned him. He pulled and barked again loudly, then tugged at his lead in the direction of the abandoned takeaway. 'No,' I said sternly. 'Come over here a minute.' I took out the packet of ham from my bag and fed him a couple of slices. He was hungry and ate them up voraciously, looking at me for more. I gave him another slice and then put the packet away, despite his whimpering.

I sighed. A day or two of this, and I would probably think about throwing him in the canal, too. I wondered how much food a dog needed every single day. He was about a quarter the size of me, but I knew his metabolism was quicker and so he would definitely need more than a quarter of what I ate. And water! I'd almost forgotten about that. His tongue was already looking a little dry as he panted along beside me.

When we got back to the centre of town, I reluctantly tied him up outside a public toilet while I filled up a bottle with water. Giving it to him was more awkward than I'd thought, though. I ended up pouring the water as carefully as I could onto his tongue, which was aggressively lapping around the top of the bottle, and half of it ended up on the floor. I filled the bottle up again and put it away for later, which meant leaving him outside again for a minute. I realised the most difficult part about owning a dog would be keeping him, because a lot of homeless people would snatch up an unattended dog – for warmth, for begging, for security, or for the company.

A couple of people looked at us – Tatum and me – as they walked past. But I didn't care. People always wanted to look at somebody and think to themselves, 'That could never be me.' Because they were special and hard-working and talented, because they came from better stock than that, because they'd listened in school or because they had all of these brilliant ideas running around their brain all the time, they would never know what it felt like to live in the trash heap and not to care about catching fleas any more. You saw the satisfaction on their faces that they had something worse to compare themselves with, even if they weren't as clever or as talented or as good-looking as they thought.

That need to remind themselves how good they were in comparison to everybody else arose, I knew, from fear. Deep down, everyone was afraid that they weren't good enough. Most of all they were afraid, like chimpanzees, of being ejected from the tribe.

I was starting to realise that if you managed to wade through that fear and emerge unscathed on the other side, you could end up stronger than everybody. That was why people who had been shot at during wars or had smuggled their family across multiple borders seeking asylum managed to become successful doctors, lawyers, authors or businessmen. It was because they'd managed to conquer all the fear that holds most people back their entire lives.

People were afraid of walking home in the dark. People were afraid of having to find food to eat, or of having to find a way of keeping warm. How could I be frightened of those things any more? I had fended for myself in a big city full of danger. I would never have to worry about what would happen if I didn't pay the rent on time – at least, not in a speculative way. Some people walked around with that burden their whole lives.

There were things to be frightened of, but they weren't the basic things like finding food or shelter or water. They were the bigger things, the spiritual things, the search for a purpose. I couldn't seem to find my way. And what scared me most was the thought that there wasn't one; that there was no path ordained for me, that there was no *fate* or anything more important than this, that I might perish by the roll of a dice without ever knowing what the life I was given was all about: on the corner of a street in the rain, under the wheel of a truck, or at the hands of an idiot.

5.

'You've gone bloody soft,' was the first thing Tony said to me when I ran into him outside Sainsbury's on Deansgate. He directed an uninterested frown at Tatum and nodded to the fellow sitting beside him, who gave a grating cough. 'What do you think this is, "Animal Hospital"? Where'd you pick that thing up?'

The man sitting next to Tony was called Jonesy. He was a bum who kept to himself and nodded along to everything. You couldn't be sure if he understood you sometimes because he never had anything of note to say – and even when he did speak, you never knew what he meant.

'It's a bit of a long story,' I said.

'Always is, lad, always is,' Tony said. 'Thing is, it's another mouth to feed, at the end of the day. And don't think it cares for you or anything soppy like that. First time it gets hungry, it'll run off on you. You know that, don't you?'

'He's got better teeth than you, Tony,' Jonesy murmured. He laughed with a rasp which rattled and tailed off, then he held his hand out to Tatum. The dog sniffed him warily and allowed him to stroke his head.

Tony grumbled to himself. He made an effort to keep a

distance away and stood there, shaking his head and watching the people walk by.

When Tatum blinked, he looked old and tired, but I knew he was a young dog by the tone of his muscles. He sat down on the concrete and licked his fur. He was old before his time, I realised as I watched him, just like many of us were getting. There was that *us* again; I shuddered, recoiling at the thought. I wondered what he had seen or done – what other names he'd had, what other owners.

Could a dog experience post-traumatic stress? I supposed they could. People had dogs with all kinds of conditions, didn't they? In a lot of ways, Tatum reminded me of myself. He didn't seem to bark very often, and he spent a lot of time looking out into empty space, with some untold thought reflected in his eyes. He'd had that look this morning in the park when he first approached me, and he had it again now.

I had got so caught up in the morning's events that I'd almost entirely forgotten about the night I'd spent in Jenny's apartment, or the plan I had formed in the morning to turn my life around. It had all just started flooding back to me, and I was about to mention something to Tony, when a security guard came out of Sainsbury's and stood over the three of us. He was a big bald man with a G4S badge sewn onto the breast of his black waterproof jacket. I was looking down at his feet and noticing how the polish covered up the undeniably cheap leather of his black boots when he spoke with a loud, deep voice that almost sounded too put on to be real. 'You, you three – yes, you! You need to leave now!'

Tony was already on his feet. He took a couple of steps back along the side of the shop next to the cash machine. Jonesy seemed to meld in to the wall, his woolly hat pulled down low over his face, covering his eyes. Normally, I made a pretty good job of being inconspicuous. I waited for the security guard to approach Jonesy and tell him to move, or to ask Tony to keep on walking further away from the shop. But then I realised it was me he was looking at, blocking the path in front with his huge figure and motioning down the street.

'Alright, alright, we're going,' I said, bending down to pick up my backpack from the floor. I noticed the way the security guard was looking at Tatum, with an apprehension I hadn't encountered before. I backed off a couple of steps, while around us a small crowd had started to watch. Another store attendant was standing at the shop doorway, asking the G4S man whether he wanted him to call for help.

Jonesy, meanwhile, hadn't moved an inch. He was still sitting with his back to the façade of the shop, head down, arms folded. The security guard noticed him next, bellowed at him to move. Jonesy registered it slowly but didn't manage to get himself up at all. I wondered how much he might have had to drink that day. The security guard turned, grabbed him by the shoulder and tried to pull him up onto his feet. But Jonesy's legs had turned to jelly. Whether he had intentionally relaxed or whether he was simply too drunk or cold to muster any energy into them, I didn't know.

The security guard wasn't wasting his time. He half pulled, half pushed Jonesy away from the shop, his feet dragging along the floor.

'Come on, Jonesy!' Tony said, taking hold of his arm and trying to help him up onto his feet while I watched the whole thing unfold like a useless spectator. The security guard stepped forward, his confidence bolstered by the small crowd that had gathered. Jonesy apparently wasn't moving on fast enough for his liking. He cocked his leg back as he stepped forward, and swung it, the steel-capped toe making contact with Jonesy's leg with a solid crack. I saw Jonesy's usually relaxed expression stiffen up, and he closed his eyes gently before falling to the ground in a heap.

That was when Tatum kicked into gear.

It happened out of nowhere, an explosion from deep within the quiet brain of the animal that had been sitting calmly by my side. All at once he let out a series of deep, ferocious barks, baring his canine teeth and lunging forward, almost ripping the lead from my hands. The security guard's eyes opened wide and he took a step backwards, holding his hands up in case Tatum lunged at him.

And I thought he would. He snarled loudly as I dragged him back, his powerful hind legs digging into the pavement. By now, everybody on the street had turned to look. I could hear Tatum's barks reverberating off the walls of the buildings, the echo making it sound as though Cerberus himself had woken up from hell.

'Get back! Get that thing back!' the security guard shouted.

Dragging Tatum backwards, I looked further up the street. Tony had managed to help Jonesy to his feet and along the street a little distance. He shouted after me to catch up with them. I hauled Tatum out of there, running through the wide gap in the crowd which had formed in front of me.

'Come on, let's get going,' Tony said as I caught up. 'You've caused enough trouble for one day.'

The people watching had started filtering off into the crowd.

I noticed one of them had his phone out, recording the whole thing, and I glared at him for a second until he put it back in his pocket and moved along. The security guard had taken up position on the corner of the street and was speaking into his radio, keeping his eyes fixed firmly on us, and especially on Tatum.

We turned around a couple of corners and found a quiet alleyway to rest in. Jonesy sat with his back against the wall and Tony flexed his leg backwards and forwards to assess the damage.

'I'll never walk again,' Jonesy said.

'Don't be daft, man,' said Tony. 'He's just bruised your shin. Not even broken.'

'Tell him, boy,' he said to me. 'Tell him I need a doctor.' I looked at Tony, who rolled his eyes at me. Meanwhile, I noticed Tatum had taken to guarding the alleyway entrance, watching out for trouble. I patted him on the head to calm him down.

'Did you see the way he looked at him?' Tony said.

'Who?' I asked.

'The dog.'

'Oh. I mean, yes. When the guard came towards me . . .'

'Should've seen the way he kecked himself!' Jonesy cackled. 'I thought that pooch of yours was going to tear him apart. It's a shame he didn't, really. Would've made a change from getting kicked about by another know-it-all.'

'And where would that have got you?' Tony said to me. A serious look had come over him. 'You being charged under the Dangerous Dogs Act, and him, well,' – he made a finger-across-the-throat gesture– 'say no more. I'm telling you, a dog's trouble, and you don't want to be getting yourself into trouble at your age.'

'Oh, leave him alone,' I said, rubbing Tatum's head. 'He was just looking out for me.'

Jonesy had managed to sit up and was rubbing his shin. His leg would be purple by tomorrow morning, and if we were ordinary people we'd be giving witness statements right now, and the police would be charging the security guard with assault.

But we weren't, and I knew Tony had a point about Tatum.

'Whatever you say,' Tony said, 'only keep him away from us, will you? You've seen what's happened to Jonesy.' I could see he wanted to add *because of you*. And for the first time, I saw the other side of him: the side that would do anything for his own self-preservation. The Tony who was so afraid of losing the nothing he had that he couldn't love anything, couldn't trust anyone – not properly, not any more.

'I need to go,' I said. 'Get him something to eat. I'll see you later, Tony.' Jonesy nodded at me, and I made a mental note to check up on him later.

'See ya,' Tony said.

I left him there with Jonesy, in the shade of the alleyway. The clear sky of the morning had greyed over, and it cast a grim look over the paving slabs of the street and the dirty bricks of the building next to the canal. Tatum looked up at me, his strong features calmer now, an eager furrow appearing across his brow. There was something stirring in the city.

'I don't know, Tatum,' I said. 'Look at this place. Look at you. You should be wandering through the woods sniffing for rabbits, and I should be out cutting logs for the fire. We should be walking down to the lake together, you and I, and you could have a swim in the cold water, and I could fish.' He looked up at me at the word *fish*, and then he got fed up of waiting and barked loudly. He didn't have time for my existential problems.

I fed him a few slices of cooked meat and then we walked together for a while. We passed the old Victorian buildings which were due to be torn down – tall buildings with lots of old, dirty windows and cracked chimneys – along the arches of the railway bridge. The workings of the railway looked down on us, built by men of a different time who believed in bricks and furnaces and a world made from iron and sweat. There were people sleeping under them now, small bundles of fabric tucked in among the drains and in the shadows.

On the other side of the road they were busy building some new apartments. There was the tall concrete spire of the lift shaft sticking up out of the earth, but the cranes sat stationary for now. The fence along the site was covered in computer-generated drawings of the new apartment building, with little computer-drawn people walking around among the potted trees and sitting in the plaza.

How civilised could a place be, I wondered, that built luxury high-rises for the rich while the poor literally slept under their shadow?

We passed a taxi rank with the taxis all setting off for their fares as day turned into night, a laundrette bathed in a pale blue neon glow, a burger shop with the smell of chips and greasy fried chicken being blown out of the front door. Tatum nudged his head towards the smell; I pulled him away again. Further on there were more tower blocks, but the streets were narrower and the shadows darker there, and I would not go. We passed a couple of people walking with their hoods up, heads down, hands in pockets, hurrying on their way home. We followed the path right along the river and then back across a footbridge, in the direction of our territory.

I walked Tatum back along the black abyss of the canal, still in the evening light. There were no stars visible – not here, so close to the bright lights of the city – and tonight there was no moon, either. In the gloom I thought I saw the fluttering shape of a bat fly out from the corrugated roof of a factory, and then it was gone. Under the bridges that crossed the canal were dark corners filled with graffiti and piss.

Normally, I'd have been hesitant to walk on my own down there. There were disappearances down by the canals, rumours of a person called the Pusher who targeted young, usually gay, people on their way home during the early hours of the morning. But I didn't feel half as afraid with Tatum by my side.

We neared the bridge I had called home ever since Tony had invited me to stay there one night in June. In a way, it really was home to me. At least, it was more welcoming than any place I'd lived before, that brick archway which sheltered me from the rain. The place looked quieter today, though, without Tony. I sat down next to the canal and threw a couple of pebbles in, watching the lights reflecting off the ripples. Tatum was quiet.

I don't know how much time passed before Tony found me there, silently looking down into the water, but he came up on me unawares. He stood next to me and lit a roll-up cigarette which he'd drawn out of his coat pocket. 'Hi, lad,' he said, flicking the ash into the still water of the canal.

'Hi, Tony.' I didn't know what he wanted me to say. I was just a boy with nowhere to go, and he was a man who had used up all of his choices, and right now I felt he and I were different in so many ways that it was impossible the two of us could be friends. I laughed out loud; it was absurd, really, this whole thing, living down by the canal in scruffy clothes and asking people for change as they walked by. If I was tired or if the lighting hit the walls in a certain way, I could sometimes be convinced that the whole thing wasn't real. Because how could it be?

'I wanted to apologise, Cam,' he said. 'I didn't mean to upset you. I just don't want you to get too caught up in all of this. It's far too easily done. And I thought you'd have been gone by now, mate, if I'm being honest with you.'

'Gone where?'

'I don't know. Away from here. Selling paintings on the streets of France, picking berries on a farm in Spain, anything.'

I didn't know how to tell him that all I saw was walls all around me, and that there was a huge void in front of me whenever I thought about the future. I couldn't see anything beyond that. 'I know you're right about Tatum,' I said, finally. 'But he doesn't deserve to be thrown in the canal. You of all people must understand that.'

'Who, him?' Tony said. 'He's a good boy. Like you. But I don't want you getting too attached to him. I don't want you setting yourself up to fail. It won't end well. Nothing ever does.'

'I think having him around is really helping me. Having somebody else to look after instead of myself.'

'But it's still just passing the time, isn't it?' Tony said.

'What do you mean?'

'I don't know what you've got. Whether you want to call it depression or whatever. With me it's different, I've had my chances,' Tony said. 'But you? You haven't even started yet. I'm telling you, you should get away from here.'

'I know what you mean, Tony,' I said. 'But I can't just fix everything overnight. It's taken me this long to realise that I never had a proper childhood. I thought I had it all under control, but the reality is, I just got numb to everything that was going on. I think the way I cope with some of it is to not have a hope or care in the world. Do you understand?'

'Yes.' Tony understood all too well. 'But look at me. Do I look like a role model to you?'

I laughed. 'I guess not.'

'Well, then. What I do know is that nobody can help you except yourself,' he said. 'You can't shut yourself away. I can see in your eyes that you really want to make something of yourself. You're not dead yet. But you have to find a way to get past it, Cam.'

'I know.'

'Do you fancy a smoke?'

'I'd better not.'

'Come on. There's a couple of pasties in my bag that want eating.'

I followed him away from the canal bank and we sat down under that old familiar bridge. The night was quiet. Tony was humming the Bob Dylan song 'Like a Rolling Stone', and the sound echoed around us quietly. These were the moments I liked best. I fed Tatum the remainder of the meat from my backpack, and Tony told me about the time he took his kids to see Robbie Williams at the Manchester Arena. He didn't say it in a wistful way, you understand; these were just his memories, and they made him happy. I kept my hand over my face so he couldn't see the tears running down it.

I didn't know what I was crying about. I thought it was for Tony, but maybe he was right – maybe it was that deep down

I still felt the desire to be loved and happy. Although I might not have had much left inside me, there was still something buried in there that was worth clinging to. Or maybe it was because I knew mine and Tony's time together was coming to an end; that I would, before all of this was over, know again what it was like to feel completely alone.

6.

The long days I'd spent walking around the city with Tatum became shorter, and instead of sitting in the park we spent our nights surrounded by the orange glow of the street lights, watching the steadily increasing flow of shoppers who came in the dark evenings after work, and waiting in the long, cold mornings for the sun to come and heat us up.

The one thing I can say about Tatum is that he kept me warm during those freezing nights. Sometimes I would watch his chest moving up and down while he slept, and his calm face would twitch as he dreamt about something I couldn't imagine. Other times I slept while he stood watch over me, looking out for trouble. If he'd been a person, he probably would have complained all the time, but Tatum was steadfast throughout. Only through that time did I finally learn the meaning of the phrase *man's best friend.*

In the first week of December they set up the Christmas markets all across town. There were festive lights in all the shop windows, and the people walked home with bags full of clothes from Debenhams and Next and Marks & Spencer, chatting to each other, laughing, taking in all the festivities. To me, it was like being on an alien planet. I didn't have anything in common with anybody, it seemed. The festive season also marked a new chapter in my life: this would be my first Christmas away from home.

January seemed to disappear straight after Christmas, and then it rained for three weeks straight. It rained as if Biblical floods were coming to wash away all the filth of the city, a never-ending drizzle coming from a grey blanket of sky which hung over the place like grey static. Some days the rain came down in a thin sheet all day, and other days it poured down in thick, cold torrents that bounced off the pavement as people dived into whatever cover they could find. It ran off the roofs of the shops and gushed down the drainpipes and formed rivers which rushed down the streets and ended in big puddles around the drains, and the people ran through it or walked with their coats held over their heads, or hid underneath shop awnings, smoking and waiting for it to calm down before they finally made a break for it. It ran off the umbrellas and it made droplets on the windows and the cars drove through it with their wipers going, and the people packed into the buses and the windows of the buses were all steamed up because of all the people.

I don't know about other places, but in Manchester when it rained, the city came to life. There were always places you could find to shelter in, and the temperatures tended to be a few degrees warmer because of the cloud cover. Of course, the rain dripped off the greasy ends of your hair and down into your socks so that your feet squelched everywhere you went and you couldn't feel your toes any more, and Tatum followed me everywhere smelling permanently of wet dog. But weather, to me, was the great leveller. It didn't matter whether you earned four hundred thousand pounds a year or four pounds a day, whether you were a politician or a policeman or a scally from a council estate; the rain treated everyone the same.

Sometimes it rained all night. I liked the way it sounded when everything was quiet save for the constant sound of the rain hitting the pavement. It sounded like white noise on a television tuned to a dead channel. At one point the canal swelled because of the rainfall, and looked like it might drown Tony and me right there while we were sleeping. We were sharing our bridge with more rats now that everywhere else was wet, and at night they scurried around us in the dark.

I woke up as the sun rose above the silhouettes of the factories. Tony was nowhere to be seen; he'd been missing for a couple of days. I rolled up my sleeping bag and fitted it into a nook in the corner of the bridge. Tatum stretched himself out as the mist rose off the surface of the canal. Although I didn't know it as I walked with him into town, that day would turn out to be one of my last in the city. The rain clouds had reduced to a murky darkness far away on the horizon, but the city was still damp from the night before. There were puddles everywhere, and the last of the rain was finding its way down the drains and into the rushing waters of the canal.

On Saturday I'd heard about the death of a homeless man who sold the *Big Issue* outside Victoria Station. News of things like that travelled around us quickly, but for most other people it was something you might hear about in the local news if it was a particularly slow day. The man who had died the night before was called Ant, although nobody could be sure that was his real name. I'd seen him a couple of times with a stack of newspapers in his hand, offering them out to the crowds of people walking past with their hands in their pockets. He was Polish, Latvian, Lithuanian – something like that.

There was a wave of spice going through the homeless community at that time. A lot of people said they took it because of the rain and the cold, but mostly they took it because they were hopeless. You could see in somebody's eyes if they were on it. There were different types, too: some that would make you fall into a coma-like sleep in the middle of the day, and others which would make you agitated, paranoid and twitchy. It was the second type that scared me the most. The sleepers were scattered all across town, and people nicknamed them 'spice zombies' because of the way they fell asleep in awkward positions – standing up, or with their head tilted at a near-impossible, *Exorcist*-like angle.

The news stories about spice had one unexpected effect: they made everybody else hate us and wish we were dead. It was the perfect excuse, really, for reaching the conclusion that all of us were there by our own choice and deserved what was coming to us. That was about the time I realised a large portion of the population would be glad to be rid of the homeless by any means necessary, given half a chance.

There were always some people who tried to help, of course. There were social workers and teams of volunteers roaming around in the late evening, handing out flasks and sleeping bags and offering hostel beds for the night. But everybody knew the hostels were full of spice addicts and psychopaths. For most, it was safer outside in the cold. If you were lucky, the volunteers came around with hot food and cups of coffee in the night-time, but during the day I had never felt more alone. Nobody wanted to give handouts any more because of the spice problem. And nobody bought the *Big Issue*.

I'd decided a walk to the station would be in order. I don't know whether it was morbid curiosity or some sort of need to pay respects that made me decide to go down to the place where Ant had died, but in any case, I was always looking for something to do to break up the monotony of the days.

'Come on, Tatum,' I said. He walked alongside me contentedly, without a clue in the world where we were headed. Tatum never questioned anything.

By the time I arrived at the station, the place was packed full of commuters streaming out in all directions. There were railway workers in yellow jackets, newspaper sellers milling around between them, people queuing up outside Greggs for bacon sandwiches and coffee, managerial types buying newspapers from the stands. I walked around the perimeter of the building, and then I saw where it must have happened; somebody had lashed a small bunch of flowers to the railings near to the spot. There was hardly any sign of anything untoward, save for a piece of police tape still flapping in the wind where, earlier in the night, an ambulance must have carried the poor bloke away.

I was standing on the other side of the road taking it in when a man with a long grey beard and a hat shuffled over to me. He smiled warily at Tatum as he approached.

'Don't worry,' I said, 'he won't bite.'

'Who d'you hear it off?' the man asked me. There was a sickly smell on his breath and a crumpled, sodden newspaper in his hand. He had this awful twitch every few seconds, where he tilted his head to one side and shut one of his eyes in a terrible grimace.

'A friend,' I said. I didn't use Tony's name wherever I could avoid it. It was better not to attract any attention towards us.

'Oh, aye, aye. Was awful, you know. I saw it from over there, near that thing.' He meant the Football Museum. It had a long sloping roof which looked like Jackie Chan could have slid down it in an old nineties film. 'Terrible, terrible shame. Saw him a few times a week, you know.'

He shuffled weirdly, then carried on. 'Poor Ant. What a terrible mess. I saw them carry him away. I was sat over there. Oh, would you look at that.'

I looked over and saw a girl take out a camera and aim it at the corner of the building. It must have been her assignment for the morning. She took a few photos from further back so she could get the police tape into her shot, and then crossed to our side of the road, glancing at us briefly. After making a few notes, she crossed back over and went inside the station, presumably to ask one of the staff members if they could tell her anything about it.

'What happened?' I asked the bearded man. He was still twitching, holding the newspaper up at me as though it were a weapon. All in all, he made quite a sight. I wasn't quite sure if he had heard me. 'What happened?' I said again. 'Was he killed?'

'Killed? Oh, no. What an awful, awful shame. No. I saw them cleaning it up afterwards. Thought nobody could see him do it. But I could. I was sitting right over there. No, he wasn't killed. He did it himself, the poor bastard.'

'I'm sorry,' I said.

And then the man sat down on the pavement and started to cry. He took off his hat and sobbed into it for a minute while

I stood there, not knowing what on earth to do. His shoulders heaved up and down and I could hear him saying something, some indiscernible words of grief for another stranger. I stood there in a stunned silence. After a few moments he stopped, but he didn't speak to me again. I was not sure either of us wanted to restart the conversation.

I could guess the worst of what had happened. Ant, or whatever his name really was, all alone in a foreign country with no future, no job prospects, wondering what the hell he had done wrong in his life and who would help him now in his current sorry state. Probably drunk on vodka, cold and miserable, having spent Christmas freezing and alone, with no prospect of anything better to come. A lot of people came to Britain thinking the streets were paved with gold. I could picture him lying there lifeless in his sleeping bag, like so many others who were found by the street sweepers as they came to move them along in the mornings. These were dark times we were living in.

I walked around the station past the front entrance, where the girl with the camera had emerged. Now she was asking passers-by if they had any comments about the homeless for her newspaper piece. I felt like going up to her and asking her how on earth anybody could stand by while other people lived out this wretched kind of existence, here, in a first-world country. I felt like grabbing her by the shoulders and demanding to know why nobody was doing anything about it. Not just a page-nine story in a print edition – why was nobody helping us? We needed counsellors and GPs and jobs and girlfriends, and things to do which would give us fulfilment. I wanted to tell her this life I had been living for the past few months was unfit even for stray dogs. I wanted to tell her that what was happening here was just as bad as anything the Nazis had done. But I didn't. I walked past her and kept on walking, pulling Tatum along with me at a striding pace.

When I was finally on my own, I found a skip and kicked the shit out of it. The bangs echoed along the alley and disappeared into the nothingness.

'I don't know, Tatum,' I said. He looked up at me with compassion, but in a way that told me I just had to keep going. 'I just don't know.'

Food, warmth, shelter, companionship. The hierarchy of needs. I felt calmer with him by my side, that was for sure. I was sure that if I had been on my own I might have jumped off the roof of a multistorey car park by now. I wondered why animals didn't feel like giving up in the same way people did. They just kept running until their legs stopped. I wondered if that was the way people had been a long time ago, before they started giving themselves up and worrying about everything all the time.

'You're a good friend, Tatum,' I said, 'even if you don't know much about anything.'

We walked back along Corporation Street, where a group of Chinese tourists were standing outside a hotel with suitcases, waiting for their guide to arrive. I must have looked like something from *Blade Runner* by this point. Shoppers, handbags, people sitting in doorways, overflowing bins, traffic, pigeons, people on spice; the sight of everything in the city had become stale to me. I didn't even feel like eating.

I found some leftover pizza for Tatum at lunchtime, and he scoffed it down and then lay down in the sun, watching the pigeons.

I woke him up after an hour and took him back through the alleyways towards the canal. The evening sky was ablaze. What I needed was a change of scenery: a beach, mountains, a fresh running river stocked with fish, forests full of birds and fruit. I could sense that was what Tatum wanted, too. We were all of us being made grey in our souls by the city and the clouds and the concrete. I needed to get away, and I was struck by the irony that it was that feeling which had made me leave home in the first place, only to end up here.

As we turned the corner, I was so lost within my thoughts that it took me a minute to register Tony with his back against the wall, Sam holding him up by his collar, and the long knife in Sam's other hand.

7.

I didn't have any time to process the scene, but I took a moment to adjust to the vision in front of me of Tony and Sam, the latter red-faced and in some sort of wild rage, the gleaming six-inch blade in his hand reflecting the light off the canal. Neither of them had noticed me yet, and Sam was holding his fist up in front of Tony's face, pulling him forwards and throwing him back against the wall while shouting something about money.

But while it took my reflexes a second to adjust, Tatum's synapses had already fired up. Before I knew it, he had lunged forward, nearly ripping the lead straight out of my hand. Tony and Sam turned around in unison to see the cause of this new commotion. I must have been unable to hide my fear, or maybe it came across as anger, because they both looked as though they'd seen something horrific in my face.

'What the fuck are you looking at?' Sam said. Tatum was barking louder than I'd ever heard him before, a guttural, primeval roar emanating from his jaws. The fact that Sam hadn't seemed to register his presence at all was unsettling. Tony flashed me a lightning look that I took to mean *Get the hell out of here, Cam.* Sam grabbed him and threw him back against the wall again.

'I told you, I don't owe you anything, you stupid bastard,' Tony said.

Sam hit him in the face, hard, and he kept quiet after that. A minute ago I had been walking around stewing in my own misery, and now it felt as though all my worst fears were about to come true. This was how I was going to die, then – next to the canal, probably along with Tony – and even worse was the idea that nobody would investigate it, or even care. Just another couple of bodies dredged up; homeless guys, probably junkies, they would say. I had to think of a way to move Tony and his current predicament to somewhere more public. I could deal with Sam if there were people around.

Then, just as I decided I didn't want to add any fuel to the situation, my feet gave way to Tatum's pulling and I stepped forward.

Without looking over, Sam hissed out of the side of his mouth. 'Get that piece of shit away or I'll cut his belly open.'

Tatum was straining at the lead, and I dug my heels in. I realised I hadn't seen the true strength in his muscles before, and the question crossed my mind as to how he had managed to get so strong living off bags of crisps and leftover kebab meat.

'For Christ's sake, lad, will you get out of here? I'll sort this out on my own. Go on!' Tony said.

And for a second I actually believed he would be alright if I just left. But the mere idea that Tony could defuse the situation obviously got to Sam. He dragged Tony to the floor, brandishing the blade centimetres away from his face. 'Sort it out! Go on then, you toothless prick, sort it out!'

'What do you want, Sam?' I asked, hoping he didn't notice the wavering in my voice. He walked towards me, glancing at Tatum as I held him back. His barks were echoing around the walls next to the canal, and I wondered how long it would be before the police showed up. Sam stopped just short of the perimeter of Tatum's leash and stared at me with two twitching eyes.

'You still owe me, remember?' he said. It wasn't true at all, not in the slightest. 'Pay me what you owe, or I swear to God I'll throw him in the fucking canal.'

'I don't have anything on me.'

'You're lying!'

'I swear I don't,' I said. 'Just leave us alone, Sam.' His arm dropped to his side, and his voice suddenly changed to a whimper, which was even more terrifying.

'Haven't got anything, has he?' he began ranting to himself. 'Might be lying, might not. Has a big dog on a leash, doesn't he? Big hard man with a big dog.' He kicked the ground, flinging dirt and pebbles towards me and Tatum. Sam's sullen face suddenly fired into a glare again. I realised he was off his face – on spice, probably. Tatum was pulling forward relentlessly, and I realised that I was now holding him close enough for Sam to swing a boot at him.

Just as the thought crossed my mind, Sam threw it: a swinging arc which caught Tatum in the side of the face and landed with a smack that I was sure would have killed a person. And then, before I had time to react, he rushed at me.

I had just enough time to look at the rays of light falling off the bridge into the shadows underneath. In a way, none of it felt real. And yet this was real, my story, which was about to end in the most pointless of circumstances. *What a way to go*, I thought.

Sam gripped me by the shoulders. I managed to get a hold on his knife hand, gripped it as hard as I could, and simultaneously let go of the leash with my other hand. Tatum leapt forward and sunk his teeth into something. Then the three of us were scrapping at the edge of the canal, Sam's blade lunging in and out of view, both of our feet scraping on the floor as he tried to get his other arm around me.

I felt that nothing in my life had meant anything up to that point. That being depressed and not knowing what to do with my life were such petty little worries compared with fighting for real survival, with a brick wall on one side of me and the deep water on the other. In a moment or two I'd either be drowning in the canal or bleeding to death on the concrete. Sam was screaming at me to let go.

Finally, my strength gave way and his hand broke free. There was a sudden blurred movement near my face, the thud of the blade hitting flesh, and a frightened yelp. Then I struggled to get to my feet and saw Sam running along the length of the canal, disappearing out of view, his black tracksuit bottoms fading into the shadows further along the bridge.

Tony waited a second for Sam to get out of sight. The side of his face was starting to swell up where Sam had hit him. He came over, crouched down beside me and looked at my leg. There was a patch of blood on my jeans where I must have scraped my leg on the floor.

'I'm alright, mate,' I said, looking around for Tatum. I saw him lying on the floor with his tongue out, panting. 'Please, look after Tatum,' I said. I tried to stand up but my leg kept giving way.

'Never mind the f—' Tony started, but I grabbed him by his

jacket. 'Please!' I said again, and tried to crawl over to where Tatum was lying. The patch of blood on my jeans had grown to the size of an orange and I sat down on the floor again. Tatum stood up, slowly.

'I said never mind him,' Tony repeated, and I was in no shape to disagree. He carefully rolled up my trousers. I could see a river of thick blood running down my leg, while further up, the skin was moving against itself like an optical illusion. When I moved my foot in a certain way, the wound came apart and blood poured out of it enthusiastically. Tony took a rag out of his pocket and tied it around as best he could.

It took a minute for me to process what was going on. Tatum walked over to me slowly, and although he'd taken a boot clean to the face, I could see no real signs of him being hurt. He looked at me, whimpering, and I realised that the thud I had felt of Sam's knife plunging into flesh had been my own. The cut was a couple of inches deep, but the knife must have cut into the muscle, which simply refused to cooperate. Every time I tried to put weight on it, the whole thing gave way.

'Take my arm,' Tony said. 'Give it a minute. Now, take a step. Gentle. There we go.' He helped me along for a few steps, then up the stairs, away from the canal and back up to street level. Tatum was following behind with his leash trailing on the ground, and there were people looking at us as we emerged onto the pavement.

'Where are we going?' I asked.

'To the hospital.'

'Don't be daft. I'll be alright,' I protested.

'No, *you* don't be daft,' Tony said. 'You've got a deep cut, and I don't think my dirty rag is going to help it heal. You need to get it cleaned up and dressed.'

'What about Tatum?' I asked. I knew there was no way they would let him into Accident and Emergency. Tony let out a frustrated sigh. 'The dog. Of course,' he said. 'I tell you what. I'll look after him while you're in there.'

'Are you sure? You won't let him loose, will you?'

Tony laughed. 'I thought you trusted me by now?' he said. 'No, he'll be fine. Just this once, mind you. Don't think I'm taking up work as a dog-sitter any time soon.'

Every step was a slow, concerted effort which made my calf throb. Tony's makeshift dressing was soaked through with blood. The evening faded slowly into night. All I remember is endlessly walking beneath the orange glow of the street lights, with Tony helping me along, and the odd passer-by looking at us funny, as if to say *That's what you deserve for not getting a job.* I was losing my grip on reality, and I knew then that I had to get out of here before I got any more caught up in this life of poverty and grime. If you stayed here, you were certainly dead; it was just a case of when and how. I held on to Tony.

When we arrived at A&E I left him and limped in on my own. The room was full of people sitting on the benches under the pale white light, all of them turning to glance at me as the automatic doors opened and I staggered up to the front desk. I gave my name, and the receptionist asked me a few questions to update their records. She asked me to confirm my address, but I shook my head; they had the old address on file. I asked her to change it to 'no fixed abode'. She told me to sit down and wait for a while.

I found a quiet corner and focused on the deep, throbbing ache that was now pulsating through my leg. The other people waiting glanced over at me, but none of them wanted to make eye contact, apart from a little girl who kept staring at me. Her face was full of so many questions, and I didn't know many of the answers. I guessed she couldn't understand why my clothes were dirty or why my leg was bleeding or why I was sitting away from everybody else. And who could blame her?

The pain came back when I least expected it, abruptly reminding me that it wasn't all a dream. I waited in the hospital for a good two or three hours, losing track of time as I fidgeted around on the steel chairs, trying to find a comfortable position to rest my head in. When they called for me and I tried to stand up, the muscle spasmed and my leg nearly collapsed. I suddenly wondered about the bacteria on Sam's blade.

After the nurse had seen me through triage, the on-call doctor called me in, took Tony's rag off and bandaged the wound up properly. She was a lovely woman in her late thirties. As she dressed my leg, she gave some sympathetic *Mm-hmms* as I told her I hadn't seen who had stabbed me in the leg and answered her questions, as briefly as I could, about where I lived and what I got up to. She advised me to report the incident to the police, though I don't think she believed I would, and then finally she agreed to let me go with a packet of painkillers and a couple of spare bandages.

'I can't give you more than a packet, you understand,' she told me. 'If the pain gets bad and you've run out, you can see a GP out of hours. Here, I'll write the address down on a piece of paper for you.'

'Thank you,' I said. She smiled, contemplated my appearance for a second longer and then showed me out. I felt as though I had just experienced some supernatural power, someone pure and somehow immune from the moral judgements I had been dishing out about the rest of society. A doctor treated people no matter where they came from or what their background was – heroin addicts, terrorists, you name it. There was nothing more she could possibly have done for me; she was simply too busy.

When I got outside, Tony was long gone – and Tatum with him, I hoped. The street was empty and quiet, and the pain had started up properly around my calf muscle: a sharp, tearing feeling which radiated out whenever I put pressure on it. I tried to bear it for twenty minutes, but had only made it halfway back to town when I made for the painkillers. My throat was dry and I had nothing to drink but I chewed them up anyway, despite the foul taste, and sat down for a while on the street corner, waiting for them to kick in.

This was surely what rock bottom felt like. I watched the taxis driving up and down full of young people who had been on their nights out, all laughing and stumbling around together; the girls with short skirts and bare legs, the lads wearing T-shirts, all of them tanned and gelled and full of money, as far as I could tell. Further up towards town, they were jumping out of the taxis and queuing up at kebab shops and cash machines, sitting down on the kerb or throwing up in the corner. None of them even so much as looked at me.

I'd managed to cover up the bandages, but they left an awkward lump under my trousers. I was dreading the thought of removing them at some point to wash them out, but I knew at some point I'd have to. Then my thoughts turned to Sam, still roaming the streets and probably right back after me and Tony once he'd recovered. I had a feeling he wouldn't bother us for a few days at least, though, after what had happened.

Good boy, Tatum. He'd probably saved my life in the heat of it.

The night seemed to go on and on, one of those cold, echoing, pale kind of nights, and I was reminded of my first night sleeping rough just half a mile away from home. Once you lost your footing in life, you kept falling forever, it seemed, to places which made those that had once looked like the furthest you could fall seem like decent prospects.

And what about Tony? There was still a chance for me, but for him things would be like this forever.

When I finally got back to the canal it was silent, and they were both gone – or so I thought, until after sitting there for a moment I heard a quiet voice call out to me from the darkness. It took me a second to be sure I wasn't delirious. I heard it again, and then I found Tony in a dark little alcove around the corner. He must have decided to keep out of the way for tonight. There, next to him, was Tatum.

'So, you made it,' Tony said. He let Tatum go, who excitedly ran up to me and leapt up, licking my face.

'Good boy, Tatum! Get down, get down!' I said. I smiled at Tony, who sat down, clearly exhausted. In the gloom, I could just about make out the bruise spreading underneath his eye.

'How is it?' he asked, nodding at my leg. I rolled up my trousers to show him. The dressing had a damp, dark spot in the centre where the blood had seeped through. Tatum whimpered at me, his tail wagging. I sat down and patted him on the head to calm him down.

'I'll live,' I said, then paused for a moment. 'The bastard was trying to kill me.'

Tony laughed, taking me by surprise. 'And me. You're alright, you know, Cam. You're alright.'

With that, I put my head down and slept until the morning. My head was throbbing so much with tiredness that I couldn't even feel the cold that night, or hear the sound of the water lapping along the banks of the canal a few feet away.

8.

When I woke up, there was a scene I could barely adjust to. Somebody was kicking – well, nudging – me with their foot, and I shaded my eyes with my hands as I leant up to see what was happening. Two men stood there, telling me to wake up. I had a splitting headache and I didn't understand what on earth was going on.

'Keep the dog on its leash, alright?' said one of the men. The sun was in my eyes, but I could see their black silhouettes standing wide-legged between me and the canal. 'Now get up slowly.'

I staggered to my feet, and the leg threatened to give way completely. Only now did I realise that somebody had managed to bother us without Tatum raising all hell. He must have still been concussed from Sam's boot the day before.

I got my footing and looked at the two men. They were police officers. I suddenly felt sick to my stomach. The police always left us alone if we stayed out of sight, down here by the canal. The two of them eyed me up warily. I noticed they were keeping their distance from me.

'What's the matter?' I asked. The body language of the coppers was tense, as though they were ready for a big confrontation. The whole situation felt dangerous; I wished I could calm them down, because there was really no need for it. Tony had just woken up, and the policemen asked him to step away – a command which he ignored. My brain was doing overtime trying to work out what exactly was going on and how to defuse the situation.

'What do you know about an incident that happened last night?' one of them said to me. I started to panic. Clearly, they knew about Sam. If I told them anything, Tony and I would be in much bigger trouble with him than we were already.

'I don't know anything,' I said. The two of them looked at each other, and then another couple of officers came down the stairs. Tony was flashing worried looks at me. We had our backs to the corner of the alcove, with nowhere to go.

'Is that your animal?' the second one asked.

'Yes,' I said. 'Well, in a way,' I added, and immediately regretted doing so. Trying to answer their questions felt like tying your own noose. Tatum barked, probably feeling the growing tension of the situation, and the policemen who were closest drew their batons and told me to calm him down.

'Shh, boy, Tatum. Stop,' I told him.

'There's been reports of an incident down here last night. Somebody bitten by a dog, says it was yours,' one of them said. The truth hit me all at once. It hit me like a knife to the stomach, and I started shaking my head, pushing Tatum behind me.

'No, listen,' Tony said, 'you've got it all wrong. We were the ones who were attacked last night. Show him your leg, Cam.'

I knelt down and pulled up my trouser leg, but the coppers looked on apathetically, both they and I part of the same process which was already ticking down to its inevitable conclusion. My legs started to tremble. There was a barrier here that I couldn't climb over, or run from, or break, like a tsunami threatening to wash us all away.

'You can't do this,' I said.

'Are you saying it *was* your dog, then, last night?'

'You don't understand. Someone tried to kill me, he was trying to throw me in the canal,' I said. 'Tatum would never hurt anyone.'

'Do you know you could be prosecuted under the Dangerous Dogs Act for harbouring an illegal breed?' the second one said. I had no idea about dog breeds. They could have been making it up, for all I knew.

'Look, I got stabbed last night. You can check at the Royal Infirmary,' I said. 'Someone tried to kill me! Why are you going after the wrong person?'

'If that's correct, then you'll need to make a report — we can do that down at the station,' said the policeman. 'But for now, we're going to have to ask you to bring your dog to the van. Do it calmly, and nobody will get hurt.'

'Please,' I said, 'what do you want with us? Just leave us alone.'

'Listen, Cameron,' he replied; I had no idea how he knew my name. 'We're giving you a chance to do this quietly. We'll take you down to the station and get to the bottom of all this. But if you don't comply, we'll be forced to bring someone down here and shoot him. And you could end up facing prison time.' The pit of my stomach was turning over and over. Tony stood silently by, looking at me as though trying to tell me something telepathically, but the helplessness had overcome us both. I stuttered and tried to play for time. One of the officers started to speak into his radio again.

'Wait! Stop! I'll do it. Please,' I said. The policemen stepped aside to make room for me, but my feet were fixed to the spot. Tears streamed down my face. They were waiting. Slowly, I took Tatum's leash and walked him past the police officers, up the stairs and around the corner.

Tatum gazed up at me with his usual look: *Where are we going today?*

As if to answer him, there was a police van parked with the doors open and another officer standing by the side. The back of the van was caged, and Tatum stopped for a minute when we got to the doors. He looked at me again, confused and unwilling.

'Come on, boy,' I said. 'It's going to be alright. Come on.' He didn't budge, and the officer by the van looked at me impatiently. 'Please, Tatum,' I said, but when I realised he wasn't going anywhere I had to stoop down to grab him around the belly and heave him up onto the floor of the van. When he saw the cage he pushed back, resisting me as I threw my weight behind him and forced him inside. Then, as his feet gave way and he stumbled inside, the officer at my side quickly leapt forward and slammed the door shut.

Tatum leapt against the wire, barking. The rest of the officers were coming up the stairs, with Tony following them at a distance. Tatum was howling at me and the officer, and after they closed the doors to the van I could still hear him throwing himself against the sides of the cage. The bangs echoed inside the van.

The policemen came at me from all angles at once.

'Put your hands behind your back for me, please,' one of them said. I numbly complied, the cold steel pressing against my wrists with a sudden, resolute click. The policemen were saying something to me, but in my mind I was already somewhere else, somewhere far away from here, and Tatum was with me. We were walking across a great plain, with herds grazing far off in the distance. It was late afternoon, and as evening drew in we'd light a fire to sleep next to, down by the lake, and we would rise with the sun and walk together through the morning mist.

Around the corner, another police car was waiting, its lights flashing in silence. 'You can't do this,' I said, but they marched me to the back of the car and put me inside. The car followed the van out of there and down the road.

They didn't speak to me until we got to the station. We drove through a set of electric gates at the side of the building, and the car stopped, but the van carried on. I watched it drive through a set of garage doors around the back; it disappeared inside and the doors closed behind it. That was the last time I ever saw Tatum, disappearing through the gates at the police station in that unmarked van, and the sight of it driving away was one I was sure I'd remember for the rest of my life.

One of the officers turned to me. 'Right, let's get this over and done with.'

Shortly afterwards, in a white-walled reception area, with the air-conditioning turned up too far, a burly policeman and his colleague took my details and filled in a form, which they handed to the receptionist. I was taken into an interrogation room, where I waited some fifteen or twenty minutes before the two of them returned and sat down opposite me. I stared at them head on.

'Hello, Cameron,' the lead officer said. He had a hard face

which was clean-shaven, and his eyes were impenetrable. 'You say you ran away from home, and you've been living on the streets for nine months, is that right?'

I shrugged. 'Give or take, yes.'

'Been in any contact with your family?'

'No. I don't see how that's any of your business, though. As I tried to explain before, I was attacked. My friend, too – have you spoken with him yet? He'll confirm everything I'm saying. I—'

'We've not had any reports from your family of you being missing. Why do you think that is?' He glanced at his colleague, who gave him a congratulatory look.

I did not have time to deal with any of this. 'Beats me. Why don't you ask them?' I needed to get out of here. 'Can we just get on with this quickly? I don't need a sympathy party.'

The policeman looked again at his friend, who shrugged. 'Alright,' he said. 'We'll need a statement from you. *If* your story turns out to be true, you'll be free to go. If, on the other hand, any evidence emerges that your dog was involved in attacking an unarmed passer-by, you could be facing prosecution under the Dangerous Dogs Act, as well as potentially assault and actual bodily harm. Do you understand?'

'Perfectly,' I said, numbly.

'Do you have a contact telephone number?'

I nodded and scribbled my mobile number at the bottom of the blank witness statement form on which I now had to justify the existence of Tatum and myself against the word of a lying rogue like Sam. The scariest part was that I didn't know which of us the authorities would rather believe. Somebody like Sam was consistent – a bad 'un, the epitome of a villainous character, like Bill Sikes – and the police probably had a lot of dealings with him. A kind of Stockholm syndrome developed, I had noticed, over time between the worst of society and the people who had to deal with them on a daily basis.

Who was I, though? Someone not good enough to be redeemable, but not evil enough to be admirable? I sighed with defeat. The officers got up from their chairs and turned to leave.

I stood up, too. 'Excuse me,' I said. 'But what about Tatum? I understand you need to do your investigations, but after that . . . ?'

The policeman nearest the door turned and gave me a look, and his colleague did likewise. It struck me as odd for a moment, because it looked as though they were preparing for a confrontation again, and I couldn't think of any reason why there might be one.

'I'm afraid, regardless of whether you were attacked or not, your unregistered dog was responsible for biting somebody,' he said. My face felt as heavy as stone. 'It's already been sent to be destroyed.'

'Destroyed? Does it help you sleep better at night, calling it that?' I said. My hands were trembling.

'You understand, we can't take the risk of letting a dangerous animal back out onto the streets. Once you've completed your statement, bring it back to the reception desk, and we'll arrange for you to be released for the time being.'

'You've killed the one thing I cared about,' I said.

He paused for a moment, ready to leave. I could feel the tears building up behind my face, and it took all of my strength to hold them back. What was I supposed to do now?

'If I were you, I'd get back in touch with your family. Try to find a place to stay. Sort your life out. I hope we won't see you back here again.' The two of them walked out of the room, and the door closed behind them.

The silence surrounded me like a wall of steel, and at last I couldn't hold it back any longer. I cried for Tatum, my tears falling onto the blank sheet of paper and discolouring it in small, damp circles, my chest heaving with quiet sobs.

After a while I felt calm again. I wrote as little and as factually as I could about what had happened. I gave a description of Sam and of the doctor who had seen to me in the hospital, and then I left.

Some time later I found myself back out on the street, alone. I wandered away from it all; away from the city centre, away from life itself, past the faded brickwork, the wind picking up and rattling the broken shutters of the takeaway shops. I'd lost track of what day it was, and something seemed lost forever – not just to me, it seemed, but to everyone. You could call it the sense of direction, the hope of man going to the moon, the dream of world peace . . . or maybe it *was* just me, after all, with no sense of belonging on 150 million square miles of planet Earth.

I stumbled into one of the shops. There were people lining up at the checkout to buy cans of beer and packets of cigarettes. I bought a box of plasters and a bottle of antiseptic, then withdrew all the money I had left from a cash machine in the corner. I stuffed the notes inside my shirt and zipped my jacket up again.

With what I had left, I stepped into the future. It wasn't much: a couple of hundred pounds, a phone for emergencies, a toothbrush, a change of clothes and a sleeping bag. Twenty years of dead weight had been cut loose and allowed to sail on down the river. I hoped to Christ it would never find its way back to me.

The only regret I had was not saying goodbye to Tony. He was a good man – good enough, anyway – and I didn't know whether I would have made it this far without him. I struggled with the thought of going back down to the canal to say thank you, at least, but in the end, I couldn't do it. It would mean facing everything again. I hoped he would understand.

The city was the same as ever, but the steady hum of its machinery was fading in my head. Manchester, a place that kept going even as it broke you, over and over again, still hopeful even in all of its imperfection, still dreaming of something better. Sirens echoed in the distance of the night. I could see the outline of the Hilton Hotel, its solitary red light blinking across the top of the city. I was already making ground. I crossed the motorway and kept going, one foot after the other, past the estates and the houses with their curtains shut, through parks and under underpasses. I felt light on my feet, and I knew I would keep walking until morning.

PART TWO

9.

This was how things had to be, eventually. For every day I'd spent running away from my existential problems, for my failure to act decisively, for the ten pounds I'd stolen from Jenny, I was severely owing. And after nine months living a less-than-proper existence on the streets of Manchester, I'd arrived at a dead end. Tony was right: there was no soul on earth who could provide me with an answer except myself. I didn't know where the road ahead of me would lead, but I knew that whatever road I took would be a long one.

Somewhere between Levenshulme and Stockport, I fell into some luck. A van driver stopped at a set of traffic lights and shouted something at me across the street. I ignored him and carried on walking, but when the traffic lights turned green, he pulled over to the side of the road after the junction, just in front of me and tried again. 'Where are you going to, mate?'

He must have seen me walking a while back. Though he didn't look as if he was going to feature on University Challenge any time soon, his face was pleasant enough, and the van was modern and clean. 'Come on, hop in,' he called out. The bus driver behind him was beeping his horn. Quickly, I made my mind up and climbed into the passenger seat.

'Where are you off to then, exactly?' he asked as we pulled off the kerb. The air in the van was warm and slightly stale. The radio featured a pundit talking about a football match from the other day, and the driver turned it down so we could speak.

'I'm going to London,' I said, 'if I can.'

'I see. You have mates down there or something?'

'Something like that, yes.' I didn't feel like discussing much with a stranger.

'You won't get there today, I suppose.'

'No. It doesn't really matter, though. I can look after myself.'

'I can see that. I can take you as far as Birmingham, anyway. After that you'll have to sort yourself out. Is that OK for you?'

'Yes, that'd be more than fine, thank you,' I said. Then, not wanting to create an awkward silence, I asked what Birmingham was like.

'Shithole. Just like here, really. Do you want one?' he replied, holding out an open packet of cigarettes. I shook my head but he lit one for himself, ash falling onto the seat and smearing onto the gearstick as he drove. I realised, as I watched the city fade out of view in the mirror, that I might never see Manchester again. All those places and people were far away from me now. I marvelled at how long it would have taken me to have walked this far.

'What is it you do?' I asked.

'Deliveries, you know, for companies and that.'

In the back of my mind, I remembered I was supposed to be waiting for the conclusion of the police investigation. I thought about sirens and helicopters. In a minute, I thought I would see roadblocks up ahead; the whole *Daily Mail*-led fascistic regime come to put a stop to whatever spiritual excursion I was trying to embark on.

'Actually, go on then,' I said, gesturing at the cigarettes. He passed the packet to me and I slipped one out and put it in my mouth. I laughed for a moment as he held the lighter out to me, and I watched the end of it trembling in front of me. Home was far behind me now, but I was still a long way from feeling free.

On the way the driver told me about his job, and his ex-wife, how he used to work down in Bristol a lot before Amazon took over and sapped all the jobs off the smaller companies. I nodded, but for some reason I was thinking of the scene in *The Matrix* where Morpheus tells Neo that anybody still within the system is an enemy. After a while, we stopped at some services for petrol. The driver came back five minutes later with a McDonald's coffee and a cheeseburger.

'Here you go, mate. You look as though you need it.' I nodded gratefully, noticing for the first time in a while that I was really, really hungry. 'We'll be in Birmingham in about twenty minutes. Where did you want dropping off?'

I hadn't really thought about it until now. 'I don't know,' I said. 'Somewhere near the centre?'

'I'll try my best,' he said cheerfully.

We arrived in the centre of town and merged into a flood of cars. The city itself didn't look much different to the one I'd just left. There were blocks of flats and shopping centres, churches and kebab shops. Finally, after a busy intersection, the driver pulled over onto the pavement with a thump.

'Thanks,' I said, grabbing my bag and hopping out of the van. The pain in my leg – which I'd temporarily forgotten about

— came shooting back all of a sudden, and it took me a minute to compose myself, taking in large lungfuls of breath. The van driver looked me over with some concern. He unfastened his seatbelt and leant across.

'You OK from here, mate?'

'I'll be fine. Thanks for the lift.'

'Here,' he said, leaning over, 'you can get a Megabus from over there the rest of the way to London. That should cover it.'

'You've already been a massive help, honestly,' I said.

'Don't be daft. Here.' He thrust a ten-pound note into my hand, and I stuffed it away quickly in a pocket. 'Best of luck,' he said, and with that he started the engine again and pulled out into the flow of traffic.

I lifted my bag onto my shoulders and looked around. A few shops along, I saw a fellow sitting in a sleeping bag, his woollen hat pulled down over his eyes, an empty cup on the street beside him. People walked by without turning their heads.

Well that was England for you. Or at least, it was the England I knew.

I found the bus station around the corner. The ticket to London cost eight pounds, but the bus itself didn't depart for a couple of hours. I picked up a copy of the *Metro* and read it for a while on one of the benches. There were pigeons nesting between the spikes in the alcove above. Opposite me, a young woman was looking after a little boy in a pram. I smiled at her, and she gave me a stern look. I wondered what I would do when I got to London.

The question answered itself almost immediately: I'd keep moving. I had at least another twelve hours of energy left in me before I collapsed, and more than anything, my desire was to cross the sea. Then I could say farewell to all the brick walls and alleyways, and feel the breeze weave its way through the trees. I could see ancient woods and white sandy bays. That, at least, was my intention. I had to draw a line under the past, and I knew I could only do that by letting go of everything I had ever known.

On the bus I daydreamed, watching the open fields and farmhouses pass by the window. It became dark. There were not many people on the bus, and the night-time gave the journey an eerie feel. My head and neck ached from sitting uncomfortably. At some point I must have fallen asleep, because I woke as we came into the outskirts of London. There were taxis everywhere, and people milling around on the pavements. It was around half past eleven at night.

As we approached the city centre, I pulled myself off the squashed seat fabric and waited for the bus to arrive at the station. When we finally stopped at Victoria, I queued to get off and stepped out into the cool night air. The other passengers collected suitcases from the luggage compartment and disappeared into waiting taxis or cars.

I wandered around the bus station. The bus for Dover would be setting off at nine the following morning. Short of ideas, I found the toilets and washed my face in the sink. I could barely recognise myself in the mirror any more. My face had become buried under a deep-set stubble, and there were dark circles underneath my eyes. I decided to look for a shop where I could find some food for the trip ahead.

Making a careful note of the station so I could find it again, I set off wandering the streets of London. It was a different place here, for sure, and I felt slightly out of my depth. There were plenty of shops nearby, though. I found a Sainsbury's and bought myself a couple of bottles of water, some packets of instant soup and a tin of corned beef. I gazed longingly at a couple of hotels I passed, and sat down on a bench next to Eaton Square Gardens for a while.

Tentatively, I lay down and tried to sleep, but the terror of being alone in a dimly lit park in London was too much for me. After half an hour of it, I moved again. Not wandering too far for fear of getting lost, I eventually found a quiet corner behind a tenement building. I was reminded of my first night away from home. It felt colder than the nights had for a long while; I realised it was because Tatum wasn't around any more.

In the early hours of the morning I ate the corned beef straight out of the tin, navigated my way back to the bus station and sat down to wait for the nine o'clock bus to Dover. Some time passed, and a few other passengers arrived.

Just then, I heard a strange noise coming from my backpack, and I realised my phone was ringing. I rummaged around for it, glanced at the unrecognisable number on the screen, and answered.

'Hello, can I speak to Cameron, please?'

'Who is this?'

'My name's Vicky. I'm calling about the job you applied for at our Manchester offices?' I did not recall having applied for any job. Even worse, I had no idea where the woman had got hold of my phone number.

'Which job is it, sorry?'

She explained that the company was a Manchester-based estate agency. 'You applied for an admin vacancy here a few days ago. We'd like to invite you to interview later in the week. How is Thursday for you?'

I held back my laughter as my brain tried to work out what was going on. There was no possibility they'd got the wrong Cameron with my telephone number. I had not caught the name of the company Jenny worked for, but I did recall it was an estate agent. Could she have put in an application on my behalf?

The mystery would have to wait for another day.

'I'm really sorry,' I said. The bus driver had started the engine, and people were queuing up to get on. 'But I won't be available on Thursday, actually. I've . . . taken up another offer.'

The woman on the other end seemed puzzled. 'I see. Sorry for troubling you. Have a great day.' She hung up.

I stood up and scratched my head. The bus driver was smoking a cigarette next to the open door. I stowed my bag in the luggage compartment underneath the bus, and got on.

The traffic out of London wasn't bad, and the bus made good speed. It left the city behind and sped onto the motorway, through the flat, green countryside, and it wasn't long until I saw signs for Dover out of the window.

The sea air hit me first, coming up the hill from the port at the bottom of the cliffs, and then I heard the horn of a ship heading out into the blue. It was less than half a mile's walk to the port from where the bus had dropped me. There were rows of cars and lorries queuing up at the freight entrance. I could see a ship in the harbour. I pulled my bag straps up and walked down the hill towards the port entrance.

10.

The road from the village of Saint Laurent was lined on either side by trees with painted white trunks, and fields of grass and potatoes with deep forests behind them, and the odd dirt path which led up to a small farmhouse or ran out of sight behind the trees to places unknown. Though the road was well used, there was not so much traffic that it was unpleasant to walk along; but the speed limit was 80 kph, and the cars and lorries often flew past in a roar, without stopping.

I could hear the sound of church bells coming from the small, shallow, tree-covered hills; nestled in among them were small villages and hamlets, connected by smaller roads. I walked along the road from the village I had just passed through, and after a quarter of a mile or so I stopped for a drink of water. I sat in the shade of a chestnut tree, away from the road. The blisters on my feet were aching. I took my socks off and allowed them to dry out in the breeze.

While they did so, I took out my notebook. It had been sitting in the bottom confines of my bag since Manchester until, somewhere halfway between Dover and Calais, I had decided in a sudden frenzy to write about everything that had happened – from the encounter with Jenny in Piccadilly

Gardens, via Tatum and our run-in with Sam, through to walking out of Manchester that fateful evening, after the police station. I took out the notepad from my bag, my head all full of it and raring to go, before realising I didn't have a pen. I looked around the deck I was sitting on. There were families and some people on their own, some toing and froing and some sitting looking out of the windows. Finally, I spotted a half-completed crossword puzzle on a table next to a woman in her mid-forties.

'Excuse me? Do you mind if I borrow your pen?' I asked, gesturing to my notepad. 'I need to write something down, if that's OK.'

The lady looked at me and smiled. 'Not a problem, help yourself,' she said. I sat opposite her and paused for a moment.

'What are you writing?' she asked.

'A letter to my parents,' I lied. I started and tried to get down as much of it as I could. The lady looked on with interest, but I decided not to engage in further conversation. She would want to know who I was and where I was going, and the trickiest thing about that would be that I didn't know the answers myself. I lost my train of thought and thought about Tony again, and whether Sam would get hold of him again. Somehow, I felt sure he would be OK. People like Tony had ways of surviving, miraculous means of keeping going while everybody else around them . . . the boat lurched slightly. I felt like I was about to be sick.

'Here you go,' I said, handing the woman back her pen.

She smiled at me. 'Thank you, but you can keep it. You might want to add something else later.'

'Thanks. That's very kind.' I turned to leave.

'Where are you from?' she asked.

'Manchester.' It felt strange to say it. I felt no more a Mancunian than I did an English person, or even a human being, at this point in time. I was painfully reminded that while you could change where you were going, you couldn't change where you were from. Could you?

'I thought so. I could tell by the accent,' she said. 'I'm sorry, I don't mean to intrude, but are you alright? I can usually tell when somebody is at the end of their tether.'

I laughed. 'Thank you, but I'm really fine. At least, I think so. I'll be happier once my feet are back on dry land.'

She smiled and nodded, and I left the compartment to look over the railings at the open sea.

It was quite a view. There was a big liner some distance away on the horizon, and I could make out the shape of the English shoreline slipping away behind me. Something had stirred within me. You could call it a death wish, and you wouldn't be too far from the truth of the matter. I dreamt of mountains and deserts and forests going on forever. It was as though all of my life had been building up to this final, spectacular half hour, and it would be flying-by-the-seat-of-your-pants stuff right up to the end; a Hollywood blockbuster, the big finale.

That was my frame of mind as I had crossed the sea.

An hour or so must have passed now, and the traffic on the road outside Saint Laurent was starting to build up. I had been daydreaming. Under the trees, away from the road, it was calm and comfortable and there were all the signs of life: flies buzzing around, insects and beetles crawling through the grass, and birds singing high up in the trees. A few cars passed by on the road while I hastily scribbled down a few more notes.

It had been ten days since I'd arrived in Calais. If it was warmer here, I didn't notice it. The nights were long, cold affairs in my sleeping bag, and during the day I travelled further south. What was I doing? I had something close to a hundred pounds to last the rest of my life, and my feet were already starting to blister.

I tucked the pad away in my bag, fastened my shoelaces and stood up. My bag was getting heavier, and hauling it up onto my shoulders took a big effort. My back seemed to ache permanently since I had arrived in France. I made my way back to the road and waited for the next car to come around the corner.

It came from the village not long after, an old blue Citroën with a couple of old-looking farmers sitting in the front. It must have been doing no more than thirty. I stuck out my thumb, then watched the driver glance at me and say something to his friend as they crawled past me and disappeared around the next bend. The sound of the engine faded away and was replaced once more by the chirping of the birds.

Until a week ago I had never known about hitch-hiking, except for what I'd seen in American films about serial killers and young wayward teens. I don't think I had ever seen a hitch-hiker in Britain, but on my second day in France I'd seen a young couple sticking their thumbs out at the cars passing by; they were picked up in under an hour. It seemed like people did this sort of thing in Europe. So I waited, cheerfully. The next car to come along pulled up beside me; the driver, an old man with a short white beard and a flat cap, wound his window down to ask me where I was going.

'Bonjour,' I said. My French sounded right out of an *Only*

Fools and Horses special. He gave a dry smile and shook his head at me.

'No Anglais, no English,' he said.

'*Direction à la Marseille?* Are you going to Marseille?' I tried to ask.

He sighed and shook his head again, forced the old gearstick of the car forward with a crunch and pulled away, leaving behind a trail of exhaust fumes. I turned back towards the village and waited as the sun rose higher in the sky.

Beep! Beep-beep!

I turned around. The old man had come to a stop about twenty metres further down the road. He was sounding his horn loudly, but it took my brain a minute to click into gear. I grabbed my bag off the floor and jogged towards him. The car's reversing lights came on and he came back towards me in a cloud of pebbles and dust. I arrived at the passenger side, panting.

'*Allez-vous a Marseille? Le sud?*' the man asked. I nodded, catching my breath. He gestured at me to get in. I opened the door and hauled myself, backpack and all, into the passenger seat. The man nodded, smiling at me with brown teeth, and we set off again. The car was full of cigarette smoke, and there were paper bags of vegetables – potatoes and cabbages, by the looks of it – stacked on the back seat.

I wound down the window a couple of inches and felt the breeze on my face. It felt good to be moving again. I knew enough French to thank the driver. Instead of saying anything, he offered me a cigarette from a packet on the dashboard. I took it gratefully.

'*Je ne peux pas te prendre le chemin,*' the man said. I didn't have a clue what he meant, but he smiled and continued. '*Je peux vous emmener vers Montpellier.*' I could only assume we were heading the right way. *Le Sud:* the South.

The road took us through a series of small hills. I inhaled a lungful of smoke and looked out of the window at modest farmhouses with little French cars parked outside, newer houses with clean brick walls and electric gates, patched-up cottages that had weathered many winters and looked as though they'd fall down at any moment. The old man didn't speak much, but he seemed pretty comfortable. Every now and then he hummed a tune, or said something to me in French and waited for me to react. I tried to smile or laugh or nod when I felt it was appropriate.

I had no idea where we were going, but I hoped the weather would be warmer the further south I travelled, so my goal was to reach Marseille on the Mediterranean coast. The hills grew steeper and the car struggled up some of the inclines; we were overtaken a couple of times by other cars, and even once by a lorry. Then the road descended again, and the small road we were on joined a dual carriageway which led straight down towards a couple of towns in the distance.

At the next junction, we pulled off the road onto the gravel, and the old man gestured down the road to me.

'*Le chemin de Montpellier,*' he said. 'Marseille, after.'

'*Merci,* thank you,' I said. I understood well enough what the man meant. I climbed out of the door and picked up my bag.

'*Voilà,*' said the man, tipping his cap to me as I shut the door. He pulled back onto the road and turned off at the junction, headed in some other direction.

I sat down and drank the last dregs of water I had. It was

lunchtime, and I was starting to feel hungry. In front of me the road carried on straight, and in the distance I could see the town I assumed must be Montpellier.

Further along the road, maybe a kilometre or two away, I could make out a petrol station. A lorry whistled past me in the direction of the town. I looked around for a minute and decided to walk for it. Walking here was more of a mental challenge than anything else. The roads seemed to go on forever, and my feet complained furiously each time I placed one in front of the other. I had stuffed tissue paper into my shoes to cushion where the skin had been rubbed raw, but the backs of my heels still felt as though they were on fire.

After a while I got to the petrol station. The lone teller sitting in the kiosk looked at me as I walked around the side to fill up my water bottle from the tap, then watched me leave again.

I passed the first buildings, which marked the beginning of the town: worn-down houses with walled gardens with dogs or chickens, and washing hanging on the line. If I carried on the way I was heading, I assumed I would reach the town centre. I caught sight of some factories running parallel to the street I was on, and having started to get a sense for the way French towns were laid out, I headed towards them. On the outskirts of town you could usually find a supermarket or two, and as I turned the next bend I saw it: a white, glistening building stood out from the industrial buildings I was walking past. It was a Carrefour.

Inside was quiet, not like the bustling aisles of Morrison's or Asda back home but cool and large and open. I walked straight past the fruit and vegetables I couldn't afford – kept clean and glistening with a constant spray of mist – and instead bought a baguette, a small block of cheese, and a couple of wafer chocolate bars from the discounted aisles. At the till I dumbly waited for the checkout girl to tally up the bill. She smiled at me sympathetically as I handed over a couple of euros, then gave me the change.

Outside, I made myself a sandwich and ate it on a concrete step overlooking the car park. All of my meals were lonely now that I had left Tony behind, and the people walked past without looking over at me. Still, there was no point feeling sorry for myself. I had to eat.

After packing up I set off again, staying close to the outskirts of town while I looked for the highway which surely must lie on the other side, towards Marseille. I must have walked for an hour before my feet gave in again. I had passed a road which went north and eventually cut through the mountains to Geneva, but it had taken much longer than I'd anticipated to get to the other side of Montpellier.

There were blisters forming everywhere: on the side of my foot near the heel, on the bottom of my big toe on the other foot, and a few on the backs of my ankles that were smaller but hurt the most. Finally, the pain was too much to bear walking on. I sat down to take off my shoes and socks carefully.

There was not a chance I could carry on walking today. I patched my feet up as best I could and put my shoes back on loosely. Limping a little, I took a road heading away from town and climbed up a small hill which led into the trees. Below, nestled in between two steep inclines, was a factory of some sort, with people working out in the yard.

At the top of the hill I cut into the treeline, away from the road. There was a chain-link fence which went around the perimeter of the factory and blocked it off from the forest; I traced it, looking for a gap, and when I found one I squeezed through, catching my coat for a moment before managing to free myself. Along the top of here I found a flat clearing, with the woods sitting behind me. It was out of sight from the path, and it was a place nobody in their right mind would really think to go.

I laid my bag down, opened it up and took out my tent. It was a cheap one I'd bought in Bourges, and I had still not learned to put it up properly. I fed in the two poles through the sleeves and propped it up, pegged the outside into the soft ground and placed my sleeping bag inside. The tent looked flimsy, but it would do the job.

From here I could see the customers leaving the building below and driving off back towards the town or out towards Grenoble. I sat outside to eat a bit more bread and drink some water. I thought more than once about lighting a fire, but the risk of attracting attention made me decide against it.

I waited for a while on a fallen log, alone with my thoughts, until the workers shut up shop for the day and left. Finally it was quiet and I was alone. If you'd looked at me from afar, you might think I was comfortable up there on my own, but in reality nothing could have been further from the truth. I was worried about my vanishing funds and the zero sense I had of where I was going or what I would do when I got there, and the hours I spent alone in silence seemed to last forever. Somewhere off in the distance, a dog barked, as if at me, and reminded me once more of Tatum. At least up here things felt honest. I felt better off alone in the woods than I had done trying to cling on to society in the city.

I wrote down the details of the day's journey in my notepad and watched the sun set behind the buildings opposite my camp. The factory glowed orange in the fiery light and cast its long shadow across the car park below. As the evening set in, the cold came quickly and the mosquitoes started to whine around my head; it only took a couple of bites to drive me into the tent for the rest of the night.

11.

In the morning I reached the highway early and hitched a ride with an early-morning van driver to Aix-en-Provence. Moving so quickly from one town to another kept my mind off thinking backwards, and instead I kept focused on my next ride towards Marseille. I walked a kilometre or two to the next slip road and repeated the process. Luckily, I didn't have to wait for too long.

I was picked up shortly after by a couple in a little black hatchback; it stank of cannabis, but I was grateful for any lift I could get. The man was in his late twenties, wearing a baseball cap and tracksuit that made him look like some of the scallies back home. The mixed-race girl in the passenger seat must have been his girlfriend. She had braids in her hair and a face that reminded me slightly of Jennifer Lopez.

It became clear very quickly that the two of them were high as kites. They kept asking me questions in broken English and laughing at my answers. We sped down the highway to Marseille with French hip-hop playing, switching lanes this way and that, undertaking and overtaking. I held on to the door handle and tried not to be sick.

'Are you a student, no?' the girl turned around to ask. Her

boyfriend was studying me in the rear-view mirror.

'No,' I replied.

'Working?' she asked.

I shook my head.

'Where are you going?' the man asked.

'To Marseille,' I said.

'Why?' asked the girl.

'Why not?'

The two of them looked at each other and laughed again.

'It's dangerous to travel on your own,' the boyfriend said in the mirror.

I said nothing.

'Do you have any money?' asked the girl.

'No,' I said, but then had a sudden change of heart; it was better to be believable than an obvious liar. 'Well, a little.'

The girl nodded, and the boyfriend gave me a full-toothed smile.

'You're crazy,' he said. 'You will like Marseille, I think. It's full of crazy people.' He took out the CD that had been playing and changed it for another from the glove compartment. The beat started off and it made me laugh. It was 'Straight Outta Compton' by NWA. He turned, saw me grinning, and nodded with approval.

The highway to Marseille passed through some rough-looking areas with graffiti spray-painted on the underpasses. I saw gangs of lads playing football in cages, and schools which looked as though they'd feature in a film about young teens, alcoholic parents and drugs. As we neared the tollbooth on the highway, the driver passed his girlfriend a small green packet. She tucked it away in her bra.

The journey from Montpellier had given me time to think about what I was going to do next. As I saw it, there were two options. Going west would bring me, eventually, to Spain. From there, I would have to find a way through Barcelona or Madrid to reach the south coast, and scrape enough money together to board a ferry to Morocco. But from there, I didn't know what I could possibly hope to achieve. The trip through the desert was too daunting; every step would put me further into danger, increasing my chances of getting killed by terrorists, wild animals, disease or thirst. The alternative was to head east through Italy. Eventually, this would bring me out in the Balkans, and from there I could follow the roads south to Greece.

The climate and the openness of this option had a lot more appeal. Of course, there was the option of going north through Germany or Poland, but I knew I would eventually reach a dead end and have to traipse all the way back.

East meant, technically, a journey with no end. From Europe you could cross the land bridge to Turkey and then keep going, like Alexander the Great, until you reached India or even somewhere further afield, like China or Tibet. I wanted to keep moving until I found some quiet frontier where I could discover whether or not there was a God. It was as though my entire genetic code was screaming out for it; that thousands of years of evolution were telling me to get the hell away from civilisation and cut loose, like those first tribes who set off on their own across the Bering Strait, or who cast off in their canoes to discover Hawaii.

The couple dropped me just off the main highway, near a suburb close to the port. Up the hill, away from the road, there was a path which led up to some houses. The buildings were worn-down three- and four-storey tenements, and the community was quite evidently North African. There were children playing on the streets; their mothers wore headdresses, the men robes with rounded skullcaps. A few of them turned and stared, and I wondered if they'd ever seen a white person on this side of town before. I turned onto the main street and walked along it. There were a few stray cats hanging around in the alleyways.

This wasn't the direction I needed to be going in, but I was hungry. Around the corner I came to a small shop – more of a stall, really – which sold bread and some fruit. The man who ran it had a worn, bearded face that wasn't quite symmetrical. I pointed to a loaf of bread and handed him the money. He started signalling to me as though I hadn't given him enough. I wasn't sure what he meant until he came out from behind the stall, put four oranges in a bag, handed it to me and nodded. I thanked him gratefully, slightly mystified, and went around the back of the buildings to sit down and eat.

That was the first time anyone had been truly charitable to me, and I was immensely grateful. I could see the port from here, full of cranes and industrial buildings, and some tower blocks perched on the hill on the far side of the highway. I ate an orange and half the loaf of bread and put the rest away.

It was around twelve and I was already starting to feel the heat on the top of my forehead. I had a spring in my step down the hill, despite the blisters, and I made good ground cutting through the quiet industrial estates to make my way to the port. I passed cranes loading things out of boats and into ferries, men working, lorries pulling out of yards and driving up the main road onto the highway.

An hour later, and my feet once again felt like I was walking on hot coals. I stopped to take off my shoes for the second time in two days. My socks were sticking to the raw skin, and when I pulled the first one off the pain was enough to make me hop around, cursing, on the empty street. I took the second sock off with gritted teeth, to inspect the damage. The loose dead skin looked foreign, and I gently pulled some of it away to reveal bleeding, raw flesh underneath.

Carrying on walking like this was going to put me out of action for days, maybe even weeks. I held my head in my hands. It was bad enough not to have enough money left to rest, but even worse to have reached the south of France and be thwarted by something as simple as sore feet. I didn't know if I could get healthcare here if things got any worse, but I didn't even want to contemplate the possibility right now. I was about half a mile from the city centre, where there were bandages, creams – even foot massages, if you wanted them – but everything would cost money I didn't have.

I remembered Tony showing me his feet once, the soles hardened like leather, and I made a promise to myself that I wasn't giving up so close to home, because I wanted to keep hold of my money. I also decided the time to hold back from spending the remainder of my money for fear of 'cheating' was over. I had to look after myself. I loosened the laces of my shoes, put as much padding as I could in between them and the blisters, and set off towards the city.

Surprisingly, it didn't take me long to find a cheap hotel down a back alley off one of the main roads near the city centre.

The man at the reception desk barely noticed me walk in, and I leant over the desk to get his attention. If the reception was anything to go by, I was in for a treat. The chairs in the corner were covered in torn red fabric, and there was a tobacco-stained lampshade on the side table next to the reception desk.

'*Ah, pardonnez-moi, Monsieur,*' the concierge said, looking up at me and presenting a sickly smile.

'Hello. Do you have any rooms?' I asked.

'*Oui*, yes, *Monsieur,*' he replied. 'For twenty-five euros a night. Very nice rooms.'

'How much are the not very nice rooms?' I asked.

Not missing a trick, he continued. 'I can provide you a single room for twenty euros. For you, sir, not a problem.'

I wasn't in the mood for arguing further. I handed him the money and he gave me a set of keys for the fourth floor. '*Merci,*' I said, with more than a hint of sarcasm in my voice.

The man smiled back. 'Checkout at 10 a.m., *Monsieur, merci.*'

I trundled up the four agonising flights of stairs with my bag and found the room. The door took a bit of force to lever open. There was a single bed with an ancient brown blanket on it, and a broken picture frame hung on the wall. In the en suite was a dirty-grey sink and a shower that was covered in mould. It was the kind of place George Orwell would have taken a liking to.

I took my bag off and stuffed the remaining euros I had into my clothing. Like a man who had been trekking across the desert for days, I slid off my shoes and socks and wiggled my toes around in audible pleasure. The aches started to recede as soon as I elevated my feet.

In short, the room was the best twenty euros I'd ever spent.

When I'd recovered a little, I washed my face and changed into my spare clothes, hanging the rest around the room to dry. I took the stairs slowly when I came down again.

'*Excusez-moi,*' I said to the man at the reception desk. 'Do you know where I can find a pharmacy?'

'*Pharmacie, oui,*' he replied, without looking up. 'The second street on your right.'

I thanked him and left.

It was only now that I got to see the city properly. Outside, people were walking up the hill in the direction of the shops and restaurants, hanging around the cafes and bars, drinking coffee and reading the newspapers. There was a mixed array of people here: some richer-looking French people, Africans wearing kaftans and headdresses, Arab women with headscarves, and young Eastern European men with gelled hair who looked like characters off *Grease*. On the other side of the road were street stalls selling Turkish pastries and fruits. Marseille was not a pretentious city. In a lot of ways, it reminded me a lot of home.

I found the pharmacy around the corner and bought myself a couple of packets of plasters and some cheap antiseptic cream. On the way back, I spied a stall selling second-hand clothes. I took an ugly-looking shirt and a new pair of trainers for ten euros. Today I had spent almost half of my money; I would just have to be more careful from now on. Back at the hotel room I washed and dried my feet and applied the cream sparingly. Thank God, I thought, that this place at least provided soap and a towel.

For the rest of the evening, there was really nothing else to do but think. I made some notes about my journey and then stared at the ceiling for a while in silence. I wasn't unhappy, but the exhaustion had made me that way. I had spotted an Arabic prayer hung on the wall when I first came in the room, and now I removed it and folded it away in my bag, out of a mix of boredom and of genuinely needing any spiritual intervention I could get. Then I remembered one other thing I needed to do.

I'd meant to do it a long time ago, but it had simply fled from my mind; besides which, the occasion simply hadn't been right for it before. But now seemed as good as time as any. I took my wallet from my trouser pocket and emptied the contents out onto the bed. These were the only things apart from my passport that held any bearing to my old life. There was my provisional driving licence, which I'd got at sixteen. The photo looked like somebody else – some young boy with his fringe falling onto his eyes and a naïve smile. There was my college ID, the boy with his fringe cut and his face thinner, a more serious look in his eyes, the innocence gone and replaced with something else, something darker. There was my bank card granting me access to a savings account with no money in it, a library card, some others marking my loyalty to various corporations: Waterstones, Subway, Puregym. I hadn't used any of them for years, and I had no idea why I had kept hold of them for so long. I took out a pair of scissors and started cutting them up one by one. There was something ritualistic about it. I placed the pieces in the dustbin in the corner of the room. Then I put the money I had left back in the wallet, which was thinner now, and stowed it at the bottom of my bag with my passport.

For the rest of the night I didn't move from where I lay, apart from getting up once to kill the mosquitoes on the ceiling and walls. I left them stuck, splayed and papery, to the places they had been sitting.

12.

I set off walking in the morning at a slower pace than the days before, giving myself time to wear the new shoes in and stopping whenever anything rubbed to adjust my socks and make sure the plasters were properly in place before setting off again. The footpath left the road and cut its way along the coast through tunnels set into the rock, and I could see the sea crashing into the rocks below, the cliffs jutting out into the sea and the shoreline cutting back inland, somewhere out of view.

I must have walked about thirty kilometres and was well out of the city by the time it was starting to get dark, but the small towns seemed to merge one into the other, and the whole thing seemed to go on forever. I set my tent up for the night in a quiet corner of a nearby park, and was woken up by the first dog-walkers in the early morning. The sun was still below the horizon when I packed up my tent, still covered in dew, and set off again along the coast. As I walked, the first rays of light broke and turned the sea into a sheet of shimmering gold, and the waves sparkled as the first fishing boats set off, breaking through the crests of the waves.

I passed through the town of La Ciotat and followed the route around the coastline. I took my time to climb the long uphills, my lungs crying out for air during the steepest ascents, and at the top of them I stopped to compose myself under the shade of the pine trees and take in the views of the sea below. At the bottom there were steep cliffs covered in netting, with the road running along the top and tiny staircases taking you down to the small beaches, and it was on one of those that I decided to rest at midday. I climbed down to the tiny bay, a pebbled beach with seaweed-matted rocks on either side, and took off my bag to sit down on the sand. There was a fisherman sitting quietly at the far side of the inlet, but he paid me no attention.

I ate what little bread I had left and a wafer biscuit, then took off my shoes and socks and walked down the beach to dip my toes into the sea. The water was freezing at this time of year, but I enjoyed the feeling. I rested for an hour or so, lying with my head to one side and watching how the sea stuck to the side of the Earth. I felt content enough just then, when the cars were gone and it was quiet. I thought of ancient hominids searching the rocks for oysters and crabs and jogging along the sand with their bare feet. I wondered if they had all felt the same way I did. I wondered whether things ever changed at all, or was this just a permanent cosmic struggle I'd become involved in? I wondered whether anybody missed me back home.

After I'd rested, I had enough energy to keep on walking for a good while. I cut through car parks and across gravelled paths, following the coast along, and kept my head down as I passed people lurking around in the evening. There were others like me, sleeping on benches in the park or sitting on a corner waiting for life to come along. We passed each other warily, like stray cats – and there were plenty of those, too. One night

I saw a fox ahead in the gloom. It eyed me, stood still for a minute, and then dashed away into the thickets.

It was late and cool, and I could hear the sound of the waves lapping along the shoreline a hundred yards or so away. By now the ache in my shoulders had become a familiar friend, and I could feel the muscles getting used to the weight. Around the next corner I saw a police car at the end of the road, pulled in at a lay-by.

I was thrust back to the place I'd been a couple of weeks ago, being woken up in the morning to the sight of police officers blocking the way who took my best friend away from me and nearly charged me with an offence just for defending myself. I had no desire to get involved with the police again any time soon. There was nothing to do but walk past with my head forward. I glanced in their direction as I got nearer, and saw the window half-open, the officer now clearly looking in his mirror at my approaching figure. As I drew adjacent to the car, he called out to me.

'*Salut*,' he said. 'Hello?'

I looked around. He opened the car door and got out, and I stood and waited for him. He had a pistol at his side. I realised he was a gendarme.

'Hi,' I replied.

'You speak English? *Anglais?*'

'*Oui*. Yes,' I said. Had the British police put a notice out for me? It probably only took a couple of clicks on the computer these days. My heart sank.

'Where are you going?' he asked.

I told him I was heading towards Toulon. He looked at me as if to say my answer wasn't good enough. He asked me for my passport, and I set down my bag to retrieve it. I had to take out my sleeping bag and tent, aware of how vulnerable it made you feel, tipping out all your belongings at the side of the road. Dizziness hit me, making me feel like I'd had too many cups of coffee. But the policeman didn't seem phased at all. 'It's a nice night,' he said while he waited.

At last I presented my passport to him, and he glanced at my photo for a second, idly flicking through the stamp pages.

'I'm heading for Italy,' I said. He looked up and furrowed his eyebrows at me. 'After Toulon,' I added.

'Walking?' he said.

I nodded.

He handed me back my passport, and I knelt down to put it away.

'Do you have any drugs on you? Hashish?' he asked. 'Do you smoke it?'

'No.'

'How many days will it take you to get to Italy?'

I hesitated for a moment. Honestly, I had no idea. 'Three? Four?' I said.

The policeman seemed to ease up. He looked incredulously up the road in the direction I was walking.

'It depends on my legs, I suppose.'

'That's quite a walk,' he said. 'Stay out of trouble, OK? Have a safe journey.' He stood while I put my belongings away and hauled the heavy rucksack back over my shoulders. Unsure of what to do, I gave him a thumbs up and started to walk.

'Good luck,' the gendarme said. I felt him watch me for a few minutes, and then I heard him getting back in the car and pulling away.

It was quiet again. I had a chill from standing around, and there was a cold sweat on my forehead. After another couple of miles, I was about to collapse. I hadn't eaten for hours, but I kept on going a bit further until I found a place to camp.

It was at the back corner of a car park, under the shade of a couple of trees, but you would still have to be looking for the tent to see its dark blue fabric in the shadow. I sat down to survey the area for a minute before putting up camp. The waves were gently coming into the shore, but there were some bright flashes in the sky. I paused. A couple of seconds later there was another, far off, out to sea somewhere, and then after it had flared up it was gone again just as quickly. Every fifteen seconds or so, another bright light illuminated the night sky, then vanished. I couldn't work out what I was looking at – some flares, perhaps, or a meteor shower? After fifteen or twenty minutes, the flashes stopped. I got to my feet, unsteady after the day's long walk, put up the tent and quickly went to sleep.

It was only a few days later that I would realise what I'd been looking at, when I saw a television screen in a cafe I walked past showing the news about some rebel insurgency taking place in Africa. I stopped to watch what was happening. The country was Libya. The French had been involved – the whole European Union, in fact, including the British – and I realised what I had been watching were the first strikes of that war, the jet fighters which had taken off from the carriers and launched cruise missiles at the African coast from the sea.

The next day I made my way to Toulon along the coast, and then hitched a ride to Cannes with a couple of young girls who were on a road trip of the south coast. They'd travelled all the way down from Normandy and laughed a lot; they seemed almost as poor as I was, except for their car and a packed lunch. They were going to see their friend who had moved down here to live with her Italian boyfriend.

After that I was picked up by a bald man with a ferocious tan who was on his way back from a fishing trip somewhere near Barcelona. His car was old and battered, and I couldn't believe it had carried him however many hundreds of miles the journey was. He took me as far as Nice. I walked along the boardwalk where Elton John had made the music video for 'I'm Still Standing'. It was busy, even for this time of year, with cyclists and people strolling along the promenade. I kept my head down and passed them all by in a terrible mood, because it was no ordinary day. In fact, it was my birthday.

I was twenty-one, the age when you're supposed to be going out seeing your friends, passing exams, getting a part-time job or thinking about moving out for the first time. Instead, I was heading east, away from everything I knew. In the summer there were English people who'd holiday around here, the children of senior managers or doctors or lawyers, bringing their young, blonde-haired kids down here to their holiday villas – kids who had cars bought for them and were on Mummy and Daddy's insurance and who had never had a hard time growing up – and they would eat in the restaurants and swim in the sea without so much as a care in the world. It all seemed so natural, and yet there were people like me who had never even stepped outside of Manchester. Manchester, where it always rained. Manchester, where you tried to scrape a life together and the only way to cope with it was either getting pissed or getting stoned, and the rest of the time you spent trying to finance it without getting your head kicked in.

As you can tell, I was in a terrible mood. Nobody would pick me up on the other side of the town, and I had to walk most of the day around the rocky points until I reached Villefranche-sur-Mer. From there I managed to hitch a ride to just outside Monte Carlo. There was nowhere to put up a tent, and I ended up sleeping on a piece of cardboard around the back of a group of houses, praying that nobody found me there and reported my presence to the police.

I was cold and hungry when I woke up. I followed the road downhill, with pine forest on either side of me, until I reached the city of Monte Carlo proper. I found the port down below, and the Formula One track that I recognised from so many races, and on the street there were shops selling clothes and perfume, watches and diamonds. There were boats sitting in the port: small sailing dinghies and enormous, grand yachts with polished wooden interiors and widescreen TVs and stacks of radar equipment up above, all finished in gold trim and with names like *Atlantis* and *Tyrol* and *Illes Balears* emblazoned upon them. I could see fish swimming around the bottom of the boats in the clear water.

At lunchtime I tried to fill my water bottle up at a nearby restaurant and was refused, loudly and rudely, by the bartender. By some miracle I found an ordinary supermarket and bought a can of ratatouille, which I ate outside on the floor. I didn't mind the looks from the people walking past.

I wanted to leave this place as quickly as I could, but on the way out of town that afternoon I was once again stopped by a couple of gendarmes at the side of the road. They looked as though they were going to give me a load of bother, but they didn't seem to care once they realised I was leaving Monte

Carlo. As they were getting back in their car to leave, I asked how far it was to the Italian border.

'Less than fifteen kilometres,' the policeman replied. Fifteen! I couldn't believe how far I'd managed to travel in the space of a week. It had taken all of my effort to get this far.

Before I turned the corner out of sight, I craned my neck back to take in the view. I could see the city encircling the bay below, a cruise ship docked a short way out to sea, the restaurants, Dior and Bulgari and Breitling shops with hardly any shoppers in. It was an absurd place, I thought— a playground for the rich. There were cliffs all the way around so that the people here could pretend there was no such thing as the real world. For my brief time there, I had enjoyed reminding them that it existed.

When it was quiet, I took out the cash I had left in the depths of my bag and counted it. There were two twenties, two tens, a five and a handful of coins. I held them in front of me like the bloody hands of Macbeth.

'Shit!' I exclaimed to no one in particular. I felt like someone in the desert who was sipping his last dregs of water. Of course, I had managed fine without money before. But that was different; I had Tony then, and the places I was heading towards now weren't as kind to the penniless as Manchester had been. It wasn't much, but that was the first time I had something you might call a positive thought about home.

Then my mind drifted off into things I could do once I had spent every penny I had left: working in a village or on a farm picking fruit, or learning how to fish and trap, and finding some huge forest somewhere to lose myself in and living off the land. I carried on daydreaming as I walked, losing all sense of myself as my feet carried on in their automatic rhythm, until sometime later I looked up and realised I was about to cross the border.

13.

On the 15th March, thousands of protestors gathered across Syria to call for an end to the regime of Bashar al-Assad. People were rising up in Yemen, Libya and Tunisia, there was tension in Burma, too, according to the news, and the Korean peninsula seemed to be on the verge of a nuclear war. Everybody, it seemed, felt the same way as I did. There was something deeply broken with the world, no longer sitting dormant but starting to break through in the places where the veneer of society felt weakest.

Was it simply anger at a consumerist, money-obsessed civilisation, which cared more about branding and profit margins than helping people lead happy, fulfilled lives? Was it a sense of dissatisfaction with working for measly pay and trying to pay the bills on time while millionaires did absolutely nothing and sat around on their yachts all day?

Those would be the simple answers, but for me they were too obvious. Yes, I found all of that intolerable and depressing, but for me capitalism wasn't the problem; it was just a distraction that allowed people to avoid thinking about the *real* problem by shopping and feeling good about themselves instead. The real problem was that we – humanity – had achieved everything we'd set out to achieve, and were none the better for it. We had been to the moon, and it hadn't brought about a new golden age of space exploration. We had won the war against fascism, but democracy hadn't made us any freer. We had Facebook and e-mail, but we felt further apart than ever before.

I, on the other hand, was making great progress. I had part walked, part hitch-hiked through San Remo, walked around the coast and up through Alassio and Albenga, and finally reached the large town of Savona, which marked the end of the Cote d'Azur and the start of Italy proper.

I'd changed my schedule around so that I could walk during the night, in part because it was a different routine, but mostly because I was fed up of looking at all the resorts. In the evenings the towns of the coast were different altogether. I saw, quite regularly, the women standing on the street corners dressed in miniskirts and fishnet stockings, and the police driving up and down the main streets of the little towns, moving them along. Other evenings were quiet, and the small villages seemed deserted. I liked those times the best. I liked to pretend I was in one of those apocalyptic films where everything had been wiped out, and the protagonist has to fend for himself among the rubble.

I passed through all those places like a ghost, not leaving a trace, and the people sitting outside the cafes glanced at me only fleetingly – some without any expression at all, others with a curiosity that was soon expended by the time I stepped out of view. When I stopped to eat or rest for a while, I spent the time alone, lost in my thoughts or writing a few more notes in my diary. An hour with absolutely nothing to do could feel like an entire day. I spent time watching the light hitting the leaves on the trees, looking at the way they built their houses here, studying the way the hills sloped up with the Alps rising up behind them, and I took in as much of it as I could, because I assumed that these were among the last of my days.

Eventually, the clear skies I'd enjoyed for the past week or two vanished, and the weather that had been so kind to me this far turned cold and rainy. That managed to put an instant dampener on my journey. It drizzled all day, and I spent most of it waiting for the rain to clear, until I realised there was nothing to do but make a move, so I set off walking anyway.

It didn't take long for the rain to get into my shoes, my trousers and even the inside of my bag. I took the sodden things off when I could and tried to dry them inside my tent at night-time, but it turned out to be mostly a useless endeavour. Oh, those nights I'd spent in the dry with Tony and Tatum, listening to the sound of a downpour from the shelter of our bridge next to the canal!

I wrapped my things up as best I could with plastic bags, and whenever I found a secluded place away from the footpath, I would change hurriedly out of my wet clothes and into the other set, which were merely damp. One day I found a shower block attached to one of the beach resorts, which was closed for the winter season. The door was unlocked. I found the shower inside working, but the water was freezing, and I had to rush for fear of getting caught there.

The environment took some getting used to. We'd never been to the beach when I was younger, except maybe once or twice; I had some foggy memories of windy days and sandy towels, and those were the things I remembered on the journey along the coast from Marseille. The sand and rocks were unattractive to me, the sea felt angry, and the places I passed through were half-towns, resort-places without a soul. I desperately wanted the whole thing to end. I kept my head down and kept walking, promising myself there were better things to come.

In my notepad I had sketched down a few maps for the next portion of my journey. I had become good at memorising the shapes of the countries and their main roads. After another day's trek, I anticipated arriving in Genoa. From there, you had to cut across the country somehow to Venice, then follow the coast around to the border with Slovenia. There was nothing to it except waiting for rides and walking when you couldn't find any. And having enough to eat. I had limited myself to spending no more than a pound a day on food.

A pound a day doesn't sound too bad until you realise that in France and Italy it barely buys you a loaf of bread in most of the supermarkets. So I did what I had to do. I sneaked some fruit or a block of cheese or tin of sardines into my bag when I could, but most of the supermarkets had security guards at the entrances, and I was too afraid of getting caught. The easiest way to steal, I discovered, was to do it forgetfully. Once, I managed to pay for a packet of crisps and walk past the girl on the till with a loaf of bread in my hand, clear as day. She didn't even look up at me to notice.

I also bought myself a lighter, and when I found a quiet place in the evening to camp I boiled up water for packets of instant soup or those two-minute pasta sachets that office workers ate during their lunch breaks. Some of those meals, at the time, tasted like the best food I'd ever eaten. Sometimes I fell back to my old tricks of looking for food in people's rubbish. One time, I found a plate of seafood dumped out back of one of the seafront restaurants. The previous diners had not done a very good job of cleaning out the shells with their forks, and I ate lobster and mussels that day.

All kinds of rubbish got washed up by the waves. Among the debris I found a couple of cans of Red Bull that must have fallen off a container ship or wound their way across the Mediterranean somehow. The cans were a little rusted, but they opened up fine, and you couldn't even taste the seawater. It amazed me to see what else the sea brought in. There were flip-flops and bits of polystyrene and plastic ring pulls and carrier bags, and one day I found the corpse of a rat bigger than any I'd ever seen lying on the sand. It had hollow sockets for eyes, and its fur had been bleached entirely white by the sea.

Just after ten o'clock the next night, I turned a corner and saw the city of Genoa lit up along the coast. There was a big port on this side, closest to the sea, and another one far away, maybe another ten or twenty miles away. I could see the lights of the ships reflecting on the black water. I had been walking for several hours, and my feet were aching, as were my shoulders under the weight of my bag.

There was no beach here, just a pile of large rocks to stop the waves from reaching the street. The houses were four or five storeys tall, with nice balconies, and further along there were palm trees planted in blocks of concrete. I could see blinking lights – an airport, maybe – up the hill on the other side of town. After I had walked along the street for a while, I came to the fenced area of the port. Inside, through the railings, were cargo containers, and torches moving around in the dark. The rocks went around the outside of the port, and if you wanted to you could have clambered your way along them, but I worried there would be something blocking the way and I'd have to come all the way back.

I turned left away from the sea instead and followed a set of concrete steps up onto the next street until I wound up on the main street, Via Don Giovanni. Though the shops were shut, there were still a few buses and cars driving by. I stopped to look in one of the windows at house prices, then walked uphill until the road took me right into the middle of town. I kept looking for a side street to cut back in towards the sea, but the port carried on and on. There must have been a freight train straight into the port, because I could see the power lines up above the warehouses, and later on I saw carriages on the other side of the fence, covered in graffiti.

These kind of challenges were the worst thing about walking. Once you'd committed yourself to entering a place, you generally had to keep going until you'd got out of it, and in this case it looked as though I might have bitten off more than I could chew. That meant I'd end up sleeping in the city, and of all the things I wanted to avoid, that was number one. You could be woken up by the police, or kicked, or set on fire by a malicious stranger – and even if nothing happened, it never made for a comfortable night. I could never sleep because of the anxiety of what might happen to me if I did.

Just then I looked up and spotted something I hadn't seen before on my journey. I thought I must have fallen asleep because there, on the other side of the road, was someone who looked exactly like me. The man – or boy, because he really looked not a day over eighteen – was carrying a medium-sized grey backpack; he had a windbreaker jacket on, and what looked like walking shoes. His head was down and he was walking in the same direction I had been until I stopped. In all the places I had passed, I had seen policemen, prostitutes, restaurant owners, street cleaners, all kinds of people, but I had never seen anybody like this. It was like looking in a mirror.

I looked on incredulously as he kept on walking away, getting smaller.

'Hey!' I shouted. I grabbed my bag as quickly as I could and started running with it, fighting to get my arm through the straps. The traveller was already some way ahead. I found it hard to run with the bag, and I could hear the thump of my shoes hitting the pavement. My heart was beating in my chest and I could barely breathe. 'Hey, you! Wait!'

The stranger had almost turned the next corner when he heard me calling and looked around. He must have had a shock as well, to see me running after him with all my stuff bouncing up and down on my back and my face full of sweat. When I got closer, I realised he was wearing headphones. He took them out and looked me up and down, waiting for me to gather my breath.

'Hello,' he said. An English accent.

'Hi,' I said. 'Where are you going to?'

He sighed and pointed around at the gated fence. 'I'm trying to get past the port,' he said. 'But look. It just goes on forever. It's a bloody piss-take, that's what it is.'

I laughed and looked around. 'That's not what I meant,' I said. 'What's your name?'

'Jacob,' he said. 'Yours?'

'Cam.'

'Well, nice to meet you, Cam. It's getting late,' Jacob said. 'I need to get out of the city. I should really keep walking.' He glanced at my belongings, which were now on the floor. 'What are you doing – stopping or carrying on?'

'I wasn't sure' – I picked my bag up – 'but I'll walk with you, if that's OK.'

'Sure,' he said. 'It would be nice to walk and talk.'

We set off again. I watched Jacob, though his eyes remained fixed on the road ahead. He had folded the headphones inside his coat and I had the impression he had forgotten how to talk to anyone. But his feet never missed a step. There was a crazy determination in his walk.

'Where are you from?' I asked.

'Me? I'm from Stoke. You?'

'Manchester.'

'Cool.'

The road was quiet, and all you could hear was the sound of our footsteps and the noise of the sea, over in the shadows somewhere. We didn't walk long before Jacob stopped again. He looked at the port in deep contemplation and then turned to me.

'To answer your question, I'm heading towards the Balkans,' he said. 'Sorry. I'm not great at talking. What about you?'

'I don't really have a plan,' I replied. That old feeling sank in that I was way out of my depth with everything, and that nobody in the world could understand me. 'But I wanted to go east, maybe head towards Greece.'

He was quiet for a moment. I wanted to say something to break the silence, but then he finally spoke again. 'You know, it's a pretty big coincidence, running into you like this,' he said. 'Actually, I intend to travel through Turkey to the Middle East. It's a similar route to yours, for a while.'

'That sounds like quite a journey.'

'Look,' Jacob said, 'over there you can see the port. They drop the containers off here and then the trains carry the freight all over Italy. I've been thinking about it for a couple of hours.'

'Thinking about what?'

'Train-hopping. They used to do it in the thirties. The hobos, I mean. All across America. But the trains are checked every once in a while for illegal immigrants. You have to be careful.'

I looked across at the freight yard. There was a fence about eight metres high around the outside, beyond that the maze of containers, and then the loading bay itself. I realised Jacob had stopped here on purpose. I couldn't see anybody now, but I knew there were people working there in the shadows, and if we were caught inside we were sure to be arrested.

'You know, I've had some pretty good success with hitch-hiking,' I said.

'Oh, come on. Are you afraid? You don't look like somebody who would be.'

'No, I'm not scared of getting caught. But . . . that's crazy,' I said. Really, I was scared of being sent back to the UK. I didn't say it at the time, but I had a feeling Jacob already knew, somehow.

'Well?' he said.

Of course, it was crazy. But then so was my life, and the even crazier thing was that I was starting to like it. And Jacob had a sort of religious conviction in his voice that made you think anything was possible. It was such a chance meeting, in the middle of the night in an Italian city, him coming from some forty-odd miles away from Manchester. I wanted to know more about him, and a part of me already knew that Jacob was going for the train.

There were two options. Number one: leave him here to disappear forever or get arrested by himself. Part of me had a feeling that without me, this ridiculous plan was never going to work, that he needed me as much as I needed him. Or number two: climb the fence, sneak through the containers and get on a train which would take us out of Genoa, maybe even all the way across the country to Venice on the other side.

There was also the possibility of getting caught or killed, my brain reminded me. But there was the possibility of that half a mile down the road, too. Jacob had already taken a navy blue woollen hat out of his bag and put it around his head. He knelt down and tightened his shoelaces.

'Alright,' I said. 'I suppose I'll give it a try.'

14.

Jacob tested the fence with his foot, then slipped his bag off his shoulders and handed it to me. It felt heavy, at least a few kilos heavier than mine. He was reaching upward, about to heave himself up onto the spikes at the top, when I heard the sound of an engine approaching from the city.

'Get down!' I hissed.

Headlights came around the corner and into view. I knelt down quickly and held still with Jacob's bag in front of me while the lights passed over us. Jacob, meanwhile, had dived onto the floor and now lay there motionless. With the dark grey of his coat, and his hat pulled over his head, you would think him a pile of ordinary-looking rubbish. The car drove out of sight.

'Shit,' he said quietly once the danger had passed. 'Right. I'm going for it this time. Throw my bag over once I'm on the other side.'

I nodded.

He clambered up onto the fence, then slowly raised his legs over the sharpened points and onto the other side. Then he pulled his weight over and landed on the other side with a thump in the darkness. I heard him whisper, 'Psst! Throw my bag over.'

My arms and back were already aching from the day's walk with the backpack on my shoulders. I took a step back and hurled the bag with all my might. It was a clumsy throw, and for a second I was sure the straps were going to hook onto the fence at the top, but somehow they narrowly avoided getting caught, and I heard Jacob catch the bag on the other side.

'OK. Good. Throw me your bag first, then climb over,' he said.

Already the time we had been here, all too visible at the side of the road, felt like a lifetime. I looked around and threw my bag at the top of the fence as hard as I could. The backpack flew up in an arc, then fell onto the fencepost and hung there at the top by its strap, like a flag announcing our presence to everyone. I froze, unsure of what to do.

'Come on! Get a move on!' Jacob whispered.

I put my foot up and pulled myself up to the top of the fence. From here I could see the freight trains clearly, and the people working on them by torchlight. It was dark where we were, but if a car were to come around the bend I'd be lit up like a bomber plane. I reached over and tried to unhook the strap, carefully balancing above the spikes between my legs; if I slipped now I'd be skewered straight through the middle. My fingers reached the strap. I eased it up and free, and my bag fell into the darkness below. I turned and pulled my other leg over quickly. I felt a tear in the seam of my pants, but then I was over the other side, climbing down, and I landed on both feet in the shadows. Jacob wasn't there. I looked around frantically while my eyes adjusted to the darkness.

'Over here,' he whispered. 'Keep close and stay quiet. There's a train already loaded on the tracks over there. See it?'

'Yeah,' I said, putting my backpack on my shoulders again. I could see the train through the gaps in the containers, and the warehouse lit up behind it. 'But what about the workmen?'

'They've finished with that one. They're working on the other containers out of the warehouse. Over there.' Sure enough, the men were packing new containers in the light of the warehouse. A lone torch was moving slowly up the length of the train. It was probably a security guard, checking the spaces in between the carriages for stowaways.

We crept along the back of the containers until they no longer provided any cover, and then kept low next to a pile of steel girders which led along the side of the tracks. From here there was a short decline and a set of tracks to cross. We waited until the security man's torchlight had made its way along the length of the train. I felt a mosquito humming away in my ear, and resisted the urge to try to smack it in the dark.

'Look, Jacob,' I said, scraping my foot on the floor, 'it's gravel.'

'Yes. If you try to run, you'll make a shitload of noise. Take your time, OK? Don't panic. Just walk over to one of the carriages and make yourself invisible.'

'Alright,' I said, but in reality I had no idea what I was doing. 'Now?'

'Wait. Just a minute . . . OK, now.' He took a step forward onto the gravel. The noise of the stones made my heart stop, and I thought everybody in the whole yard must have heard us, but Jacob kept walking. The men were loading in the distance and I could hear them hammering bolts into the tops of the containers. I followed him, trying to place my feet as carefully as I could and riding out the movements as the shale shifted under my feet.

We crossed over the first set of tracks. I could still make out the shape of Jacob up ahead in the darkness, and I hurried for fear of losing him entirely. Then we crossed the second set of tracks and came up to the side of the carriages. I thought we were going to jump straight in, but Jacob started walking along the length of the train, away from the warehouse.

I tried to catch up, my footsteps crunching louder. 'What are you doing?' I called. But Jacob was too far ahead to hear, and I didn't dare try to run on the gravel. I prayed with every ounce of my soul for him to stop and board the train. He paused and checked out one of the spaces in between the containers, then carried on to the next one. Then I saw his arm reach up and grab the handles of the train and pull himself up out of sight. I walked up and grabbed hold of the iron handlebars. Somewhere up ahead, the engine was already running – I could feel its vibrations through the metal. I climbed up, half expecting to see a torch light me up at any minute.

'Jacob? Where are you?'

'Down here,' he said. He was lying with his feet tucked away under the walkway and his bag stuffed in at one side.

I pulled myself down and tried to hide as close as I could to him. It was a tight squeeze, and my leg muscles complained at the lack of space. I took a deep breath. 'Can you hear that?' I whispered. 'It sounds like the train's about to set off.'

'It's been checked once, so they shouldn't bother again,' he said. 'Did you see the markings on the crates?'

'No. What markings?'

'The containers. I could be wrong, but they look as though they're marked for Trieste. Do you know what that means, Cameron?'

'It means we literally couldn't have picked a better ride out of here,' I said.

'Exactly. Hopefully this will take us all the way through Italy.'

'That was mental,' I said, my hands still trembling. I could still barely control my breathing, and I was sure that another check of the train would ruin us completely. And what about dogs? Surely they would pick us up in an instant? And what would happen to us for breaking into a train depot in the middle of the night? 'I said, that was mental, Jacob.'

There was no response. Whether he was asleep or not, I didn't know; maybe he was merely pretending in order to get me to shut up. I didn't try to get any further response from him.

The train engine revved up and then I felt the first slow movement of the carriages pulling forward. From where I was lying, I could see through the gaps in the metal the gravel moving underneath the train, and there was a cold draft blowing up from underneath the carriage. The train pulled through the warehouses, and I kept perfectly still as we began slowing to the last set of signals at the exit from the port. I could only assume Jacob was still there, lying like a stone in the darkness. The train pulled to a stop again. I couldn't hear any conversations or any noise at all except for the train engine rumbling. Then the signal changed and we started pulling off again, out of the port. I saw the gravel change colour as the train left the yard. We started picking up speed fast.

Then it got faster, the hedges flying past, the buildings and the road, until the tracks must have broken away from the road and through the suburbs, and then out of the city the train tore away with us on it, under bridges and running along parallel to the sea, I guessed. I couldn't make out much; the darkness and the fact that I was wedged underneath the platform, with my head leant on a piece of metal, still afraid to stand up, meant there wasn't really much of a view. My legs were aching, the wind still blew, and I felt cold – proper cold – for the first time in a while.

There were no checkpoints or stops at all for a couple of hours, and I had no idea which way we were going. I had some idea of a joke, that I was going to fall asleep and wake up at Euston. I tried to gauge our direction by the lights of the roads and the outline of the sea, but soon that too was gone from view, and trying to work out where we were was futile. The train carried on through endless hills and plains which could have been anywhere in the world.

It wasn't yet light when I woke up. There was a deep, cold cramp in my leg, and the draught had frozen a cold sweat on my forehead. I sat up, stretched and looked at Jacob's form lying in the place where he'd fallen asleep. The train wasn't moving. Either side of the train there was forest, one side lying closer than the other. I paused, then nudged him with my foot.

'Jacob,' I whispered, 'wake up.'

He sat up and rubbed his neck, then looked around. I signalled for him to stay quiet, and then when I had built up the courage I leant my head out of the side and looked up and down the length of the train. In front the signals glowed red in the darkness. I could see the small ember of a cigarette near the driver's compartment.

'What's up?' Jacob asked.

I shrugged. 'Cigarette break, it looks like. Any idea where we are?'

'No idea. But we should get off soon,' he said. 'No point in risking it any further.'

He was right. Taking the train until it arrived somewhere was a bad idea. In fact, we were lucky to have woken up here, where it was quiet. I picked up my bag and stood up, ready to get off, but Jacob stopped me.

'Not yet,' he said. 'When it starts moving again.'

Soon after that, the driver must have climbed back into his cabin and started the engine. I felt the vibrations and leant out again to take a look. The signals changed, and the train started moving off smoothly. It crawled past the signals, and I motioned to Jacob to get ready. The stones were already moving by pretty fast. 'Give it a good jump!' I called out to him. I faced the line of trees and stuck my head out again to make sure there were no posts coming towards us – but in the dark, I couldn't really tell for sure.

Jacob went first. He climbed over the side of the carriage and tried to let himself down to a running stop. I saw his feet quickly slide away beneath him, then he rolled out of view. The train was picking up speed now.

I leapt for it. For a second the train and I were moving as one, and then it quickly moved ahead of me and I saw the ground rushing to meet me. I threw out my shoulder as well as I could to shield myself from the fall, but I hit the gravel with a heavy thud. I tried to roll with it, stones and branches sticking into me, carriage after carriage whooshing by until the last one rushed past me, and the train was gone.

I had no clue as to how well or badly I had landed. The next thing I knew was Jacob helping me up to my feet and pulling me into the treeline, out of view. 'Are you alright?' he asked.

I felt myself up and down. I wasn't sure, but everything seemed intact, apart from a couple of scratches on my arms and legs where I'd hit the ground at speed. 'I'll be fine,' I said. 'What now? I don't have a clue where we are.'

'It doesn't matter,' he said. 'All we have to do is follow the tracks for a while until we find the next town.' He was right; if we kept following them we'd surely arrive somewhere eventually. Despite having slept on the train, I felt incredibly tired. There wasn't much point complaining to Jacob about it.

We followed the tracks as best we could, staying a few feet into the trees to avoid being seen, and it was hard going in the pale light of the early morning. I stumbled over brambles and fallen branches, and once or twice I felt the tingling of nettle stings. If Jacob had any signs of wear and tear, he didn't show them. Once, another train approached, going in the other direction. We stopped for it to pass and for a second the forest was quiet except for the sound of birds in the trees above. Then the train came past with a rush of wind which shook the trees and sent the birds and squirrels fleeing, and faded away just as quickly.

My calf muscles were complaining, and I was about to ask Jacob to stop for a rest when, after a couple of miles, the trees broke clear and I spotted a road at the bottom of the hill, running parallel to the tracks. The road ran across what looked like a big, flat plain, with hills lying far off, maybe thirty or forty miles away. There was a crossroads about a quarter of a mile ahead. We found the nearest way down through the trees and started half walking, half jogging down through the foliage to the road.

I caught up with Jacob on the pavement next to the junction. His trousers were ripped and his legs grazed from the jump. I looked at the road signs ahead. They showed the way north to

Trento and Innsbruck, south to Bologna, and east to Venezia and Trieste. But what luck we'd encountered! We had covered almost the entire breadth of Italy in a single night, and Trieste was less than a hundred miles away.

Jacob looked as exhausted as I was. It was early morning still, and we waited a while for a car or truck to come along. From there we got a lift to Padua, not far from Venice, and in the afternoon we hitched another lift to Trieste. I'd thought that hitch-hiking as a pair of young men was going to be harder, but we didn't wait long to be picked up. The men who picked us up both chatted to us in broken English: the first on his way back to his farm, the second, wearing a shirt and sunglasses, who told us about his own adventures hitch-hiking years ago during the seventies. I sat up front both times and chatted with the drivers while Jacob sat in the back. He was quiet, and I didn't have any opportunity to talk to him that day until the evening, when we were alone.

15.

'Robbie Williams,' Jacob said. 'He was from Burslem. There are six towns in the city of Stoke-on-Trent. Hanley, Tunstall, Stoke, Burslem, Longton, and Fenton. I grew up in Hanley. The other thing Stoke is famous for is pottery. You know, like the Potters.'

'The Potters?' I said.

'What, have you been living under a rock? The Potters! Stoke City?'

'I'm not really into football,' I said.

We had found a place to camp, at the foot of a steep hill which was littered with pines. Further up the road there was some sort of gated facility, and below us the city of Trieste clung to the hillside as though trying not to slip into the sea. The road was steep; it had taken us over an hour to climb up away from the sea to here. It was a good vantage point, but there was a stiff breeze blowing up the hill. I had my woolly hat pulled down as far as I could, and I was breathing into the collar of my jacket.

'Well, I never liked Robbie Williams, either,' Jacob laughed. 'But Manchester is a pretty cool place, isn't it? You have Oasis, the Smiths, the Stone Roses, Manchester United . . .'

'I'll give you the music,' I said. 'But there's nothing special about Manchester, honestly. It pisses down all the time. Outside of the centre it's just council estates and off-licences, and in the city there are homeless people everywhere. It's a joke.'

'Well there's more jobs than there are in Stoke,' he said. 'It's getting chilly. Shall we light a fire?'

'A bit risky, don't you think?' We were in the quietest corner of town, but still I wondered how far the smoke would carry. I had just added breaking and entering to my rap sheet, as well as shoplifting. Jacob didn't seem phased in the slightest. I couldn't make him out; there was something about his confidence that seemed thin and flimsy, like it could fizzle out at any moment, and I reminded myself that out here, you could choose to be anybody you wanted. I would need to be careful.

'We'll keep it small, head into the trees a bit more. Get us some firewood, will you?' He had picked up his bag and was moving a bit further into the trees. I looked around and knelt down to pick up some small sticks, snapping them in two to make sure the wood was dry in the middle. After collecting a handful of those and a couple of larger branches, I brought the wood to where Jacob had cleared some of the leaves away from the forest floor.

'So, does your family know where you are?' I asked.

'More or less,' he said. He took the smaller twigs and built them up in a pyramid shape, then took a tissue out of his bag and ripped it into pieces, stuffing the bits in among the wood. I sat down with my back against the nearest tree. Jacob produced a lighter and lit the edges of the paper, the small flames flickering in the wind. He sheltered it with his hands as the fire took hold, then he blew gently into the core of the pyramid, making it glow until it finally caught properly. The twigs crackled and the thin wisp of smoke dispersed up into the trees without being too visible.

I wondered how long I would stay with this person. I half expected to wake up in the morning with the barely warm fire still smouldering and Jacob long gone.

'Yours?' he said.

'My what? Oh – no,' I said. 'I haven't been in touch with my parents for a while. I've been away, doing other things.' I didn't want to tell him about any of *that*. 'I suppose you think it bothers me. It doesn't. It's not important.'

'I think that sort of thing would affect anybody,' he said. 'You can pretend it doesn't, if you want. You can be anybody you want to be out here, I suppose.' There was a quiet moment as he blew into the fire once more. 'Sorry, ignore me. I'm just talking rubbish, as usual.'

'You don't have to apologise,' I said. 'But I barely know anything about you. I'm willing to bet you aren't as sure as you make out.'

'Me?' he said. 'You're having a laugh. I'm a mess. I'd stay away if I were you.'

'Why?'

'You'll melt your shoes,' he said.

I noticed then how close my feet were to the fire, and withdrew them quickly. The flames were crackling steadily now, but the fire was not too big. Jacob went away to pee. While he was gone I moved closer to the fire, feeding it small twigs and prodding the glowing centre. There was something primeval about watching the flames jump and cast dancing shadows on the trees around our campsite.

When he returned, Jacob rummaged through his bag and took out a steel teapot. He filled it up with water from a bottle he had carried up here, and placed it on the hot ashes. I understood now why he had been so keen to light a fire in the first place.

'Cup of tea?' he said.

'Oh, that would be bloody lovely.'

He took out a couple of teabags and placed them in the pot. I wondered what else he had in that magic bag of his. He stirred it with a tent peg for a while until steam started coming off the top of the kettle and the water started bubbling. Jacob took the kettle off the fire carefully and poured me a cup. I had to wait for a long time until it was cool enough to put to my lips.

'How is it?' Jacob asked.

I sipped, trying to avoid scalding my mouth. The air was getting cold, and I would have drunk anything hot at the time and enjoyed it. 'It's good,' I said. 'Now we just need a telly. What time's *Coronation Street* on?'

'Look, over there. The bright-looking star is Venus,' Jacob said. I looked where he was pointing, and made out the twinkling light in the sky. 'There's something great about seeing the stars, isn't there?'

There was. It reminded you of how small you were, sitting in a corner of a planet, feeling very far from home but in fact right at home – on the soil that was every bit as much yours as it was anybody else's, because it was the soil your ancestors had walked long before anybody thought of having borders or social classes or currency. I watched the flames for a while in quiet contemplation, and then I boiled another kettle of water on the red embers. When it was boiling I tipped in a packet of instant chicken soup and stirred it around until it was piping hot.

Nothing else needed saying— not for now, at least. We had some brief, trivial conversation about the town before I retreated to my tent for the night. I heard Jacob entering his tent about ten minutes later, and I only spoke to ask him if he had put the fire out properly.

I woke up when the sun hit the tent and the inside started warming up. I unzipped the door and, balancing awkwardly to put on my shoes, stood up to look around. There were no dog walkers, no police shining torches into the tent and asking for our passports. It was a pleasant campsite. Birds were singing in the trees. Jacob's tent was already lying flat on the floor and he was kneeling down to roll it up.

'Good morning,' he said.

'Morning. Did you sleep alright?'

'A bit. My neck's killing me. I must have slept on a root or something. You?'

'I slept like a baby,' I said, noticing that Jacob was packing away at some speed. 'What's your plan for today, then?' I left the question as open as I could, but deep down I felt a little rejected. Maybe that was the idea.

'Get moving again? There's no point hanging around, is there?'

'No, there isn't.' I unpegged the outer sheet of my tent, then took the poles out and folded them up on the floor. Jacob's tent was already rolled up and put away, but he sat and waited for me to pack. His bluff was gone, and I felt relieved. I packed away as quickly as I could, but without rushing too much. Then I picked up my backpack and waited for him to stand up.

'Down the hill and then left,' I said. 'That's the way to the main road.' He nodded, and we set off.

Little did I know at the time, but there are two very different routes out of that region. The southern route runs down the Croatian coast, eventually taking you past Split and Dubrovnik and into Macedonia or Albania. While it's a perfectly feasible route, for us it would have meant more time spent ambling along the coastline, skirting past tourist resorts on one side and forests laden with landmines on the other, along the long, thin strip of land which takes you past Bosnia. The other route heads north to the border with Slovenia. It is generally an easier route. Ljubljana is a lovely city, and from there you can easily get to Zagreb, Belgrade and Sofia. I say all this now, but at the time all I knew was that Slovenia was the next country on our journey. We took the SS14 highway towards the border, and later on the decision at Kozina would lead us up this northern route. But things could have been very different. I had no proper map at the time, and despite all of Jacob's bravado I discovered he didn't have much of a clue where he was going, either.

Energised in the morning, we walked up along the forested hillside above Trieste to a town called Rozzol. By then I could see the seaside towns behind us some twenty or thirty miles back, and the air had become light again, the way it was when you were gaining altitude. We crossed under a motorway bridge and past some ugly blocks of flats which must have had beautiful views of the coast from their balconies. Jacob walked ahead. It was tiring work climbing up what seemed to be one big permanent incline away from the coast, but the way he carried himself told me he had something to prove, and I didn't want to get in the way of it for now.

Eventually, around eleven in the morning, when I had sweat running down my forehead, Jacob started to slow down, and I was gaining ground. 'What time do you want to stop for a break?' I asked from behind.

'I'm keeping going for a bit longer yet,' Jacob said. There was the royal *I* again. 'No use stopping now. We've barely made any progress out of the city.'

'OK. No worries,' I said. I did understand why we were walking; we were walking because there was no point in trying to hitch a ride until we were on the right road. In order to get onto the right road, you had to walk until there were no options left for drivers except the road you wanted. Still, I thought a rest after the climb would have been a good idea.

We had barely walked for ten minutes more when Jacob decided to stop all of a sudden, contrary to his earlier position. 'There's a shop,' he said. 'I'm going to get something to eat. Do you want to look after my bag a moment?'

'Yeah. No problem.'

'OK. I'll be back in a jiffy.' He took off his backpack and left me at the side of the road. A few minutes later he emerged from the shop with a small bag filled with a couple of apples, some film-wrapped focaccia and a bottle of water. He put the apples and the water away and ate the bread.

'Aren't you going to get something?' he asked, mid-mouthful. I shook my head and took a swig of my water. He looked at me as if I was insane. There was a lot to explain, and I didn't feel like going through my sob story with him at that very moment. While he finished eating, I set off walking. We'd reached the outskirts of town when he caught up with me again.

'Currency,' he said in between breaths. 'I knew there was

something I'd forgotten about. In Slovenia they use euros, but in Serbia the currency is the dinar. I can't remember Hungary's, but it's something else too.'

'I'm sure there'll be a place for you to change some in Slovenia. I presume the road will take us through the capital.' The word *Ljubljana* had escaped me for the moment.

'I suppose so. But how much should I change into dinars, or roubles, or whatever? What do you think?'

'It's up to you,' I said.

'Well, what are you planning to do?'

I sighed. 'I don't know, Jacob,' I said. 'I don't know what I'm planning to do at all. Do you know if there are any good jobs going around here?'

He came up level with me. 'Wait a second. Are you trying to tell me you don't have any money at all?'

'No, I have a bit,' I said.

'How much?'

'Thirty, forty euros.'

'Are you serious?' he said. 'What on earth are you planning to do, exactly? Go into the forest and live off squirrel meat? You don't look like the Ray Mears type.'

'It's really not your business,' I replied. 'Why do you care? We barely know each other.'

'Charming. So it's like that, is it? Nobody asked you to get on the train with me out of Genoa. You could still be walking your way across Italy for the next three weeks.'

'Look, Jacob—' I was cut short. A car had torn over onto the pavement in front of us and screeched to a halt. The driver's door opened and a man got out and started shouting at us. Completely stunned, I thought for a second it was because we had been walking on the road. Then he pointed frantically at the car, and away in the direction he had been travelling.

'I think he's offering us a lift,' Jacob said.

'*Non stare lì tra le nuvole! Dai! Vuoi venire, o no?*' the man cried, jumping up and down.

'Yes, *sì!* Wait!' I called out.

We ran together to the car. The man, who was somewhere in his mid-forties, scolded us like a couple of schoolchildren for holding him up. '*Va bene. Entra,*' he said, finally. I opened the car door and hauled myself into the back.

The seat fabric was old and covered in cigarette ash, and the car stank of tobacco. The man had some prayer beads hanging up around the rear-view mirror, and a worn picture of a Catholic saint stuck in a crack in the dashboard. The car was at least twenty years old. The interior was made of plastic and everything was either broken or hanging off, and the windscreen was so dirty with smoke and dead flies that it was a wonder he could see anything out of it.

He set off. The road went up the hill and round a couple of bends. At one point I thought we must have been at the highest point for miles around. The sea was very far away now.

'We're going to the border, to Slovenia,' Jacob said. The man nodded and smiled, but neither of us had any idea whether he had understood.

The road flattened and cut through the trees; there was deep forest either side now, and trucks and cars on the road in quite some frequency. We passed a sign for a rest stop: it wasn't in Italian. The man pulled in at the lay-by ahead, where there was a van selling hot food and cars parked up with their windows open having a rest on whatever long journey they were on. He made it clear that it was time for us to get out.

'Come on,' I said to Jacob, 'it looks like this is our stop.'

The man got out of the car with us and pointed up the road ahead.

'*Buon viaggio, e buona fortuna. Ciao.*' He gave us a salute, got in his car and drove away.

I sat down on a step and adjusted my shoelaces. There was a tap on my shoulder, and I looked up. Jacob was holding an apple out for me. I took it and bit into it gratefully. After a minute I exhaled and everything was alright again. I found a tap around the corner which I used to fill up my bottle of water, then we set off down the road like the two riders in the Bob Dylan song, between the lines of trees, towards the border.

16.

We crossed the border and a load was lifted from my mind. Yes, Slovenia was still a part of the EU – but my escape from the urban, BMW-infested, aristocratic European conglomerate felt closer now than ever before. The border guard had given us a cursory once-over while checking our passports, but no warrant had been issued; there was no extradition awaiting me and I wasn't on Europe's Top Ten Most Wanted list.

Jacob's mood had lifted, too. He was cracking jokes and laughing as we walked along the road away from the border crossing. A stray dog came jogging up and started barking at us. We threw stones at it until it turned tail and ran.

The place names had changed, but besides that there was very little immediate difference on this side of the border. I did notice the motels and restaurants littered along the road were much cheaper, and there were strip clubs at some of these pull-in areas – for the truck drivers, I assumed. Road signs showed the way to Ljubljana, Zagreb and Split, with distances in the hundreds of kilometres. It felt at once like the whole of Eurasia had become opened up to us. What once had been a fear of being imprisoned in a society I didn't understand was starting to be replaced by a different thought: that nobody would, in fact, notice or care that I had gone away.

The road left the small outpost town and, after a few houses on the outskirts, carried on through brush land and trees, a landscape with remarkably few features away from the road. There was no pavement, so we kept as close as we could to the edge, away from the traffic. A car beeped at us as it passed, but showed no signs of stopping. Then a second driver shouted something and waved his arm around as he sped past. I think he thought we were gypsies.

When I was younger, reading *The Lord of the Rings* for the first time, I fantasised about one day going on some magnificent quest into dangerous lands. Is that need for adventure ingrained in every child growing up? Is it something we repress until these crisis points in our lives? What I did know, there on the Slovenian border, was that times were going to get harder from here on out– and I was OK with that. Jacob and I were even starting to look the part of adventuring hobbits. Our faces and hair were more rugged, and our clothes were starting to turn black from all the traffic pollution on the roads we walked.

At the side of the road we saw things thrown away: mostly bits of plastic and old, rusted cans. I picked up a used shotgun shell and put it in my bag. I had started a little collection now.

'Just think,' I said, 'Roman legions marched through this way towards Greece and Asia Minor. Crusaders took these roads to Jerusalem, all those hundreds of years ago.'

'Conquerors, you mean,' Jacob replied, 'marching off to wage war on some poor uncivilised tribe for money and power.'

'I suppose so.' I pictured caravans of horses crossing the plains, this ancient landscape where the Austro-Hungarian

Empire once met with the frontier of the Ottomans. 'The world must have been a lot bigger then. You could travel hundreds of miles and come across only wilderness.'

'You don't like this world very much, do you?' Jacob said.

'Does anybody like the time they're born in? Nowadays everything is crowded, polluted. We've made a mess of the planet. What one person does rarely ever matters, unless you're some sort of celebrity.'

'Oh, sure,' he said, 'things were a lot better when whoever had the largest army could do whatever they wanted. Don't you ever think that things are just the same as they've always been? That history sounds glorious just because they wrote down all the juicy bits. What you do matters just as much as it ever has done. It's always been a struggle, finding yourself.'

'Maybe you're right,' I said, but I didn't believe it.

We passed a sign for Kozina. I had hoped it would be a town, but it just turned out to be a couple of slip roads onto the highway. One sign pointed towards Ljubljana; the other led to Rijeka. I had no idea where that was, but I assumed it was somewhere on the southern route to Croatia.

'Look, here comes a car,' Jacob said.

I stuck out my thumb at the approaching Audi, which was already indicating to go onto the highway. I waved as it drove past, the driver looking at both of us with a vacant expression on his face.

'I guess we'll have to wait for another one,' I said.

'Oh, fuck off!' Jacob shouted after him. 'Stick your ride up your arse, you stupid twat!'

I looked at him in disbelief.

'What?'

'Calm down,' I said. 'There'll be plenty more.'

He shook his head. 'What a prick. You could tell just by looking at him.'

At that moment I realised Jacob and I were very different people. Could you teach somebody like that, who was so strong in themselves, anything at all? I hoped I could. I knew that I was already changing from being in Jacob's company – but when a stronger person met a weaker one, was it always the weaker one who gave way? Or could this journey be a healing process for both of us?

A few more cars drove by without stopping. It was late afternoon, and the sun, having broken through the clouds at around lunchtime, was dipping in the sky. Jacob and I had our bags down and were taking it in turns to stand by the road and stick our arms out at the vehicles going onto the highway. This time it was me standing and Jacob sitting down away from the road.

A faded orange minivan pulled in a couple of yards in front of where we were waiting. In the front were a middle-aged couple – local, judging from their looks: the husband in the driver's seat wearing an old black blazer, his wife wrapped loosely in a shawl, her hair trailing out of it. She flashed me a brief smile. In the back a young blonde girl was leaning forward to take a look. She grabbed hold of the door from inside and slid it open.

'Jake! Come on,' I said, nodding at the driver gratefully for picking us up. I bowed my head as I got in and sat down on the worn leather seat. Jacob followed. The girl in the back smiled. She had a worn backpack on the floor next to her, and the piercings in the top of her ear gave me the impression right away that she was some sort of traveller – a student, perhaps.

Jacob made his way past her to the back of the van and sat down as we set off. They said something in Italian to the girl, and she spoke back. Then she turned to me and said in a surprisingly upbeat American accent, 'Hey. Where are you guys from?'

'Hi,' I said. 'We're British. My name's Cameron, and this is Jacob.'

'Cam, Jacob. I'm Amy. It's great to meet you.' She was odd, really, and far too smiley to fit in with my current journey. She had a tendency to raise the inner ends of her eyebrows when she spoke. Her hair, though blonde at the bottom, was darker at the roots. It reminded me of a wheat field in the shadow. 'Are you headed for Ljubljana?'

'Yes, we—' Jacob's scowl was enough to stop me telling her too much. 'We're travelling that way. What about you?'

'*Si* – I mean yes, sorry.' She laughed. 'Europe has so many damned languages. I just got used to a bit of German, and then Italian. God knows what I'll do when I get to Budapest.'

'What brings you here? Are you on holiday?'

'I wouldn't really call it that. I guess you could call it more of a soul-searching journey. An escape from the forbidden thrills of Minnesota.'

'*Il tuo amichetto va allo stesso modo?*' asked the man in the front.

Amy laughed. '*Si, vanno nella stessa direzione. Grazie mille.*' She turned to look at Jacob for a moment. 'Hello.' Getting no response, she turned back to me. 'Your friend doesn't talk much?'

I looked at Jacob, who shrugged. 'Not really,' I said. 'How long have you been travelling, then?'

'A couple of weeks. I started off in Ireland, you know. Then I got the ferry across to Liverpool, Manchester, London, and then through Amsterdam and Berlin. Your accent sounds like you're from Manchester. Am I right?'

'Yes, you're right.' I smiled. The sun was beginning to set. I didn't like the idea of arriving in the city late in the evening. 'Where are you staying tonight?'

'Probably in a hostel in the city centre. I have a couple written down somewhere.'

'And where are you travelling after that?' I asked. Jacob gave me a look, and I realised the main difference between us was that I wanted, somehow, to get better.

'I might stay here a day or two, depending on the town,' she said, 'and after that, Budapest, Prague, maybe Warsaw or St Petersburg. As long as I still have enough money, that is. What about you?'

'Towards . . . well, I'm not sure,' I said.

'You have that damaged look about you, Cameron,' Amy replied. 'I can tell. There's only two types of people in the world – people who have the look and people who don't. Actually, you both have it. I guess that's why you two are such good friends.'

Slightly embarrassed, I smiled. 'And what about you? What's your story?'

'My story? Well, I had an uncle who looked after me in the town where I grew up, and he was inappropriate with me once, and nobody in the whole town would believe me because my uncle was a cop,' she said. 'He even tried to have me arrested for it. So I ran away from that town. I don't know where I'm going yet, but I won't go back there, ever.'

I'd never heard somebody tell a story like that to two strangers in such a casual way. 'Wow, that's heavy,' I said. 'I hope you find somewhere you can feel like you belong.'

'Thank you, that's so sweet. What about you, Jacob?'

Jacob, who had been pretending not to listen, looked around. 'Oh, I'm sorry to disappoint you, but there's no deep enigma to me. No exciting story to tell. It's nearly half past five, Cam,' he said. 'By the time we get into town it'll be dark.'

'We'll sort something out,' I said.

Amy was still staring at him. 'I don't believe you. There's more to you than meets the eye, Jacob,' She smiled back at me, with so much intensity in her eyes it was like staring down the barrel of a loaded gun.

17.

As evening fell over the forest, the driver of the minivan slowed to a stop at a junction which marked the outskirts of Ljubljana, although I couldn't yet see anything of the city for all the trees. But we soon pulled off onto a dual carriageway and began to pass buildings and people on bicycles, and soon we were into the built-up part of town.

The place was much quieter than I'd expected for a capital city. The conversation with Amy in the back of the van had gone quiet; Jacob had sat in silence for most of the journey until we reached the outskirts, when he made an attempt to ask her about hostels in the city centre. It seemed as though he had made an executive decision to stay in one overnight.

'Are you sure?' I asked him, as if he'd forgotten about my little financial problem.

It seemed my lack of money had to be an unspoken area for us both. 'I don't fancy trying to walk out of another city now,' he said. 'It must be getting near four o'clock. And I could really do with a shower.'

'There are a couple,' Amy said, pointing at a small city map she must have printed off somewhere. 'This one here is Parkside Hostel – but I think I'm probably going to try this one. Hostel

Ljubljanica. It's nearer the centre, so in the morning I can wake up and eat breakfast near the river.'

Jacob nodded. 'Either of those looks fine. Cam, which do you prefer?'

I shrugged, not keen to get involved in any decision-making with money that wasn't my own, and conscious that following Amy for the sake of it was both unnecessary and impractical. It was already clear that Jacob felt uncomfortable with her around. She said something in Italian to the couple in front. They had been silent the whole time, except for when they spoke to Amy, and I wondered if the reason was that they didn't know a word of English.

After a couple more junctions, we pulled up next to a set of water fountains and got out. It was already evening now, with the street lights illuminating the shops and businesses along the street and some sparse traffic moving through the centre, with people walking home or into town, perhaps for a drink at one of the bars. I stepped out first, followed by Amy and then Jacob. We thanked the driver and his wife. Jacob looked around at the city buildings.

'Thank you for picking us up,' I said to Amy. She'd waited, maybe not wanting to be the first to set off, or maybe waiting to see what Jacob and I wanted to do.

'It's been wonderful to meet you both,' she said. 'Do you know the way from here? The Parkside Hostel is a few blocks away. I'm heading down to the river.'

'We'll work it out from here,' Jacob said. He took out his phone – to look at a map of the city, I assumed. Amy nodded, smiled at me and then, hoisting her backpack up onto her shoulders, strolled off in the direction of the river. I watched her turn around the corner, her confident stride leaving me a bit sad to see her go. But as I said, it was Jacob's money.

Jacob was staring at me. His hair had been pushed out of shape by the long ride in the van. 'Don't tell me you really liked her.'

'What? Of course not. I thought she was nice enough. You didn't have to be so rude, that's all.'

He sighed, then looked in the direction Amy had pointed us in for the other hostel, the one she wasn't going to, down a road dimly lit with street lights. There was no guarantee we'd get a place to sleep either way, of course. If push came to shove, we would be putting our tents up in the first quiet green space we could find, or sleeping in sleeping bags in a doorway, like the homeless people back home.

'Come on,' he said. He put his phone back in his pocket and crossed the road. I followed him and together we set off – in the direction of the river.

We found the hostel on a road overlooking the river. It was a glorious-looking building, as they all were near the water. Further across were the lights and sounds of people dining and drinking in the restaurants – a tempting orange glow – but there was not much more indication of the hostel's existence than a sticker next to the buzzer at the front door. Jacob rang the bell and we waited. After a moment, the lock clicked and we went inside. The staircase was clean and modern, made of actual hewn stone. We made our way up to the third floor, where we found another door which led into the hostel itself. The door was wide open, and there was no sign of Amy anywhere.

The reception was empty for a few moments until a young man with dark hair and a short-sleeved shirt came to the counter. Jacob asked him about the rooms. There were double rooms available for forty euros per night, or a bed in a shared room available for fifteen. He paid for two of the latter, and internally I breathed a tiny sigh of relief.

The man led us through a small corridor and showed us the communal bathroom, a kitchen and dining area, complete with a sofa and television, a dining table, and the Wi-Fi password on a handy printout stuck to the wall, along with flyers for local museums, art galleries and the like. Finally, he showed us the bedroom. There were eight bunk beds in total, with a locker at the side of each one, and there was somebody asleep in one of the beds, next to a pile of clothes.

Jacob took off his walking boots and pulled some clean clothes out of his bag.

'I can pay you for the room,' I said.

'Don't be daft. Keep your money safe, for an emergency. I'm going to grab a shower. Do you mind keeping an eye on my stuff?'

'Not at all,' I said.

I used the time to write in my notepad. There was so much to keep track of, and I felt like the world was speeding past me again, too quickly for me to keep up. After a while the door opened. I expected to see Jacob, but instead in walked Amy, with a small bag of toiletries in her hand. Her hair was wet, and she was wearing a vest and shorts. She smiled. 'Cameron! I'm glad you could make it.'

'Me too,' I said.

She sat down on the opposite bunk and brushed her hair. It was only then that I realised her boots had been sitting by the side of the bed. She took a wet cloth and cleaned the mud off them.

'Sorry about Jake. He's . . . not very sociable.'

'I can tell. Did you meet on the road, or were you friends back home?'

'No. We met in Italy. Jacob's been very helpful to me so far. But he has his moments.'

'How's that relationship working out for you?'

'It's a bit one-sided,' I said.

Jacob walked into the room, shirtless and damp. 'Shower's free,' he said, ignoring Amy. 'Do you mind if I have top bunk?'

'Help yourself.' I took my soap and toothbrush out of my bag, along with what spare clothes I had, and left him and Amy there. I entered the shared bathroom at the end of the corridor, undressed and turned on the warm water.

The weeks of grease and grime took a great deal of scrubbing to wash away. My skin was caked with dirt and pollution from the exhaust fumes of all the cars that had passed us as we walked along the side of the road. Having watched it all run down the drain, I looked at my barely recognisable body, which was thin and pale-looking without the dirt. I ran my fingers through my hair; I hadn't realised how long and messy it was without a mirror.

Back in the room, Jacob was lying on the top bunk with his headphones in. I glanced across at Amy, whose shape was concealed under the cheap sheets of the hostel bed. I couldn't see whether she was awake or asleep. I sat down on my bed and put my things away, then took out my notepad and wrote again for a while. Some time later, Jacob stuck his head around to see what I was doing.

'What are you writing?'

'Just notes, stuff,' I said. 'Just to keep a record, more than anything.'

'A diary?'

'I suppose. I have this idea of writing a novel one day, maybe. Have you ever stayed in a hostel before?'

'A real treat. The full commercial experience,' Jacob said. 'Make sure to redeem your EU train pass at the desk. The Wi-Fi password is *complacency*.'

'You don't have to try and be so edgy all the time, you know.'

Jacob smirked. 'Terrible habit, I know—but I don't see yours as any better. Stop hiding away from yourself all the time. Live a little! Stop caring what everybody thinks of what you do all the damned time.'

I laughed; you had to, with Jacob. 'I appreciate the life lesson.'

'I'm going to get some sleep. We should set off early tomorrow morning.'

'Goodnight, Jake.'

I didn't dislike Jacob. But I was becoming dependent on him—and maybe even, dare I say it, attached. It was a frightening feeling, and a decent part of me thought I would be better off on my own, without a care in the world.

While he went off to sleep, I thought deeply. That was the first time I strongly felt the urge to grab my things, slip out, hit the road, put my tent up somewhere and find the first ride away from there in the morning.

Some other people came into the room and shuffled their things around before going to sleep in the other beds. I could hear Jacob's slow, steady breathing in the darkness. I don't know how long I lay awake there before she came over.

'Amy?' I whispered. She climbed quietly into the bed with me. I could feel the closeness of her body against mine, the warmth of her breath on my skin.

'Shh. Don't talk.' Beneath the blankets, her hands moved cautiously but intentionally. She prised her way into my underwear. I held her to me, close enough to press my lips against the arch of her neck. She bucked her hips up against me. The rest of the room was quiet. Underneath the sheets, we managed to undress and then, after a moment, we found our place together. If the other people in the room were awake, they pretended not to hear anything. Afterwards, we stayed together for a while.

'You don't have to go with him,' she whispered. 'Stay with me. Tomorrow we'll check out the town, and then you can travel with me to Budapest by train the day after. We could go anywhere we wanted, together.'

'I don't have any money,' I said.

'It doesn't matter. We can find some volunteering work somewhere for a while.'

'I don't know . . . It's a big decision.'

'Is it? What were you going to do, follow your friend around forever?'

'It's not like that,' I said.

Amy pulled away. 'Do you trust him?'

'Yes. I trust him.'

'Why? What's his birthday? How many brothers and sisters does he have? Can you even tell me where he's travelling to? Come with me instead. He doesn't even have to know.'

I had to admit I didn't know the answer to any of those questions, but . . . 'We can't just sneak out of here in the morning.'

'Yes, we can. And that's exactly what we'll do.'

18.

During the early hours of the morning, two skulking figures slip out of the doors of Hostel Ljubljanica, cross the river and pass quietly through the main square, heading out of town. One of them is wearing a pair of tough walking boots and a backpack, and has all the determined march of a soldier going to war. The other, wearing a pair of dirty waterproof trousers, his face bearing the beginnings of a beard, looks hesitantly back in the direction of the city.

They walk under the closed balconies and across the stone cobbles, their footsteps echoing off the stone in the narrow streets – two ghosts from some other era, perhaps – and they are gone before the early morning mist has faded from the streets. Nobody sees them leave, just as nobody saw them arrive, and no record of their existence survives save for a passport number and a time scribbled in a checking-in book. By the time the city wakes up, they are already long gone, following the road which heads east out of the city across the plains.

From a bird's-eye view, they can be seen reaching the cross-roads on the outskirts and flagging down the passing cars; once or twice the targeted vehicles drive past, leaving them to pace back and forth, exchange a few comments and kick the dirt.

Not long after, a nondescript vehicle pulls over to the side of the road. They pile in with their backpacks, and the car sets off with the pair inside.

It crosses the furthest of the city limits, drives through Višnja Gora and stops in the middle of town, where it stays for fifteen or twenty minutes. The driver can be seen exiting the vehicle to purchase something from a small shop nearby. He gets back in the car and quickly changes direction; north, into the mountains. A glimpse of the car's interior reveals he is alone, the two passengers gone without a trace, off on some other route.

A look down the southern road picks them up once again, walking in the direction of Trebnje as the morning warms up. They walk side by side for a while without saying anything and then, when it is quiet, one of them calls out to the other to stop for a while. One of the travellers takes out something white from their backpack and walks off into the trees. They squat down and then cover the ground over with dirt until all that can be seen are the corners of white paper protruding from the ground.

They continue for another kilometre or so until they reach a petrol station at the side of the main road, where they start flagging down cars once more. A few minutes later, a man comes out of the petrol station, shouting and cursing. He chases them off a little further down the road.

The next vehicle to stop is an old brown van with a white rooftop box and a family in the back: two young children, a niece or older sister, perhaps, a mother and a possible aunt and two men sitting up front. The travellers jump aboard and the van rumbles up the road to Bič, then to Trebnje. It stops in a dusty lay-by before a junction, and the two travellers jump out of the back. They have a brief conversation with the driver before the van pulls away and turns off the main road in the direction of a small village nearby.

The two travellers wait for half an hour. They are picked up next by a red Opel doing less than thirty with an old man at the wheel. He smiles and nods but does not speak a word of English, and the only communication he can manage is to offer them each a cigarette. One of the travellers sticks his elbow out of the open window and exhales. This journey takes them as far as a little place called Novo Mesto.

After he drives away, they set off on foot and walk a couple of kilometres along a quiet road that runs parallel to the highway. They stop to look at the road signs for a moment and then carry on along a smaller road alongside a little river. Further ahead, the river widens. There is deep forest on either side of the road. They sit down for half an hour to eat and drink, one napping, head down, the other with his feet up on a fallen branch, bare toes wiggling in the sun.

Half an hour later the sleeping one wakes up, and the other laces their boots up, and they walk down to the banks of the river. One stoops down and tries to skim a stone across the surface. There are small fish visible in the still water near to the edge; they scatter away as the travellers walk along the gravel beach.

The day wanes and the pair travel further through the woods. They enter a small clearing in between the trees and unpack some bundles from their bags. They unroll them and start assembling tent poles and fabric, and then they peg out two rectangular shapes and drape the fabric over the top.

An aerial view reveals there is nobody about for miles. One

of the travellers is lying on his coat, looking up at the stars. The other is writing something down in a small notebook he keeps with him at all times. Their fire gives off a stream of smoke which drifts over the trees and disappears into the evening.

Who are these two people travelling like nomads and hiding in the woods like wanted bandits? They are people with no place in the world, it seems, getting into strangers' cars, passing through forests and crossing roads, never stopping. One of them is a decent pool player and likes the music of The Fall and has a sister he will never talk about. One went on a school trip to the Somme. One used to go and watch the football with his dad. One can draw decent caricatures and would love to learn to paint one day. One would like to become a writer. One wonders if he ought to be a better Catholic. One misses his dog.

Silently they harbour almost all of this, talking only about place names and the road ahead, good places to set up camp and where to find food. Yes, they always talk about food, and sometimes about other things like sex and hot baths and a warm, comfortable bed.

Does anybody still think about them or wonder where they are? No one that they know of, at least. But then their world is a million miles away. Their schedule has no relation to the days of the week. Their only calendar is the seasons. Their only comfort is the warmth of the fire. Their fate is in nobody's hands. They are wild animals, who could die in a frozen river or an avalanche, or be eaten by predators without the world giving them any sympathy or thought.

That, when it comes down to it, is freedom. True freedom is a life devoid of caring, an open journey, with no catharsis to be found. Nothing to care about – that is both the great price and the great reward of being properly free.

In the morning, they wake, pack their tents away and head back to the highway. The next day takes them to the Croatian border. They cross, then carry on along a road which bends and curves through a couple of hills.

A mile down the road, a pack of huge mountain dogs blocks their path. These are big dogs with coats of thick bear-like fur, whose job it is to protect the sheep from wolves and rustlers. The travellers pause for a moment. They dare not throw stones at the dogs, for fear of provoking these roaring beasts and being ripped apart. Then a farmer appears, a small man with a walking stick who lets them pass by, his ancient authority good enough for the dogs, it seems.

They take a bus ride to Zagreb for a couple of pounds each. In the city centre they exchange some currency, eat dinner and stay in another hostel in a double room. There is no sign of the American girl. They do not concern themselves with this fact – at least, not openly.

They walk out of town the next day and wait for a ride on the highway out of Zagreb. There are yellow striped poles with red plastic hats in some of the fields and bordering the trees: forgotten landmines from the Yugoslavian war. The pair throw stones at the patches of dirt, trying to set the mines off, with no success.

From Zagreb they hitch-hike to Nova Gradiška and then to Slavonski Brod, near the border with Bosnia. They walk down the long, quiet road to the border crossing, which sits across the river.

The crossing is more difficult this time. Their passports are checked and handed over to the sergeant, then checked again. A guard bids them to enter a small hut and empties all the contents of their bags out onto the table. It takes them some time, and while one of them does it quietly, the other protests furiously, making sarcastic comments in English which neither of the guards understand.

Eventually they are left there to repack and are allowed to cross the border. There are tall grey houses on the Bosnian side, with the remains of an old concrete watchtower perched alongside the river. They carry on until a tractor with a trailer in tow pulls alongside. The driver says a few words, and they hop into the trailer, next to the hay.

The tractor takes them to the next village. There are women wrapped in shawls, and men with fierce eyes and red beards watching them pass by. A muezzin shouts out his loud, vibrant call to prayer. It is a sound neither of the travellers have heard before. It echoes around the hillsides and pierces them right through to their souls in the midday quiet:

Allahu akbar! Allahu akbar!
Ash-hadu an la ilaha illa Allah!
Ash-hadu anna Muhammadan Rasoul Allah!
Hayya ala-s-Salah! La ilaha illa Allah.

They continue on to Doboj, and then to Zenica. The road leads up into the mountains, and they catch their first glimpses of snow on the steady climb, the jagged peaks capped with heavy white drifts of the stuff, like the Himalayas. At the top of the climb the road winds through alpine forest with snow that's more than a couple of inches deep around the trunks of the trees, and at the side of the road there are thicker snow-drifts still.

The mountain path winds down to a valley nestled between the mountains, with a small town sitting in the middle. Here, they stop for a while and eat. The cold wind hits their faces like the air from an open freezer. A man asks them in English where they are going. They tell him they are on their way to Sarajevo; they do not mention the crossing to Serbia.

The man brings them outside and introduces them to a truck driver who is climbing out of his cab. He bids them to wait while he collects a couple of supplies from the town, and then he comes back and starts the engine. They climb in, squashed up on the spare seat at the back of the cab, and set off along the mountain road in the dusk. The truck driver is amiable but not too talkative. He tries to talk to them about the winter and the crops, but a lot is lost in translation.

The evening turns to darkness. The truck driver drives on stoically, hardly saying a word. He is no stranger to these late, lonely drives. The road goes on and on through the mountains, round hairpin bends and down, through valleys and tight passes. The bright headlights of the truck light up the snowdrifts up ahead. The travellers take it in turns to sleep, but adrenaline combats the tiredness as the night continues.

Some time later, before the sun has risen, the truck arrives in a large, built-up place and pulls into a warehouse in an industrial side of town. The driver tells the travellers to wait while he speaks to somebody. A serious-looking man with a bald head takes them through to an office. There is an old-looking computer in the corner, switched on, and they use Google Translate to communicate a few sentences back and forth. The man in the office tells them they can sleep here until the morning.

Gratefully, they accept, and a couple of hours later they are woken early to bowls of hot soup and bread to start the day. The warehouse owner bids them farewell and shows them the way to the city centre. They walk out of the warehouse, past the rusted gate and along the road, beyond the worn-down factories.

19.

Sarajevo was a haunted city, it seemed, full of bullet holes, and the people bore a resolute look upon their faces which reminded me of the way the British must have looked during the Second World War. That wasn't an exaggeration, by the way; the apartment blocks still bore the scars of stray rifle shots and shrapnel pieces, and on the pavement there were large holes where the shells must have landed some twenty years ago. Flowers were planted around the edges of these blast craters, probably to send some message about how life carried on growing through the cracks of the Yugoslav Wars. But I found it a grim statement, at best, and the whole place felt unnaturally quiet.

Nobody bothered us at all, in fact, and we passed through the city without leaving much of an impression. There was a thin mist hanging in the air, but by now I was well used to feeling damp. But at lunchtime, when we were almost out of the city, the black clouds overhead decided to open up.

Jacob and I found ourselves driven to cover in an empty concrete building as the rain pelted down, interrupted only by angry flashes of lightning overhead. Thunder echoed across the mountains and through the valley and reverberated around the walls of the building. I could see our breath as we spoke.

'What do you miss most about home?' I said to Jacob, in an effort to break the silence.

'Jaffa Cakes,' he said, 'and proper cups of tea. You?'

'I don't know.' I thought about it for a moment. 'It really does come down to food, doesn't it?'

'Well, I didn't want to mention family. And don't forget a pint of beer,' he added.

'It is haram,' I said. It was a joke we had started to make since arriving in Bosnia.

'What are you going to do when you get back?'

'I don't think about it. What about you?'

'I have a couple of ideas lined up. Jobs, really,' he said. 'You *are* going to get back, you know. Whether you plan to or not. This is just a blip, a software error. The prelude to the actual story, if you like.'

'Please don't start with any God stuff,' I said. There was another flash of lightning on the far side of the valley, and a booming crack of thunder followed it. I thought about how the ancient hominids must have trembled at the sound of it. How it must have been, to them, stuck to the tiny landscape.

'It doesn't need to be about God,' he said.

'What, then?' I said. 'I'm no more special than anybody else out there – I discovered that a while ago. At the end of the day, nobody really deserves anything.' Not for the first time since I'd left Manchester, I thought of Tony.

'You're wrong.' Jacob paused, trying to fit something into words. Then he smiled and shook his head. 'You're just wrong. You care about other people, and you're honest. Those are good traits.'

'Bad things happen to good people, Jacob,' I said.

He shrugged. 'Life happens. There's good and bad in it for everyone. It's what you make of what you have, that's what makes the difference.'

I shook my head and stood up, willing the storm to end so I could get out of here instead of listening to Jacob's sermon. In the distance the black clouds were racing over and through the mountains, opening up some lighter patches of sky. I could still see the flashes of lightning, but the thunder was moving further away. Torrents of rain washed away what was left of the snow down the street and into the river.

'Looks like it's clearing up,' I said.

'There you go, changing the subject. You ought to read some of the stories from Auschwitz, you know. Those are tales of real suffering.'

'What's your point, Jacob?' I snapped. 'I know I'm an entitled white British male who had plenty of chances. Hashtag first-world problems.'

'I'm not calling you entitled, Cam,' he said. 'I can tell you've had your fair share of problems, but you're letting them define you, that's your problem. Read the accounts of some of those Jews sometime. They didn't spend the rest of their lives full of anger and regret. They got on with their lives.'

'Roger that. Message received, over. Repeat, storm is clearing, over.'

'Oh, don't be such a bloody coward all your life,' Jacob said.

I picked up my bag and walked out. The rain had stopped, save for the water dripping from the trees and off the rooftops. Ahead of us the mountain pass looked clear now; there were only a few splashes of snow on the tops of the highest peaks. In front of us a long, straight road led out across the plain before it reached the mountains.

Jacob emerged from the building but didn't say anything after that for a while. We walked out of the city, down the road to Višegrad that took us the last twenty miles or so until we reached the lonely border into Serbia. Jacob kept a few yards behind me, and I walked without acknowledging his presence. I was glad we had come this way. I couldn't have borne the weight of passing through Srebrenica.

As we approached the border crossing, I took out a cigarette I had kept from one of our earlier rides, and I lit it before we walked up to the booth. The border control woman behind the glass told me to put it out just as quickly. Jacob came up behind me and presented his passport to her. She checked them both for a minute, looking at our faces through the window, and asked where we were going. Jacob told her we were on our way to Greece. She stamped our passports, then handed them over with a frown and sent us on our way.

We passed through Serbian villages with ruined-looking houses, old people tending to chickens and carrying big bundles of wood on their hunched backs, and children running barefoot through the streets, eventually hitching a couple of rides heading east across the country. The first was with an unshaven, middle-aged man called Göran, who tried to tell us a story or two about the Yugoslav Wars. He sounded strangely proud about this violent part of his country's history. The next pair didn't speak English and smoked like chimneys. The cigarettes they gave us tasted like cheap tobacco and chemicals, but I smoked them out of politeness anyway.

The road we ended up on took us within thirty miles of the

border with Kosovo, running along in between two mountains which must have been the site of some of the fighting when Jacob and I were only a few years old. We found a box of cabbages left in the street and took a couple each to eat raw. Besides these, we were living off the instant soup packets of which I kept a plentiful supply, plus bread and occasionally a bit of fruit.

Later we passed through Niš, Serbia's second largest city. At one point I saw a homeless man with one leg gone from the knee down sitting on a park bench in some sort of stupor, looking straight ahead. He looked as though he hadn't eaten properly for weeks, and I didn't think there would be much point in begging in these sort of places.

The grey communist blocks seemed like such a cold, lonely place to live. In the centre of the city there were newer buildings, renovated churches and new squares with signs which stated they had been funded by the European Union to the value of several million pounds. But you couldn't shake the ghost of the old regime; it came across in the way the people passed each other with their eyes fixed straight ahead, not daring to smile. It was an unforgiving country, I thought, but Jacob seemed to like how different it was to back home.

We camped next to the forest that night, close to Niška Banja, and in the morning we were woken by loud voices and torches shining on the outside of the tents. I unzipped the door, half asleep, and saw a police officer peering at me; he had a pistol fastened to the side of his leg. I got out slowly.

'Passport,' he said in a voice that resembled the Terminator.

'OK, no problem,' I said. Jacob had already handed his over to the other officer. I indicated that I needed to go back into the tent to get it, and I fumbled around in my bag quickly, hoping I wasn't going to get shot when I drew it out. I emerged and handed the red booklet over to the guard. The book bore its lion and unicorn emblem somewhat ashamedly; the gold lettering which said UNITED KINGDOM OF GREAT BRITAIN AND NORTHERN IRELAND had faded so much that it had almost disappeared entirely.

The policemen checked the passports and spoke into their radios for a moment, and then I waited for them to leave. They didn't. Instead they made us pack our things away while they stood over us, watching. It took a good ten minutes, even hurrying, and then they showed us the road and the direction we ought to be heading in.

'Thank you, thank you for your guided tour,' Jacob said as we started walking. 'I will be sure to recommend you to friends and family.' I didn't know whether the officers understood.

When the traffic died down, this was a nice place. The air was cool and ran through the trees quietly. The forests felt wilder here, and I wondered whether there were bears further up in the mountains. There was no sign of the officers following us.

There was no point thinking about any of it. You left all these people far behind with all of their little problems and concerns. They thought you had come here to steal something, when there was nothing of theirs worth stealing. You left behind their concerns about immigration and national security. You left behind their pride, and all of their fears and insecurities, and even their kindness or sense of comradeship. All you took with you was what was in you, and that was the thing which no amount of walking or hitch-hiking could create any distance from. I could have been angry at Jacob for our earlier conversation, but there was no point. He was only reflecting back at me the things I already knew.

There was a smaller path which seemed as though it hugged the hills around for a while. 'Shall we depart from the main road?' I said.

Jacob shrugged, so I set off along it. The footpath was made of loose rocks and gravel which shifted as I stepped on them, but I had by now become a confident walker. There were trees and bushes either side, but nothing was in fruit at this time of year. We passed a small house with a couple of goats running loose in the garden, and then the path came to another road which ran vaguely in the right direction. The sun was overhead, but I guessed the road ran east and somewhat south, which was the way we were headed.

The road climbed the next hill and then descended onto another large, flat plain which could have been the whole earth itself, it seemed, with the way it went on forever. Crickets chirped in the wild grass, and insects flew between the flowers. When I walked near to a thicket of longer grass, a rabbit shot out. I watched it leap like lightning from one bush to another, and then it was gone. There was a solitary house, perched atop a lonely hilltop, and then the large mountains further beyond. The road curved past fields which must have belonged to the owners of this house; the crops were already tall and bright green.

A small white car came along some time later and pulled alongside us. The driver said something in Serbian. Neither of us understood a word, but apparently he was telling us to jump in. He had brown skin which looked like leather and a set of crooked teeth that looked rotten from years of drinking and cigarettes. He smiled as he waited for us to get in.

'Thanks,' Jacob said.

The man nodded, then reeled off another long sentence, spat out of the window and set off. The old car rumbled along with some difficulty. There were a group of horses running in one of the fields; he pointed to them and smiled at us again.

He stopped the car no more than three or four miles from where we had been walking, next to a run-down house, and gestured at us to wait a minute. He got out, unclasped the piece of rope holding the gate together and went inside the run-down house. It was silent for miles around.

I glanced at Jacob. The place reminded me of those horror film shacks that were always filled with rusty circular saw blades and body parts.

A few minutes later, he emerged with a couple of old glass bottles filled with a clear liquid and handed them to us.

'Hajde da pijemo za tvoje putovanje,' he said. We nodded obliviously and thanked him. He took out one of the smaller glass bottles – a Coca Cola bottle from a long time ago – with a cork stuffed in the top and passed it towards me. I shook my head.

'Viskey,' he said. He kept waving the thing at me. I took it from him and sniffed the opening. It was a foul, strong spirit which burned the inside of your nostrils. 'Viskey', he said again, and laughed.

I put it to my lips and took the smallest sip I could manage. The liquid hit the back of my throat like fire, and my lips felt wrinkled merely from coming into contact with the substance.

'Here,' I said, passing the bottle to Jacob. He took a larger mouthful and swallowed it down, coughing. He went to hand it back to the man, who refused.

'I think he wants us to keep it,' I said.

We shook hands with him. He grinned, then watched us leave. As I turned back to see him, he was going back into his house in the middle of nowhere. I understood why you'd need to brew your own viskey in a place like that.

We walked on, but the road continued on for miles without respite, and there was no sign of anything. We were lost, I realised. There was a forest lying over on the right of us which started at the base of the mountain and went up onto it. I asked Jacob if we should think about setting up camp.

'I don't like it,' Jacob said.

'Don't like what?'

'This place. I think we should carry on a while further,' he said.

I looked around. The small road we were following was devoid of traffic and looked as though it wound on through the hills for days. But Jacob was right. There was a bad feeling here at the foot of the mountains. I inhaled sharply. The air was cold and stuck in the bottom of my lungs.

'On we go, then,' I said.

We walked as dusk set in. I could make out the lights of a house far away on the hilltop. Somewhere across the valley, a dog was barking. Mosquitoes and midges were starting to appear, and the forest was growing darker. I didn't fancy getting lost out here in the countryside.

'I think we should set up camp,' I said.

'Where?' Jacob looked around at the road we were on; fields off to one side, bordered with fences, and the forest off to the other. I knew he didn't like the look of the forest, but this time I stood my ground. A stiff breeze blew down from the mountain. It must have sealed the deal for him.

'Hm, fine,' he said. He traipsed over to the edge of the trees, his footsteps crackling among the twigs and pine needles of the undergrowth. He knelt down, switched on a small torch and surveyed the trees. He grumbled something to himself and started clearing the pine needles away.

Something – an owl, or some sort of large bat – flew overhead. I entered the darkness of the trees, laid my backpack down and thought about lighting a fire. It would be a good idea, I thought. I could still hear the dog barking several miles away, the sound echoing across the valley. I took the rolled-up package of my tent out of my bag and opened it up.

'Did you hear that?' Jacob said.

'Hear what?'

'Don't know,' he said.

The dog barked again. The sound carried into the trees and then it was met by another coming from the mountains. The response was cold and ancient. Jacob and I looked at each other, and suddenly I felt wide awake.

'Quick. Get some firewood,' I said.

20.

The howls came through the trees again, and this time there was no mistaking the sound. I was searching the forest floor for fallen branches when I heard the first wolf cry out, and then a couple more sang out in unison like a church choir. The dog on the farm across the valley was barking back, and Jacob and I were somewhere in the middle. He knelt down, struggling to light a bundle of twigs.

I glanced up at the dark shadows between the trees, and jogged back over to him with what I had managed to find. Everything was wet from the previous day's rain.

'Shit!' he said. 'The wood's all wet to hell. Have you got anything to light?'

I rummaged around my bag. Everything was silent for a minute before the chorus came again, hollow and mournful, a sound coming from the crypt. I realised the noise would carry from miles away; maybe ten or more. Images sprung into my head of padded feet lightly hitting the forest floor, of noses following a scent trail, of eyes in the dark. I couldn't find anything. Jacob gently blew at the smoking cinders in his hands, trying to shelter them from the wind.

The red glow faded and then went out. He let out a string of curses.

'Calm down,' I said. 'They're still a good few miles away.' Still, I was half expecting shapes to dash out of the gloom at any moment. I wished I had a knife, a gun, some *fuel*, some lighter fluid, anything to . . .

'Alcohol!' I cried. Jacob had stuffed the bottle away in his bag somewhere when we left the old man a few miles back. I reached into his backpack and felt around until my fingers touched the cold glass. I took it out and pulled on the cork, which came out with a satisfying pop. I knelt down next to Jacob and poured a liberal amount on the bundle of twigs.

'Not too much,' he said. 'What percentage do you think it is? I read anything over forty per cent should burn.'

'It's worth a try. Go on, try that. Stand back when you light it,' I said.

Sceptically, Jacob reached out with the lighter in his hand, and brushed the roller once with his thumb. With a sudden rush of wind, the pile of twigs exploded into blue flames that shot up into the air as high as our heads.

Jacob withdrew his arm and fell backwards. The alcohol was burning on the outside of the twigs like a Christmas pudding, but I knew it needed to catch properly, or it would go out just as quickly. Frantically, I broke some of the drier branches in my hands and stuck them onto the edges of the small pyramid.

'Give it a blow, quick,' I said.

Jacob gently blew into the base of the fire, and the small red embers started to come alive. I placed more broken twigs around the outside. Yellow flames started to rise up and crackle, but it was still a small fire. The flames cast light in a small circle around us and made the shadows jump in the trees.

'We need more wood,' Jacob said. He handed me the torch. 'What are you going to do?'

'Look for wood,' he said. He walked off into the darkness.

I held the torch in front of me and stepped away from the fire. I stayed close, no more than a couple of trees away from the flickering shape of the fire. With one hand I picked up as many larger branches as I could find, flinching and scanning the trees every time I thought I heard a noise. It had been quiet for a few minutes now. I half expected to hear Jacob calling for help at any second. I hurried back to the fire, but he was nowhere to be seen.

'Jake?' I said.

As I fed the fire I heard the wolves again. This time the sound was close, and it filled me with an ancient terror I'd never felt before. They could have been no more than a mile away now, or maybe even closer. I was sure they had smelled or heard us by now. The thought of the pack being so near – aware of our presence, maybe feeling us out, or watching through the trees – chilled me almost to the point of vomiting.

Jacob emerged from the treeline. He was carrying a couple of big logs on his shoulder, and he brought them to where I was standing.

'Where'd you get those from?' I said.

'There's more where that came from,' he replied. 'That is, *if* you feel like going and getting it.'

'Careful you don't put it out,' I said. He put one of the logs on the fire, and the flames dimmed and faltered. I knelt down and blew hurriedly until the bark caught fire, and big yellow flames lit up the surrounding area. Jacob was still looking at the trees; I expected to see some flash of fur in the darkness, but there was nothing.

'Those will keep it going for a few hours,' I said.

'Who's going to stay awake to keep the fire going?'

I laughed. 'I don't think I'm going to sleep tonight, some-how. Save the other log for a bit. There's plenty to keep it going for now.'

Once the fire was big and stable, I sat down beside it. The sound of the barking had stopped, and I wondered if it meant the wolves had moved away. There was no way of knowing. Jacob unrolled his sleeping bag near the fire and got inside, but neither of us dared to put up our tents. The warmth and crackling of the fire was a massive comfort. I sat there for a while, contemplating, switching the torch on and off, look-ing for pairs of eyes in the dark, but the trees were silent and forbidding. When the flames died down I put the second log on the fire and blew on it until they rose up again.

'Are you awake, Jacob?' I said. There was no answer. I sat up and tried to keep watch, but through exhaustion and some sort of miracle, I fell asleep shortly after.

I woke up in a cold sweat in the early hours of the morning. I'd had a disturbed and rotten sleep, being bitten by mosquitoes constantly; I felt the itchy lumps on my hands and neck where they had harassed me throughout the night. The fire was still glowing red hot and smoke was drifting off it, but there were no flames, and panic gripped me for a moment. I turned and looked at Jacob. He was sleeping quietly in his sleeping bag. The sun wasn't up yet, but there was some early light coming over the hills. I stood up and looked around.

It was a different scene now. The forest that had been such a maze of branches and pitfalls in the dark now looked ordinary and undaunting. The first birds were singing from the trees. I walked to the edge of the clearing and picked up some wood to stoke the fire. Next to Jacob's sleeping figure was his backpack, from which I quietly took his tin kettle. I filled it with water and made a bed for it on the fire. Jake stirred once or twice. I let him sleep, and when the water was boiled, I made a cup of tea for myself and left the rest to simmer on the fire. I had better feelings about the day ahead.

Jacob woke some time later. He stretched, looked around and then at me. 'Still alive, then,' he said.

He went to urinate against a tree while I stood up and started to pack my things away. We needed to cover a lot of ground today; there was no way I was going to spend another night in the forest.

We set off early, following the road until we reached another highway, putting the forest and the mountains far away behind us. Then we waited a while for a ride which would take us to Pirot and on to Dimitrovgrad. We covered a great distance that day, and before long we were entering yet another country.

Crossing the border into Bulgaria felt no more unusual than the previous border crossings. We camped outside a village on the main highway which seemed to be a major truck stop for the area; there were places for the lorries to park up, and more strip clubs advertised along the highway. In the afternoon we walked down a quiet road around the back of a nearby village to get away from the main road. Jacob told me to wait and disappeared for a while. This time the thought never even crossed my mind that he wouldn't come back.

After some time he returned with a couple of onions, a turnip, a chilli pepper and a handful of parsley. I gave him a frown, but didn't ask where he had got them from. The villagers went home from the fields and we kept a low profile behind a group of hedges to avoid being seen. When it was finally dark, we lit a tiny fire and boiled the vegetables up in the kettle with a little of the instant soup powder mixed in. We ate by torchlight. The soup was spicy and unexciting, but at the time I felt like it was the best thing I had ever eaten.

In the morning we hitch-hiked to Sofia, and arrived there before lunch. Bulgaria's capital city was a place of contradictions. There were big grey tower blocks with Cyrillic lettering on them next to branches of McDonald's and modern glass skyscrapers and banks. The one thing I did notice was that everything here was cheap. Jacob exchanged some money and at a local pastry shop we got a huge array of pastries, some filled with cheese and others with chocolate, for the equivalent of a couple of pounds. We sat and ate, and once again I wondered how I could ever repay Jacob for all the favours he'd done for me.

On the way across town, I had a revelation. There was a cybercafe on the corner where you could use the internet for what was a few pence per ten-minute slot.

'Wait for me here,' I said. I went in and paid the man behind the counter. He led me to a computer with all of its programs in Bulgarian. I looked at him blankly. He sat down and changed some of the settings around until everything was in English again. With a sense of old familiarity, I loaded up Facebook and my old e-mail inbox. There were hundreds of junk e-mails and a handful of Facebook messages from people I had once known. I loaded them up.

Hey, how are you doing mate? Give me a bell sometime.
Hello???

Hope you're well. Wondered if you were free for a chat sometime?
Where are you Cam? x

I paused. The last message was from Jenny. I wondered what on earth kind of impression I must have made on her. I ignored her message for a moment and clicked on to another online friend, who I hadn't spoken to for a long while. I sent him a message and waited for the blue tick to appear.

Cam is that you?? he wrote after a few minutes.

Yes. How are you doing?

Great! Where the hell are you?

Bulgaria. I realised it would be a difficult story to explain to anybody back home, and I didn't have a lot of time.

Wow! Sounds like a fun time. What are you doing there?

Actually, I was wondering if I could borrow a bit of cash until I get back.

I waited.

How much?

Whatever you can manage? I said.

Half an hour later I walked into a Western Union and withdrew fifty quid in cash. It wasn't much, but considering I hadn't spoken to any of my friends for over a year, it was quite the symbol of friendship. *Thank you. Really appreciate it. I'll pay you back soon,* I had written, before I logged off. And in my mind, things were already starting to change; I really meant to try to pay him back someday.

In the afternoon I treated Jacob to a couple of slices of pizza from a street stall. When I drew out the money, he looked at me incredulously, and then asked me if I had mugged somebody for it. I glared at him and asked him if he really thought I was capable of that.

'I guess not. But you don't need to worry about the money, honestly. Keep it for emergencies,' he said.

But the encounter in the forest had stuck in my mind. As we walked through the city in the afternoon, I found an outdoors shop and bought the biggest-looking knife I could set my hands on for ten pounds' worth of Bulgarian lev. I showed it to Jacob when I got back onto the street: a menacing serrated blade wrapped in dark wood.

'Jesus,' he said. 'I hope you don't intend using that on me sometime.'

Armed and fed, we set off in the direction out of Sofia. We passed the synagogue and the cathedral and walked along the outer edge of Borisova Park and through the districts which lay on the east side of the city. Under a bridge, I saw gypsy families who had built makeshift houses out of rubbish and lived there like outcasts in some dystopian science fiction film. They lived in the shadow of the city like animals, living off scraps, and we stayed away; they were tough people, no doubt.

Eventually we found a big highway junction with roads pointing towards Thessaloniki, Bucharest and Istanbul. We looked at each other and then parted ways, taking a slip road each. Jacob was flagging down the cars on the southern road to Greece while I stood on the Istanbul road. Whoever got the first vehicle to stop would determine which direction we travelled in; either route was good enough for both of us, and it made little difference which of us was successful first.

We weren't the only ones here; there were a couple of young backpackers with cardboard signs with their destinations written on. There was a kind of queuing system in place at the junction, which meant Jacob and I had to wait a while. We watched the other hitch-hikers get picked up until we were the last ones standing there– and then, at around four in the afternoon, just as I was giving up hope for the day, we were finally successful at getting a ride out of the city.

21.

There were fewer than three hundred miles between us and the crossing into Asia Minor at Istanbul. In the space of a month I had travelled over two thousand miles through France, Italy and the former Yugoslavian countries by train, car, bus and on foot. I had no idea what awaited us in the weeks to come. I assumed Jacob would hold to his plan to travel through Turkey, and he seemed content enough for me to join him so far. But so much was still unsaid between us, lingering in the spaces between the steps we took.

Through watching his habits, I got to know more about my travelling partner. He scowled ferociously when he was annoyed. His moods would last for hours at a time. At times it was as though he was a snake trying to swallow a difficult meal, the way those moods took him, until suddenly after a while he would get the worst of it down him and he would spring up full of excitement again as though nothing had happened. He had a nasty, vicious streak in him that came out when he talked about the people we ran into on our journey. He was not as strong physically as I was, but he was stronger in character. He had little time for idle chit-chat. When we got into strangers' cars, he would usually stay quiet in the back while I tried to make polite conversation with the drivers.

Jacob and I spent all of every day in each other's company, and sooner or later I knew things were going to break. They had to. I tried not to think about it often, mainly because I didn't have a clue what I would do without him, but when the time came for us to go our separate ways, I knew I would need to be made of tougher stuff. If it was possible to train a soul like you trained muscles, then that was what I did in the quiet moments. As for what went through Jacob's mind, much of it remained a great mystery.

The man who had just picked us up said nothing for a moment. Jacob and I thanked him in the usual way when we got into the car and he nodded before indicating and pulling back onto the slip road without saying a word. Only when we were on our way did he speak.

'Where are you going, lads?' he said.

Jacob and I were too stunned to speak at first. For a minute, I thought we had finally been picked up by some MI6 agent determined to bring us back home, but it soon emerged that the man, a cockney in his late fifties, was just a regular bloke who had come to Bulgaria after retirement to live off his state pension. A pint of beer was under a pound here, he boasted. In ordinary circumstances, I would have been desperate to escape the car and put his southern accent far behind me.

'Well, I visited a couple of times, back in around . . . 2008?' he was saying. 'And I just fell in love with the place. The people are really decent, good, honest, hard-working people. In the summer I go to the Black Sea. I go home during winter some-times – Christmases, you know.'

'We're on our way to Turkey,' I said. 'We've travelled the

whole way across Europe, and we're headed into the Middle East.' I could feel Jacob – still silent, as usual – fidgeting at the mention of our travel plans, and I felt a bit of an atmosphere developing in the back of the car.

'Sounds like a bloody good trip,' the man said, holding out his hand. 'The name's Brian.'

'I'm Cameron, and this is my friend Jacob.'

'Cameron, Jacob. Nice to meet you both,' he said. 'That sounds like quite an adventure for the two of you. Some memories that'll last you the rest of your lives. I'm surprised they're still letting people through, though, with what's going on and all.'

'What do you mean?' I asked.

'The Middle East is pretty turbulent at the moment,' he said. 'There's rioting going on all over – Cairo, Tehran, and apparently now it's starting up in Damascus as well. Haven't you been keeping an eye on the news?'

'I saw something about Libya a few weeks ago,' I said.

'What's happening in Damascus?' asked Jacob, who had sat up, and was now paying closer attention.

'Some sort of uprising. I've been listening to it on the World Service,' Brian said, 'and of course, the Syrian government won't put up with that for long. Problem is, it isn't even just the people against the dictators. It's all these factions, old tribal grudges and all that. Look at Iraq. Tony Blair took us in without a clue what we were doing, and now everything's boiled up to the surface.'

'Do you think we can still travel through?' Jacob asked.

'Hmm. It's hard to say. You'll struggle to get into Syria, the way things are going. May even have trouble at the Turkish border, to be honest. A couple of young men travelling through that way at the moment are likely to make people draw the wrong conclusion.'

'What conclusion?' I said.

'That you're jihadists,' he replied, with a calm shrug.

'Don't be daft. We look nothing like it.' I thought of the Arabic prayer in my backpack all of a sudden, and how two young men like us, headed into a conflict zone in the Middle East, might appear to a stranger.

'You'd be surprised. It's not just blokes with beards nowadays. People are getting . . . radicalised, for all sorts of reasons. Palestine. All of that WikiLeaks stuff. Or just for a sense of adventure.'

'We're not jihadists,' I repeated.

'I'm not saying you are,' he said, though the look on his face told me he didn't rule out the possibility. 'For all I know you could be Special Forces, or just a couple of lads on a camping trip. But if I were you I'd visit Istanbul and then think about heading back towards home. You don't want to get yourselves caught up in all of that.'

I glanced back at Jacob, who was staring out of the car window.

'I can take you as far as Plovdiv,' Brian continued. 'That's where I turn off. After that it's pretty much the single highway that will take you to Edirne. It costs ten pounds for a Turkish visa, which lasts for 30 days. If you want to extend it, you have to go to the British embassy in Istanbul or Ankara. If you come back through this way, you can stop off outside Stara Zagora in a little village called Yavorovo. Ask for Brian; everybody knows me there.'

'Thanks for the advice, Brian,' I said. Thoughts were flying around my head, but I couldn't put a finger on any of them. I wondered what Jacob knew and didn't know, and later on I determined to get the truth out of him, somehow.

The long road across the country passed through towns which were much of a nothingness; towns built along the highway under the communist regime to house the workers from the factories and little else. Each one felt like a frontier town, and in between them there was very little but plains and trees. Brian dropped us off at the junction near to Plovdiv.

We walked a mile or two until we found the next junction, and I turned to Jacob. 'What did you make of all that?'

'Make of what?' he said. 'Brian? It's easy to form an opinion listening to the BBC. I wouldn't take too much notice of it if I were you.'

'He seemed to know a lot about what's going on.'

Jacob shrugged. 'I knew there was rioting going on in the Arab countries. I get notifications on my phone whenever we pick up Wi-Fi. What's your point, Cam?'

'Where do you plan on going after Turkey? Through Syria? He said things are kicking off there, too. Are you sure we'd be safe to travel there?'

'That's the way I mean to go,' Jacob said, with more than a bit of impatience. 'I don't see why I should change that because Brian from Kent says so.'

'I'm just saying there might be some other options,' I said.

'If you don't want to come with me any more, you don't have to.'

'Why do you have to go and start being like that?'

'I'm not. You started it.'

'I'm just saying there are other options.'

'I helped you get this far, didn't I? I've paid your way and not asked for anything in return,' he said. 'Now you're telling me to cancel my plans and do – what, exactly? Head back to England for a cup of tea? Why can't you just enjoy the ride for a while?'

'Because I don't know where it's going, Jake.'

Jacob laughed and said something under his breath at me, then tried to flag down a car that was driving past. The driver shook his head and carried on without slowing down. I looked at him again, waiting for him to acknowledge my presence.

'I thought you didn't know what you wanted to do with your life,' he said, 'or didn't care. Why are you so bothered all of a sudden?'

'I just want to know the truth.'

'What truth? What are you on about?' he said. 'Have you lost your mind out here, or what?'

'Where is it you're going? Why are you so obsessed with the Middle East?'

'This is a waste of time,' he said, and stormed away along the road. I followed him quickly, the adrenaline building up inside of me. To be honest, I don't know which one of us had lost his mind at that moment. I stumbled on a crack in the road as I caught up with him. Jacob ignored me and carried on walking. I reached out to grab his jacket.

'Jacob, stop—'

He spun around and I saw all of the pent-up rage on his face in a split second. He swung at me. I ducked and caught the punch across my shoulder, his fist just glancing off me. In the brief moment that we stood facing each other, I could see that he was gone. I had a second to think I might have been in trouble, had he managed to hit me down properly.

Jacob turned again and strode away down the road with his head fixed forward. I didn't follow him this time. Instead I stood for a moment and watched him leave. Perhaps it would be better to give him space to think things over. I was far too agitated to think anything through or to be able to defuse the situation. My hands were still shaking.

At that moment a pickup truck pulled up alongside me. Jacob must have been a good thirty metres down the road by now. A Turkish man, young and wearing a red cap, leant out of the window and shouted something about the town of Edirne. I shook my head and carried on walking. He drove alongside me again and stopped.

'*Yala, yala! Haydi gidelim!*' he shouted.

'No, no,' I tried to explain, gesturing that I wasn't interested in his help. He looked at me as though I was mad and pulled off, beeping his horn for some unknown reason.

In the distance I could see Jacob's small figure. He must have been walking rapidly, because he had created a considerable amount of space between us in just a few minutes. Psychically, I projected all the thoughts in my head onto that silhouette further up the road. I willed him to turn around and face me like a man. He kept walking, and I started to jog up the road towards him.

The truck that had passed me drew alongside him about thirty seconds later. I could see the driver leaning out of the window, and Jacob saying something back to him. The driver beckoned to him – I imagined him saying *come on, time is of the essence, my friend* – and I watched Jacob walk around to the other side of the vehicle and open the passenger door. He stopped with one foot up on the step for a second, but he didn't look around. He took his backpack off, threw it loosely in the back of the pickup, pulled himself up and closed the door behind him. I stopped where I was. The truck pulled off the side of the road. Then it was driving away, smaller and smaller, until it was gone, and I was alone.

'Well, that's that,' I said out loud, to nobody in particular.

The road stretched out in front of me, long and quiet and empty. I felt once again like a tiny mammal on a huge spinning ball floating in space. The silence around me seemed to say *Well? What are you going to do about it, punk?* I sat down, took a swig from my bottle of water and adjusted my shoelaces. All the energy that had been in my body a few minutes ago flooded out, and I felt heavy inside.

As quickly as he had entered my life a few weeks ago, Jacob had left it. That was what the road did to you. Everything out here was fleeting yet eternal, a list of psalms. And I was tired. But the road was still there. I walked along it.

PART THREE

22.

In my head I was back at home, a year before my journey began, leaning out of an open window and looking down the back gardens of the terraces onto the industrial estate. The stale orange street lights lit up the empty street and the fences surrounding the factories, glancing off the broken glass and a heap of tyres piled up in the corner. This was the rear of the estate I grew up on. Gangs of young kids sometimes took their off-road bikes around the back of there to get to the wasteland behind the houses.

The evening air was cool. I took a drag of the cigarette in my hand, knowing my dad wasn't going to be back home until late. He was out at the Oddfellows, drinking pints of bitter and probably necking with some middle-aged bird with smeared lipstick and cheap perfume.

I still had a pain in my kidneys from the night before.

I went to the bathroom, poured myself another glass of water and looked in the mirror. If I focused enough I thought I could make out a pale yellow in my cheeks, but it could have just been my imagination. I opened the bathroom cupboard and looked to see what was in there. I paused; the empty medicine containers. I took them downstairs and put them in the recycling bin. There were dirty dishes all piled up in the sink. I left them there, and closed the kitchen door gently.

The day before, I had swallowed the entire contents of the medicine cabinet. Overdosing is a terrible way to die but, caught up in a flood of emotion, I'd failed to consider the painful, horrific nature of my death until it seemed too late. I regretted my decision almost instantly as my insides cramped up, trying to digest what I had taken. Calmly, I had decided to put on some clothes and took the first bus towards the hospital. I sat looking out of the window, my stomach a ticking time-bomb, ignoring the other passengers.

Outside the hospital it was quiet save for a few people milling around. I found my way to the emergency department and hovered outside for a minute. An ambulance driver carrying an empty stretcher gave me a quick glance as he passed.

Still lingering around outside, I weighed up the options. I had no idea whatsoever what I would say at that reception desk, what judgement and heartless looks I would get from the people waiting. Dying though I might have been, I feared how pathetic I'd appear to the nurses, giving me condescending looks as they had me whisked away down some corridor to have my stomach pumped.

Surely, after the clinicians had managed to save my life, I would be handed over to mental health services and sectioned on the spot. From there I would spend the rest of my twenties in a white-walled prison, surrounded by psychopaths and other anxiety-ridden characters straight out of *One Flew Over the Cuckoo's Nest*. Was that any better than what I had planned for myself just a few hours before?

Grimly accepting my fate, I turned around and left. The journey home was uneventful save for the heavy nausea I felt – I wondered if the other passengers could see anything in my face. At home I hurried upstairs and locked the bedroom door. The pain below my ribs came in waves, and I tried to drink as many glasses of water as I could to dilute what I had taken. At some point my head must have hit the pillow, and I fell into a deep sleep which took me straight into tomorrow.

After twelve hours of unconsciousness my mouth was dry and my head ached like a hangover from when I was sixteen, but I was alive, it seemed. I had no concept of what time it was or how I felt, but slowly I raised myself out of bed and went to the bathroom. My face looked an odd shade of yellow, and there was a slight tingling sensation on my lips. I took a deep breath in and steadied my legs.

This was it, I said to myself in the mirror. There was no way I could carry on, having received such drastic warning signs that the path I was on would lead to me being dead or even worse. Like an overly used field with all the nutrients drained from its soil, I needed something new, a fresh start. Of course, all of this had been a long time in the making.

From the cupboard beneath the stairs I picked up the bag I had prepared for such an occasion. I hadn't been bold enough to go through with my plan until now, but this time I took it upstairs to the bathroom and loaded it with toiletries, my head now fixed and determined. Finally I laid the bag down in my bedroom and looked around. The bed was neatly made; I had folded away everything I didn't need, a daft attempt to ensure I left everything behind me in a good state. Under the bed was the small bit of money I had stashed away. I reached down and took it out, stuffed it away in my clothes and turned the bedroom light off.

The house key was sitting in the front door. In the hallway I hauled my bag onto my shoulders and tested the weight for a second. Once I was confident I had everything I needed, I slipped the key out of the lock, opened the door and stepped outside into the quiet street.

I closed and locked the door behind me. With one hand I held the letterbox open and with the other I posted the key through. I paused for a second to collect my thoughts and then left, closing the garden gate behind me to begin walking.

And now here I was, trudging up a long dusty highway with trucks and cars driving past and the next town approaching; rows of white houses with red roofs covered in early morning fog and the great dome of the Selimiye Mosque and its four pointed spires protruding from the haze; the tall embankment leading to the river on one side and flat, empty fields on the other. Jacob was gone, and Tony too, and everyone I had ever cared about, and the steady tread of my feet was the only company in the world I could rely on. As well as all that, Brian had been right. The entrance visa into Turkey had cost me ten pounds, and the money I had left wasn't even enough for a night in a Travelodge.

If you'd asked me where I was going, I wouldn't have had an answer. I was running on fumes. There were houses on the other side of the road, but they were heavily fenced, with signs warning against trespassers, and I didn't dare to stop and try to ask for water. I staggered into town and kept going, past a couple of old men sitting on wooden stools outside a cafe sipping small black coffees who watched me pass, further into town and across the busy roundabout in the centre.

I had become so accustomed to constantly moving in the past weeks that now I didn't know how to stop. Only when I reached a small park did I find a tap with running water. Bending down, I rinsed my face for a moment and filled up my water bottle. I wanted to sit down and rest for a while, but I thought that if I did I might never start moving again. Instead I took the road straight out of the other side in the direction of Istanbul. The main road went on for as far you could see in both directions, with vans and trucks and small white Isuzu buses driving past chucking out exhaust fumes in an ever-flowing line.

I couldn't tell you how far I walked along that road, but it must have been at least seven or eight miles. As I continually placed one foot after the other, the sun moved across the sky and the day went on. Some dry grit had found its way into my shoes, and the sides of my feet started rubbing again. I thought I could feel blisters forming at the backs of my ankles, but I didn't stop to check.

When I was sure I was well out of the suburbs of Edirne, I started to stick out my thumb at the passing cars. The traffic was fast, though, and none of the drivers had time to do anything but sound their horns as they drove past. Finally, a bus stopped, mistaking me signalling the car in front of it, and the driver shouted something at me in Turkish. I tried to signal to him that I had no money. With a look of exasperation at his passengers, he closed the doors and left.

I was on the verge of giving up hope when a small van saw me, indicated and recklessly pulled over onto the edge of the road in a cloud of dust and gravel. I ran over as fast as I could, my backpack bouncing up and down on my shoulders, and jumped in the back.

'*Salaam aleikum,*' the driver said. He was in his late thirties, a slightly fat man with a short beard all the way around his neck. He did not smile, though at first impressions he seemed alright.

'Hello. Thank you,' I said, panting and stuffing my bag down between my knees. The driver nodded and pulled off into the flow of traffic, and then tried to ask me a question.

'Do you speak English?' I asked. 'Ingles?' I didn't speak a word of Turkish.

The driver made a gesture as if to say, *very little*, then took out a small booklet from his glove compartment and handed it to me. I read the front. It was a Turkish/English translation book. I smiled, nodded, and flicked through the pages to find what I wanted to say.

'*Nereye . . . gidi . . . yorsun,*' I tried, hoping it meant *Where are you going?*

'Istanbul?'

'Istanbul, yes. Is that where you are going?'

'Yes, I go,' he said.

The journey was a quiet one. It gave me a bit of time to reflect, and I was glad that the driver was not one of the ones who were in it for the conversation. We had barely made it out of the city and across the flat, dry land between here and the next town when he answered a phone call on his old Nokia phone and spoke with somebody on the other end for a long time. It was business, as far as I could tell.

The landscape was flat along the horizon, with plains of dry grass and sparse trees, criss-crossed with telephone wires strung up on wooden poles. We crossed a small river and I was gazing out of the window at the fields of yellow flowers at the side of the road, when . . .

'Stop, pull over here!'

The driver looked at me blankly. I pointed at the side of the road and indicated with my hands as if turning the wheel. 'Stop here, please.'

He sighed and pulled over onto the stony verge.

I leant out of the door and looked back down the road. I could still make out the town of Edirne on the edge of the plains. The driver looked at his watch and then back at me impatiently.

'Wait here a second, wait, OK?' I said. I hopped out of the van and held my hand up to shield my eyes from the sun. A few hundred metres behind us, a figure was walking into view. I left the van driver there and ran down the road as quickly as my feet could carry me.

'Jacob!'

The walker looked up at me. They gave a friendly wave and carried on up the road, with no sense of urgency. The van driver was waiting with his hazards on, but I knew he must have been getting restless. Slowly the shape of a young male came into view. He was walking with his head down and a cap obscuring his face. When he was close enough, there could be no more uncertainty.

He came up to me and shook my hand. 'Hello,' he said, 'I am Jurgen from the Netherlands. I am on a merry hitch-hike of Anatolia.'

'Stop dicking around, Jacob.'

'I want to see great beautiful mountains,' he said. 'You make a mistake. My name is Jurgen. I make bloody great walk and I need a cup of Tetley ASAP.' He punched me in the arm and I pointed at the van, whose engine was still running. Now I had time to realise my backpack was still in the passenger seat.

'Come on,' I said. 'I've left my bag in the car.'

'You bloody idiot.'

I hurried back to the van and found the driver waiting with his phone sitting in the ashtray. He gave me an indignant look. I tried to apologise as best I could, but just as I was about to try and explain things, Jacob came up alongside me and smiled at him.

'This is my friend,' I said. 'Can he go with us, to Istanbul?' He looked at me for a moment, shrugged and leant over into the back to make room. Jacob got in.

'*Salaam aleikum,*' the driver said, and nodded.

Once we started driving again, Jacob spoke to me quietly. 'I'm impressed! You carried on, Cam. Did you think you'd find me?'

'I don't know,' I said.

'What luck! An hour either way and we'd have missed each other. Have you had anything to eat?' He produced a loaf of bread from his bag, ripped off a chunk and handed it to me.

'Thanks,' I said, taking a bite. I hadn't eaten for a long time. 'But I meant what I said before, Jacob. About not keeping secrets from each other. It's not all a game for me, you know. I don't have anything left.'

'You're joking,' Jacob said. He spoke quietly so the driver could not hear us. 'Listen, do you think I'd be travelling with you all this way if I didn't think we were friends? Do you think it's all some big ruse?'

'I suppose not. I just . . . I don't think you realise what it's like for me,' I said.

Jacob took a deep sigh and looked at me. 'You think it's all one big laugh for me. That somehow I don't get it. But I do. I get it fine. There's no point in being all boo-hoo about it. This is life. You take everything too bloody seriously, yourself included. It's time to let go of it. It'll keep holding you back, honestly. I'm not saying my way is perfect. You'd probably be a better person than me if you made the effort.'

'*Bism illah, alrahman alrahim,*' the driver said. He made a gesture with his hand as we passed a mosque at the side of the road.

'What do you suppose that means?' I said to Jacob.

'It means "in the name of Allah, the all-beneficent and all-merciful",' Jacob said. 'Don't look at me like that. I learned the first verse of the Qu'ran before I started this journey.'

'What for?' I asked.

'For emergencies,' he said. He paused for a moment and then recited the whole thing, which sounded something like this:

Bismi l-laahi r-Rahmani r-Raheem
Al-hamdu lil-laahi rabbi l-'alameen
Ar-Rahmani r-Raheem
Maaliki yawmi d-Deen
Iy-yaaka na'budu wa iy-yaaka nasta'een
Ihdina s-siraata l-mustaqeem
Siraata l-ladheena an'amta 'alayhim Ghayril maghduubi 'alaihim wala d-daal-leen
Ameen

As Jacob recited the Qu'ranic verse I would later learn as the first Surah, the driver turned to look at him. He smiled, nodded and held out his hand.

'Musulman? You are Muslim?' he said.

'No,' Jacob said, 'I am a Christian – Roman Catholic.'

The man nodded. 'And you?' he asked.

'Me? Nothing.'

'You are an atheist?'

'I suppose so,' I said.

The driver turned to Jacob with a look of pity and shook his head at me.

'Alright,' I said, 'I'm not an atheist, not exactly. I don't know.'

The driver smiled and leant into the glove compartment of the car. He took out a small set of prayer beads – the kind on a small string with the larger, frayed string at the end – and handed it to me.

'No, I can't accept this,' I said.

'Yes, for you,' he replied, 'for good luck'.

I shook my head and tried to give it back to him.

'Oh, take it, will you?' Jacob said.

The driver gave me another look. 'OK, OK,' I said, defeated. I reached out and took the beads, putting them away in my pocket. The driver must have decided his work was done. He smiled, humming away as we rattled along the highway towards Istanbul. Jacob was in better spirits, too. It was funny how one minute you could be on the verge of everything breaking apart, and the next everything could be alright again. That was how things were, especially for him.

I suddenly realised that I felt alright too, for once. It was the first time in a long while that I had been able to stop worrying about the day ahead. Instead I watched the trees and the rivers and the wind blowing over everything, with the sky and the earth and everything in between, and I felt as if I had woken up from a twenty-year sleep all in that one instant. The road ahead was open.

23.

We left Istanbul along the southern road to Bursa, towards Eskişehir, and the route which would eventually bring us to the southern coast. I was relieved that Jacob didn't want to stay in Istanbul – partly because I couldn't afford to, but mainly because the main thing I wanted was to be out in the wild, away from the sights and sounds of other people.

It wasn't long before my prayers were answered, and we were surrounded by open countryside again. Soon the flat land gave way to large hills covered in pine forests, and the roads wound around them and descended into flat valleys and back up again. Summer was almost in full swing, and there were silk nests full of hairy caterpillars among the trees.

We were climbing one of those long, dull ascents which caused your lower back to ache and your legs to feel as though they had no energy left in them whatsoever. The Turks had covered their country in big highways; it was these that Jacob and I hugged the outside of when we walked instead of hitch-hiking. The steep hills sloped away on either side, giving us a choice between facing incoming death as the huge lorries came down the hill towards us, or having our backs to the traffic while we walked, with treacherous scree and the danger of rockslides on either side. Jacob had a preference for facing down the traffic.

He was walking in front, as usual. I watched him picking up one foot after the other, placing it down; there was still that determination in his walk, but today there was something uncertain about his gait that I hadn't noticed before. I had spotted something earlier in the morning, but now, halfway up our third major ascent of the day, it was obvious that something was causing him discomfort.

I was about to call out to him when his feet suddenly seemed to give way. The first step he placed slipped on a loose pebble or two, but the second almost saw him stumble off the side of the hill entirely. I watched him turn slightly as one foot gave way under the other, almost comically at first, and then he staggered away from the road and towards the steep embankment on the other side. In a second he managed to grab a handful of grass and rock, but otherwise he would have fallen straight over the edge. I ran over to him.

'Are you alright?' I shouted.

He knelt down to catch his breath as I caught up to him, and I noticed he was holding his side awkwardly. 'Jesus,' he said, 'nearly went over the edge then. Christ, that was lucky.'

'What's the matter?'

'I don't know. Feels like my back just gave in or something. Crap.'

'Here, let me help you up,' I said. There was nowhere to stop here at the side of the road, and all I could do was hope there would be no traffic for a couple of minutes while I got Jacob back onto his feet. I helped him reach his water bottle, which was hanging from his shoulder on a piece of cord. He took a few large gulps in between intakes of breath. A lorry drove down the hill and passed us in a second, kicking up dust and honking its horn at the sight of us standing on the edge of the motorway.

'Can you carry on?' I asked.

'I'll manage,' he said. 'Let's take it easy for a while uphill, though. I'd rather take my time than risk another tumble.'

I nodded and, taking his time, Jacob set off again in front of me. Below us, the hills ran steeply down into thin canyons, the edges laden with rocks. I watched Jacob closely, full of fear that at any moment he would stumble again and fall right off the edge. After a few more minutes, he stopped again. He was panting profusely, and I could see cold sweat running down the back of his neck. He was standing still, trying to come to terms with whatever he was feeling.

'Here, let me take your bag off,' I said. I slipped the straps off his arms and suddenly felt how heavy the contents of his backpack actually were. The thing must have weighed at least fifteen kilos. I set the bag down at the side of the road and waited while Jacob took another large drink of water until his bottle was empty. He stretched from side to side with his hand over the same spot as before.

'That feels a bit better,' he said. 'Sorry about that. Must have been some sort of twinge. Bloody hell. Right in the lower back.'

'Do you want me to take a few things out of your bag?'

'No, honestly, I'll be fine,' he said.

'Nonsense. Let's have a look.' I opened it up and pulled out his tin kettle, a bag of apples and the package that housed Jacob's tent, which I noticed was heavier than mine. I opened up the casing and took the metal tent pegs out, putting them away in my bag with the rest of the stuff. As I packed the things back in Jacob's rucksack, I spied a glimpse of metal underneath the roll of his sleeping bag. I reached in and grasped something large, hard and heavy.

'What's this?' I said. It was a square metal box like a biscuit tin with the label scratched away. The contents slid from one side to the other as I picked it up.

Jacob snatched it from me and placed it back inside. 'Just a few things in case of emergencies,' he said. 'I think I'll be fine now. Just needed a breather and a drink of water. Thanks for that.'

'Don't mention it,' I said.

He picked up the backpack and slung it onto his shoulders, testing the weight for a moment. The stiff look on his face had gone away now, and we set off again without any problem. At the top of the hill you could see the valley below, criss-crossed with large, open fields. Just a bit further down was a stopping place for cars and lorries, and we walked down towards it. The sensation walking downhill was unnerving; my knees jolted with every step, but if Jacob was feeling any worse about his back, he didn't mention it.

There were a couple of trucks parked up in the far corner with blinds covering the inside of the cab windows, and just a little further up the road was a sort of shed. There was a little puff of smoke coming out from a chimney at the top, and Jacob set off towards it.

'Where are you going?' I asked.

'To try and fill up my water. Do you want me to take yours?'

'Sure. You can leave your bag here, if you like.'

'I will do. Thanks.' Although his voice sounded much better

now, I knew he could not have been feeling one hundred per cent. I watched him walk down the road while I sat down quietly. When he got to within fifty yards of the building, a dog started barking from inside. I saw Jacob stoop down and pick up a stone to throw as he approached and looked in the window. Then he went around the front of the building, out of sight. A few minutes passed and the dog stopped barking. I was getting nervous when, with a casual stride in his step, Jacob re-emerged and came back up the hill to me.

'Find anything?'

'Yes. I spoke to a man in the hut. Here you go,' he said, handing me my bottle of fresh water. 'If we carry on along this road, eventually we'll get to Konya. Some lorries come through this way, but a lot of them have broken off earlier towards Ankara. That must be why we haven't had much luck on this stretch of road.'

'Did you ask about the border crossing to Syria?'

'It didn't cross my mind, to be honest. The main thing is, Konya is a big city. We might need to stop there for a couple of days. Don't worry, I'll pay for it,' he said.

'Why? What's the matter?'

'I'm not feeling too well. Might just need to rest it off,' he said. After a few seconds I saw the light come back into him as if he had just fought off some unseen force, and he was happy again. 'After that, it should be plain sailing. Except for the civil war, of course. What do you think?'

'I think we should take one step at a time,' I said. 'And right now I don't think we should walk any further. Let's wait for a lift here.'

'Fine,' Jacob said. He took the bag off his back, and instantly

I felt more relaxed. I thought that break-necking it across Turkey was a bad idea. It felt better to have time to get accustomed to the place, and a small part of me was worried about our journey coming to a premature end. I had suddenly, in the space of a couple of days, gone from feeling like Jacob's shadow to feeling as though I needed to look after him.

'How are your feet holding up?' Jacob asked me.

I undid my shoelaces and slowly took off my trainers, which were covered in yellow flaky dust, and had started to wear away at the edges. To my surprise, there were no more blisters to contend with – during my time on the road, the skin had toughened up along the bottoms of my feet, and now resembled hard leather.

'A lot better,' I said. I rinsed them and let them dry in the sunshine for a while. As the evening drew in, we decided to set up camp away from the roadside. I walked in front through several thickets of Mediterranean pines and thorny bushes as we climbed up one of the hills away from the road. Further down, you could see the road snaking its way onwards in the distance. We lit a fire and boiled up a kettle of pine-leaf tea. Jacob had run out of the proper stuff a while ago, and I knew he was annoyed by that.

'Any news about the uprisings?' I asked him as we sat around the campfire. He was staring into the red-hot, crackling embers, having put his phone away a couple of minutes earlier.

'Yeah. No good news, I'm afraid. There's been more fighting in Syria – uprisings in Aleppo, Homs. President al-Assad has sent in the army now. They're shooting protestors, rounding people up off the streets and all.'

'That's terrible.'

'It is. But it's about time the people stood up to the dictators. The rich and powerful have been oppressing people for decades all across the world.'

'So you support the idea of violent revolution?'

'If it's the only option, yes. If freedom of speech and peaceful protest is banned, what other choice do people have?'

'I'm not sure it's that simple,' I said.

'You and your moral complexity,' Jacob said. 'No offence, but everybody wants to finds reasons not to act. It's easy to do nothing. To not pick a side. So what if it's not simple? Life isn't simple, but at some point you need to put your chips down and commit to something. If I have to choose between a group of downtrodden citizens and a violent oligarch, I know whose side I'm on.'

'There are surely more than two sides to every story,' I said.

'Well,' Jacob replied, 'maybe there are. But one day, when you care enough about something in the world, you'll fight for it. Even if that means potentially being wrong.'

'Are you suggesting I don't care enough?'

'I don't know. Do you?'

'Goodnight, Jacob.'

In the morning we packed quietly and walked back to the road before the sun had properly risen. The conversation of the previous night was long gone, it seemed. The first ride of the day took us to a hilltop town called Afyonkarahisar, and shortly afterwards, in the early to mid-afternoon, we arrived in Konya. Jacob was feeling much better, he said, and although I asked him several times if he wanted to stop and rest, as he'd suggested the day before, he simply smiled and said he was happy to carry on.

As a result, we did not stay in the city, but immediately set off walking out of there, as we'd done many times before. And so we continued. We made our way across flat grassy plains and hills, and then drier plains with yellower grass, and tall, rocky hills with dry paths between them and little canyons through which the rivers ran, bringing with them channels of damp earth and greenery. On top of the flat plains were wind turbines, turning slowly in the daytime warmth, and in many of the fields there were huge automated sprinklers churning out water so that the crops could grow.

When it was quiet, this landscape resembled a place from the future, some automated terraforming project that you might expect to find on Mars. There were lonely outpost places along the highways, with the occasional small shop where you could buy a few basic amenities. Jacob insisted in the afternoon that we buy a couple of eggs. We boiled them over a small fire that evening on the outskirts of the city, and kept them for the following day to eat with the remaining bread.

As we reached the south coast of Turkey, the temperature was becoming warmer, and neither of us minded walking after dark. Our journey continued the following day, and the next, until we reached the city of Mersin on the coast at about ten o'clock at night. I don't know the exact date, but it was some-time around the beginning of May. I did not know what was going on back home, and it rarely crossed my mind, either, other than to wonder which of the homeless people I knew had managed to survive the winter.

We followed the lines of palm trees until we reached the shore and passed the port, which closely resembled the place where I had met Jacob in Italy, weeks ago. It was funny how quickly time passed while travelling; I thought a year or two could disappear out here without me even noticing it. Somewhere in the dark and not too far away, the sea gently lapped onto the shore. We walked as quietly as pilgrims, and the people we passed on the street gave us little attention.

The road left the sea for a while, crossed a small river with reeds along either side, and ran alongside the fields. There were crickets loudly chirping in the long grass. I asked Jacob if we should set up camp soon. He took a moment to respond, and I realised he had been on autopilot for the past hour or two.

'Sure. Why not.'

'Where's your torch?' I asked.

'Here. Give me a second.'

I had been there a few times too, placing one foot after the other while barely being conscious of it. You could walk off the face of the earth without noticing it when you were in that zone. At the edge of the field there was a short fence which was easy enough to hop over. I waited for Jacob to climb over and then I walked into the darkness, away from the road.

The earth was dry and crunched beneath our footsteps. It was quiet all around, and everything seemed good enough to set up camp. We started to put our tents up by torchlight. It had been a long, exhausting day, and it was only now that tiredness decided to catch up with me. I fumbled with the tent poles, desperate to climb in and fall asleep.

'Look at that,' Jacob said.

'What?'

'*That*,' he said, his hand outstretched at the night sky.

I looked up. Above us was an entire meadow of stars. I could see Sirius and Orion, and the whole Milky Way stretched out above us – a spectacular, glimmering sight. The light from stars millions of years old quietly observed us with a serenity that could not be equalled. I'd never seen a night sky so clear in my whole life.

'No wonder we've lost track of everything,' I said to nobody in particular. If only, I thought, kids from council estates could all be brought out here to see skies like that, then we might be in with a chance. Then, as if to recognise us, the flick of a meteor shot across and disappeared in a streak. I would later learn that it was the season of the Perseids.

'And you say you don't believe,' Jacob said.

We finished putting the tents up and both of us quickly climbed inside. I could see Jacob's torch moving around through the fabric as he fumbled for his sleeping bag, and then he switched it off and was quiet. I lay in my thoughts for a few minutes, listening to the sound of the crickets. Sleep came quickly, as it always did after a long day on the move.

Some time later, a dream woke me up and I stepped outside to relieve myself in the night. The sky had changed, and all the constellations were now alien to me. I could see nothing across the empty expanse of the field. The darkness was whole and absolute, and I was conscious of being bitten by mosquitoes once again. I hurried back inside the tent and zipped the door shut.

24.

Awoken by a loud, rumbling noise, I opened up the flap of the tent door and looked around. It was early light, but a thick mist covered the field we had chosen to camp in. Somewhere nearby, the ground shuddered with a loud, heavy noise. I shook Jacob's tent fabric until he woke up.

'What? What's the matter?' he grumbled.

'Get up.'

It must have taken him a moment to register the sound of the engine in the background. 'You know, it's rude to wake someone—' The sound stopped, turned around at the end of the field and started rumbling back towards us. 'What's that?'

'Come on,' I said. 'Quickly. We need to go.'

Jacob dragged himself out of bed and climbed out while I frantically rolled up my sleeping bag, looking behind me at whatever impending doom this was. Through the thick mist, I saw two bright lights emerge. They were headed straight for us, and I tried to wave at the farmer, to buy us some time. 'Hey! There are people here! Stop!'

Without a care in the world, it seemed, the tractor came towards us and our tents. It seemed huge now, a bulking leviathan of machinery bearing down on Jacob and I. I picked up the first piece of clothing I found and waved it in the air at the impending headlights. The harvester came within fifteen feet of the tents and then swerved, its heavy wheels crunching mercilessly over the dry earth. The sprayer followed closely behind it, swinging around with a dull inevitability, the closest end bearing dangerously near us in its arc. It narrowly swung past me and the edge of my tent before rumbling away as quickly as it had come at us.

The farmer sounded his horn a couple of times. The tractor, although close, had already been enveloped by the low-lying mist. I could hear it somewhere up ahead in the distance while, frantically, we packed up our camp.

Once we'd packed we hopped back over the fence, walked along the road a while further, and stuck our thumbs out for a ride heading east. The Syrian border was now no more than a hundred miles away. Then there was Jordan, Egypt and Arabia past that, after Damascus; Iran lay further east; but I had no idea how any of the border crossings had been affected by political affairs or the events of the Arab Spring. I hadn't seen the news in over a week, instead relying on Jacob to give me second-hand information which he'd read on his phone.

Jacob now showed an increasing interest in the events in Syria, as well as the wider struggle. He kept telling me that somebody needed to do something about it all, and at times I felt powerless to calm the emotions which came over him after he'd read a news article about a massacre of civilians, or the new involvement of Russia and the United States in the conflict.

A white Mercedes with a couple of well-dressed men in the front was the source of our next ride. The occupants were wearing light brown robes, but nothing on their heads, and their facial hair was short and well groomed. Jacob spoke to the pair briefly through the open window, then nodded at me to hop in the back.

'Hello, my friend,' one of them said in decent English, as I got in. 'Where are you two going?'

'Towards Syria,' I said. 'Can you take us in that direction?'

'Yes, certainly,' said the passenger. He was wearing a shemagh around his neck with a chequered pattern on it, and the interior of the car was spookily clean. There was no cigarette ash smeared on the dashboard (as was usual for this part of Turkey), and the rubber housing of the gearstick was free from even the slightest coating of dust. Even the seats looked as though they had just been shampooed. There was a cassette tape playing in the background: lairy, droning sitar over a beat, which sounded like wedding music. The two men sat looking forward without saying a word or making any indication to us whatsoever.

'What do you think?' I tried to whisper to Jacob.

'What?' he said.

'Nothing.'

'It's greener than I thought it would be. Look at all the crops growing here,' Jacob said. Then he leant forward and tapped the driver on the shoulder. 'How far is it to Syria?'

The driver, a young man, leant over. 'Maybe . . . sixty kilometres,' he said. 'Sixty-five. Approximately.'

'Are you going there?' Jacob asked.

'Yes,' said the driver. He turned to his passenger and said something in Arabic. They had a small conversation; the passenger seemed to be disagreeing about something. He spoke to us.

'My friend and I are on our way to Aleppo. He says he will drop you near the border. If you want us to take you there, it

231

is not a problem. We will cross' – he indicated himself and the driver – 'and we will wait on the other side. There is a place to stop on the Syrian side. When you have crossed the border, you can meet us there. OK?'

'OK,' I said. I assumed there was passport trouble at the border. It seemed I had interrupted Jacob; he had sat up momentarily at the mention of the border crossing but now he was looking out of the window at something in the distance, and didn't speak for a while.

The road curved south and we joined more traffic: lorries, and cars with families in, all packed full of luggage, who were heading in the same direction as us. The hills in front of us were as green as any in England, and I even recognised the purple shapes of thistles growing in the crevices of the hills. I would later learn that we were entering the fertile crescent of the Middle East – the birthplace of human civilisation.

We stopped at a service station close to İskenderun. The passenger got out of the car and went inside the building while the driver filled the car up. He came back with two bottles of water and handed one to us. I thanked him.

'Please,' he shook his head. 'You are our guests. For a Muslim, it is required.'

'Thank you,' I said. 'How do you say thank you, in Arabic?'

'*Shukraan.*'

The driver got back into the car and smiled at the conversation we were having.

'*Shukraan,*' I said to the passenger. He nodded, and I realised we had done no introductions. 'What is your name?' I asked.

'Nasir, and Abdullah,' he said, indicating to the driver. 'And you?'

'I am Cameron, and this is Jacob,' I said.

'Jacob,' he said approvingly, 'from the Bible.'

We set off driving again.

'How is the situation in Syria at the moment?' asked Jacob. At the mention of the trouble, the men went quiet for a moment, then the driver looked to Nasir to speak.

'There are many problems in the Middle East,' Nasir said. 'Many, many problems. America causes problems. England' – he smiled ruefully– 'causes problems. But if you are passing through Syria, you should be safe. This is something which does not concern you, you understand.'

Jacob nodded. I noticed they did not want to go into specifics about the unrest.

The road signs had started to show directions to Aleppo, and it felt as though we were on the verge of something new. Somewhere in front of us across the desert was Baghdad, the ancient city of Babylon, and all the places I had heard about during the Iraq War: Fallujah, Karbala, Kuwait. After that was the giant land of Iran, an ancient country, and Pakistan beyond that. You could follow the landmass all the way to the coast of China, if you wanted. I had contemplated this journey before, at the beginning of my travels, but it was something which would surely involve leaving Jacob behind. I held that thought somewhere at the back of my mind for later.

On either side the road was flanked by fields full of green vegetables, and the hills were receding in the background; it was all flat now on either side.

'Reyhanli,' said the driver, pointing at a road sign as we passed it. I assumed we were nearing the border. A police van passed us along the other side of the road, and then another.

Our friends appeared not to notice them, or at least showed no signs of concern.

The road divided into two lanes of traffic, as we approached the Turkish side of the border. The cars were queuing and being let through one at a time by the guards in the booths up ahead. Next to the crossing itself was a parking place with a couple of cheap cafes and a place to exchange money. Abdullah parked the car up before entering either of the queues, and Nasir explained to us the way the border crossing worked.

'At the first checkpoint you leave Turkey. Then you will come to the Syrian side of the border. You need a visa to enter. There is a building before you reach the place where you enter Syria. A big government building. You have to go in there to receive the visa, and then you may cross into Syria. We will meet you on the other side. Good luck. *Inshallah.*'

Abdullah looked nervous. I could see Turkish soldiers carrying rifles, and they were searching some of the cars coming through the other way. Jacob and I got out of the car. I slung my backpack on my shoulders and looked ahead at the crossing.

'What is it?' Jacob said.

'I don't know. Just a feeling,' I said. Crossing into Syria felt different somehow. We were hundreds – no, thousands – of miles away from home, a fact that had just hit me now after weeks of travelling across the Turkish peninsula. Whatever steps Jacob and I took from now on, we were taking them alone, without the protection of the European authorities. Even the international presence of Great Britain seemed remote out here.

I turned around to see Nasir frantically waving at us to move on. I had the feeling they wanted us as far away from their car as possible before anybody saw us speaking to them.

'Come on, we'd better go,' I said.

We walked past the lines of traffic and arrived at one of the booth windows on foot. Jacob handed over his passport first, then I reached across and threw mine into the mix. The guard pored over them for a minute or two, then drew out a circular red stamp and stamped them both with a thump. He handed them back without so much as a 'thank you', such as you might expect from an airport official, and looked back at his computer screen. We walked on, into the no man's land between the two countries.

Sure enough, as Nasir had said, there was a large white building before you came to the next checkpoint. There were people milling about outside, either resting or repacking their cars before they continued on their journeys. Some of them were going inside to collect their visas. A few of them looked at us, with our dusty clothes and backpacks, as we followed them inside.

Inside, we were greeted by a sign written in Arabic plastered to the window of a booth which looked as though it might have been a kind of reception desk. In the corner were some old wooden chairs with other would-be border crossers sitting on them glumly. One man was arguing with an unknown person on the other end of the phone; a crying baby was being comforted by its mother next to him. Another older man sat quietly, looking forward.

Jacob pointed at the sign. 'What does that mean?'

'I don't know. Could be an out-of-office message?'

Jacob tried to ask the old man, who looked at him blankly for a couple of tries until he pointed at the sign. The man nodded and pointed at his watch.

'It means we have to wait a while,' Jacob said. I sat down on my backpack on the floor and waited. It was some time after midday. Jacob paced backward and forward the whole time, looking up at the dusty clock on the wall, his footsteps echoing across the marble room.

I took out my passport and opened it up to the photo page. The boy there was almost unrecognisable – his face covered in spots, his hair badly kept, a half-terrified, numb look across his face – and I wondered what had happened to him along the way. I had been depressed then, and now I wasn't, but there was nothing I could put my finger on to know what had happened to change it. The depression hadn't been replaced with happiness, exactly. What I felt now was that it had become mature, a deep *knowing* that the world was far from perfect, and that everybody had their fair share of problems. I felt sure there was a wisdom which came from the lifestyle I was now living. But there was also a quiet, whispering voice which kept reminding me that soon Jacob's journey would be over, I would be out of money, and sooner or later trouble would find its way back to me. With some effort, I silenced it and waited patiently for somebody to come and speak to us.

Soon, a person emerged from a door at the back of the room and started ushering us all forward. Jacob and I lined up behind the Turkish people who had been waiting before us, and watched as each one slowly went up to the window and presented their case. The man who had been shouting over the phone shouted some more at the person in the window. The conversation went back and forth for a while, the man presenting more and more pieces of paper from his pockets until finally he was given a form and a pen and went away to fill it in grumpily in the corner of the room. The woman and her baby were given a similar form. Finally, the old man approached the window. He handed over something which was probably more accurately described as parchment than paper. The man behind the counter looked at it and shook his head. Rather than arguing, the old man simply took it back off the wooden counter, folded it away quietly, and walked back to where he had been sitting.

Jacob walked forward and presented our passports to the Syrian behind the counter. The man pored over them for a second, then scribbled something down on a piece of paper. He slipped it through the gap to us, his large writing barely legible: REASON FOR VISIT?

Jacob flashed me a look. I took the pen from the counter and wrote *Tourism* underneath. He took the paper from me, added it to the passports, and then disappeared again through a back door.

Finally a policeman – at least, he looked like a policeman, wearing a stiff blue cap and epaulettes on his black shirt – emerged from a door and walked over to us both. He handed back our passports with a calm smile on his face.

'Hello, I have spoken to the commander. At this time you are not permitted to enter Syria without written authorisation. I am sorry for the inconvenience. You may apply in writing at the embassy in Ankara for a visa which will allow you to cross.'

'What?' Jacob said. 'That's bullshit. Do you know how far we've travelled to get here?'

I stepped in, eyeing Jacob as sharply as I could to try to get his attention. 'Maybe we can reach some sort of agreement,' I said. I thought that maybe a small bit of money slipped into our forms might help us gain entry. At the time, I had no idea of the atrocities that were going to occur in the next couple of months. The authorities probably had orders from Damascus not to allow any unauthorised foreigners in – particularly Americans or Europeans – under any circumstances.

'I am very sorry' – he smiled again – 'but it can only be arranged at the embassy. There is nothing else I can do for you. Good day.' And with that he folded his arms and gave Jacob and me (but especially Jacob) a look which said *now get out of here before any trouble starts.*

'You want us to walk back to Ankara, do you?' Jacob said, raising his voice. 'Let me speak to your so-called commander.'

I grabbed his arm and pulled him out of the building and around the corner. 'What's got into you?'

His face looked as though he was about to cry. 'You don't understand,' he said. 'Since I set off from home, all I wanted to do was find somewhere I can make a difference. Do something that matters. And then when I read about the people standing up to the regime in Syria, and all of the awful things the government is doing, I decided I needed to help somehow. I know I should have told you sooner, but now it looks as though I won't get to set foot in the country, anyway.'

'Maybe it's a good thing,' I said. 'You don't know what kind of trouble you – *we* – might have ended up in.' I was still processing the fact that Jacob meant to get us into a war zone.

'But what am I supposed to do now? Turn around and go home, knowing I never amounted to anything?'

'Jacob, you've got your whole life ahead of you to make a difference,' I said.

'For fuck's sake.' He paced around for a while, then stopped and placed his hand on my shoulder. 'Sorry– I know you're just trying to help. But the fact is, we've run out of places to go. Our journey has come to an end. It feels too soon to be turning back now.'

'I know,' I said.

I tried to comfort Jacob as best I could. But the truth was that I had barely started to consider what it meant for me, or the prospect of having to go back home again.

Eventually, I helped him up onto his feet and back across the border into Turkey. I assume that Nasir and Abdullah waited for us for a short while on the other side. I do not know whether either of them survived the chaos which was to come. In the context of those events in the world which are too large to think about– which swallow up whole towns and communities, and are talked about only in terms of numbers and statistics and outcomes– I suppose it barely matters, but the fact is that our journey carried on in a different direction after that day, and neither of us saw either of them ever again.

25.

I didn't sleep much that night. There was something unsettling in the air and in the soil – it was border soil, you know – and the uncertainty which surrounded the days ahead was troubling me. I listened to Jacob snoring while I dipped in and out of consciousness, and I was up and packing before the sun had risen.

The first, overriding, desperately selfish thought I had was that I didn't want Jacob to go home. It didn't matter that he was paying our way; meeting him had given me a sense of direction. Temporary direction, perhaps, towards an elusive and meaningless goal, but direction nonetheless. Out here we were two rolling stones, free to be whatever we liked, and despite my travelling partner's erratic moods and secrets, I very much needed him. The second thought was that it was not really so far to travel back to Ankara for permission to enter Syria.

But the third thought, which sprung up purely from intuition, informed me that Jacob had given up. That was what scared me the most; if someone like him could get down and defeated, then what chance did I have? And if it was time for me to step up and find a direction of my own to travel in, was I ready?

In the morning we walked back into town from the place where we had camped overnight. Reyhanli, the town, was full of Turks and Syrians, a busy border place with tobacconists on every corner, vans and motorbikes driving around constantly with their noisy, hornet-like engines, and small shops and cafes which looked as though they pre-dated the rest of the town. Towns like this were made for trading, bartering and bustling – the kind of places that could grow into a Prague or a Singapore or an Istanbul, if the dice fell properly. As fate had decided, it had become more of a Milton Keynes.

I took Jacob to a place to eat and ordered a couple of coffees and sandwiches from the money I had left. We needed to recoup our losses, and there was no rush to be anywhere today. Unlike other places we had visited, we received no odd looks here. The people here had seen everything before.

Jacob was quiet, mulling over an invisible dilemma.

'What do you want to do with your life, Jake?' I asked him.

'Who knows? Busk my way through Europe. Ride the train to Aberdeen. Take a paddle steamer up the Mississippi. The same as everybody else.' I thought about the first time I had seen him marching up the road with his headphones in and his eyes fixed firmly ahead. Jacob was at war with the world. 'What do you want to do?' he said.

'I'm not sure. That's why I thought I'd ask. To steal one of your ideas,' I joked.

'I thought you wanted to be a writer. I thought that was why you're always making notes in that notepad of yours.'

The man in the cafe brought over our tiny coffees and the sandwiches, which were made with today's freshly baked bread.

I crumbled up a couple of sugar cubes and stirred the coffee around, watching the sediment settle to the bottom.

'Well, I suppose I do. But I meant something more practical,' I said.

'That's your problem. Stop being so doubtful all the time. You want to be a writer, then say "I want to be a writer".' Jacob frowned, as though he had no time for any of this today. 'There isn't enough room in life for capitulating every single time you have a conversation. Christ.'

'Right,' I said. We hadn't got off on the right foot, again. I supposed everybody reached their breaking point sometime – maybe it was dragging me along everywhere, or the pain in his back playing up again. All of that, and the fantasy Jacob had in his head about playing some part in the Syrian revolution, which I reminded myself would have been a suicide mission. 'I was thinking about . . . Sorry, what?'

The man sitting at the table across from us was waving at me frantically through the back of Jacob's head. I turned behind me to see who he was waving at, but the street was empty, and I was sure it was us he wanted. When I caught his eye, he nodded and pulled his chair over to us with an awful, scraping sound. Jacob flashed me a look which meant he did not have the patience for this interruption today.

'Sirs,' the man started; I had to stop my eyes rolling up into the back of my head. 'I am sorry, but I couldn't help saying hello. You are on your way to Syria, yes? My uncle is a taxi driver. I can take you to my uncle, if you like.'

'We don't need a taxi,' Jacob said furiously, 'we need a diplomat.'

The man tilted his head to one side, confused.

'What he means is we don't have the visa. We've already been turned away at the border,' I said.

'Yes, no problem. My uncle can take you, very cheap, anywhere you need.'

'No, you don't understand . . .' I started.

Jacob had turned in his seat, and I could tell he was ready for a shouting match. I looked around. In a second he would shout or throw his chair out of the way, and everybody walking past would stop to look at the commotion. I didn't like the idea of spending the night in a Turkish prison cell. The man held his hands out like an invisible ward to protect himself.

'The border is closed,' I said. 'We cannot go. Do you know what closed means?'

To my horror, the man had taken out a small, worn notepad and had started to draw Jacob a diagram. He drew a square with four wheels on it, with a man in the front driving and two figures in the back which I assumed were supposed to be the two of us. Then he drew a thick black line to represent the border. He wrote the letters T, A, X, and I . . .

'Yes, we understand your uncle is a taxi driver,' Jacob said. 'Now please, will you just f—'

To my surprise, the dotted line went up and around the line representing the border. The man was pointing at the picture, not yet frantically but with some enthusiasm in his voice. He picked it up and waved it at Jacob, who I thought was about to punch him.

'Wait, he means another way into Syria, I think,' I said, 'a way around the border.'

The man grinned at me and then sat back down. He spoke more quietly this time, which I found ridiculous given the way he had approached us before. 'No visa, no problem. My uncle will take you.'

Jacob frowned, and I could see he was mulling it over in his head. And suddenly a possibility opened up to my imagination that had been closed and dark a minute earlier: Jacob and I continuing on through Syria and Jordan, crossing the sea to Egypt, finding our way down the Nile in the summer and then . . . well, *then* could wait. This was a plan that would take up a good couple of months, and postpone the inevitable.

'Where is your uncle now?' Jacob asked.

The man pointed down the street and then gave some directions with his fingers. 'Not far. He lives here, in Reyhanli. Not now, at night-time. For each, four hundred lira.' He had pre-empted my next question. I figured that equated to around sixty pounds each.

'No way,' I said, even though I knew Jacob had the money. 'We won't pay more than two hundred and fifty each.'

'Please' – he screwed up his face a little – 'this is dangerous work. You pay my uncle, eight hundred lira, and you go to Syria tonight.'

I shook my head, offering my hand out to him as a final good-bye. I saw Jacob looking at me as though I was slightly mad.

'Two hundred and fifty each. Final offer,' I said.

The man paused for a second, then held out his hand. I shook it firmly. I still wondered if this was all a scam, and part of me was waiting for the inevitable question of handing over money up front. But the man simply took his notepad and scribbled down an address and a time for us. He folded it and placed it into my hand as though he was James Bond, and I thought the comparison was not unfamiliar to him. He gave us a wink, turned, picked up the newspaper which had been left sitting on the table behind us, and then left down the street.

'Well, that was certainly interesting,' Jacob said. 'What do you think? Undercover policeman, perhaps?'

'I have no idea,' I replied. And that was the honest truth. In the man's eyes I had seen a bit of . . . what? Uncertainty, perhaps? But then approaching two people on the street was an uncertain business. For all he knew, *we* were the undercover police. 'But I don't think so. I think we should give it a try before heading back.'

'Alright,' said Jacob. He bit into his sandwich, and I thought I saw a hint of life coming back into his eyes. Why was this trip so important for him? I saw for the first time that behind all of Jacob's bravado, he was immensely afraid of something – but what it was, I couldn't ever seem to work out.

At about half past twelve Jacob stood up and announced he would be back in half an hour. He left his backpack by the side of the bench where I was sitting.

'Where are you off to?' I asked, half contemplating the idea that he wanted to go and eat without incurring the expense of feeding me. A tiny section of my brain was still wondering if he would just disappear off the face of the planet.

'I saw a phone place on the main street before. I think I'd better give my family a ring. You don't mind watching my bag, do you?'

'No. Not at all.'

'Thanks, Cam.' He took a deep intake of breath, placed his hands in his pockets, and strode off in the direction of town. Whether it was boredom that drove him to it or whether he had some grand thing to tell them, I don't know, but Jacob was gone for over an hour. When he returned, his face was pale and he did not want to look me in the eye, but I didn't ask what the matter was. My guess was that he had received some sort of bad news.

Like all of Jacob's moods, this one lasted for most of the day. It still lingered as we walked through the quiet evening looking for the address that the man in the cafe had given us. I was more nervous than I looked, to tell you the truth. Who knew what foolish trouble we were getting ourselves into, turning up at a random building at night in a strange town close to the border? But the possibility of getting Jacob through the next leg of his journey was what pushed me on.

We found the place at around half past eight: an unassuming apartment block with the front door left open and a set of concrete stairs inside. Our footsteps echoed up them as I tried to find the apartment of the address we'd been given earlier. I could hear the sound of a mother putting her children to bed somewhere in the building. Jacob looked at me as we found the door, silent and waiting. I flashed him a look – a question, really – and he responded with a calm shrug. I knocked on the door.

The man we had spoken to at the cafe opened the door. He looked at Jacob and me, and then behind us as though checking we were truly alone. He stood to one side and invited us in.

'Please, come,' he said. 'I will introduce you to my uncle.'

The room was neatly decorated and not at all what I would have expected from outside. There was a modern-looking coffee table in the centre, a television in the corner, and some Arabic prayers framed on the wall. I brushed my shoes on the mat before entering. It was open-plan, and there in the kitchen, smoking, was a man I assumed was the 'uncle'. He stood up and came over to shake our hands.

'My name is Usman,' the man said, holding his hand out to shake Jacob's and then mine. 'I understand you are wanting to enter Syria, correct?'

The question felt like a trap. 'Can you get us there?' I asked.

'I can take you to a village across the border. If the Syrians find you there, without a visa, it is not my problem. I run a difficult business, and it is not easy to find a way across. I have a friend who works for the Syrian army. It is expensive to keep the route open, you understand.'

Jacob started to reach for his backpack. I stopped him. 'We'll pay you when we arrive,' I said.

Usman looked us both up and down and smiled, but I could tell he was quite annoyed. 'Absolutely out of the question,' he said. He folded his arms, and I noticed he was a big man when he did so. 'You may pay half now, and half on the bus.'

I didn't really understand what he meant by 'bus', but I held my ground. 'No money now. I hope we have not wasted our time coming here. It would be too easy for you to turn us over to the police and keep the money. Maybe you do this all the time. We pay you when we arrive.'

At this, Usman looked genuinely offended, although I could not tell whether it was just the most convincing impression of offence I had ever seen. But finally he caved and agreed to take us without the money up front. I breathed a sigh of relief. The two men poured us tea and we sat and drank it around the table while the night set in. It was dark, sugary tea whose very aroma made you think of exotic places. I could tell we were going to be in for a long night.

Finally, Usman bade us come with him. He put on a thick woollen jacket and his boots and he said his goodbyes to the man who had brought us here. He took us downstairs and walked us to a garage at the side of the apartment block. There were a few cars parked in the gloom. Usman walked over to a dark-blue minivan and slid open the side door; now I understood what he had meant by a bus. Jacob climbed in first, I followed after, and then Usman got in the driver's door and started up the engine.

26.

Sitting nervously in the back of the van, we headed out of town in the direction we had originally come from, Jacob holding his backpack between his knees and Usman, our designated driver, holding himself together pretty well. I didn't know whether it would be worse for him to be calm or nervous; I supposed nervous was better, as calm would mean he had something to hide, but the reality was that I had no idea what either of us were in for.

An image crossed my head of mine and Jacob's bodies dumped by a roadside somewhere. If we went missing now, would anybody have the slightest clue where we were? Would the police be able to drag up some farmer or delivery driver who could say *yes, they had picked up two people of that description a few days ago, no, they didn't say where they were headed, yes, those were the people, alright*– and if so, what difference would it make, anyway? What did life mean, if nobody in the world would notice if you dropped off the face of it? Well, that wasn't entirely true, because there were two of us, but you know what I mean.

Whether any of these things were also passing through Jacob's mind, I couldn't say. What I do know was that the atmosphere in the van was quiet, determined, like the walk up to ringside at a boxing match. And I did have an idea of Usman's route. He was taking us back into Turkey, north a bit, and then east along the main highway that ran parallel to the border. I assumed there was no way the authorities could keep a grip on all eight or nine hundred kilometres of paths in and out of Syria.

'What do we say if the police pull us over?' I asked Usman, who was humming quietly with his hands gripping the wheel a little too tightly.

'Most of the trouble here is between the Turkish army and the Kurds,' he explained. 'The best story is that I found you along the roadside a couple of hours ago and offered you a place to stay for the night. We are on our way to my brother's house in Gaziantep. I have an address there and somebody I can call for an alibi. Have you ever been arrested in Turkey before?'

'No. We've never been arrested, full stop. There was a time when we almost were,' I said.

'Good,' he continued. 'Then there won't be any records for them to check, and your British passport should give you some protection. It is me who should be worried. I risk a lot of jail time for this.' He kept on reminding us about this great sacrifice; I felt at the time that it was to justify his fee.

'Why do you keep on doing it, then?' Jacob said.

'I want to say it is for the money, but this is not true,' he said. 'I do need the money also. But mainly because many people are having visa problems nowadays. They have family across the border, sometimes they are coming here for work, in agriculture. These are Kurdish people, not Turks.' He drew a rough imaginary map with his index finger. 'You have here,

here, here, Turkey, Syria and Iran, this area' – he waggled his finger around in a rough shape – 'is the land of Kurdish peoples. Kurdistan, not Turkey.'

'It's occupied territory,' Jacob said.

'Almost correct. These are new borders from the Second World War. England and France divided everything up – Syria, Jordan, Iraq, et cetera. But we do not recognise this easily. We are still thinking, Sunni, Shia, Kurdish, and so on. This is why there is so much trouble in Iraq.'

'And between Israel and Palestine,' I thought aloud.

'Right,' said Usman.

He took us off the highway and down a smaller road past a town whose name I didn't manage to catch as it flashed by in the glare of his headlights. Aside for the sparsely placed street lighting near the highway, it was pitch black, save for those two conical beams piercing the darkness. The light bounced off some quiet, empty-looking houses, and shone over the fields near the road. Usman switched off the radio, which until now had been playing softly in the background, and a quiet voice was talking away in my head about the possibility we were about to be robbed or killed by some friends of his. He pulled up to a quiet spot on the road and turned off the headlights.

'What now?' Jacob said.

'We must wait. We are too early,' Usman said.

'Why? How long?'

'Half an hour. We must wait for the switch in the guards. Then I will take us through the small roads across the fields towards the next village.'

Jacob sighed and shuffled in his seat a little. We waited until – after a long period of silence and activity which made me feel certain that Usman had fallen asleep – he suddenly sat up, checked his watch, and took some dark grey cloth from the glove compartment. An emergency thought – *hoods for our heads?* – came from nowhere. But Usman stepped out of the van and stuck them over the headlights. When he got back in, I noticed they allowed a bit of the light through, but that the light was no longer being cast out across the fields as it previously had been. He was clearly a veteran of this sort of thing.

Usman got back in the driver's seat, but instead of starting the engine, he folded his arms and shut his eyes again.

'What are you doing?' Jacob said.

Usman didn't respond for a minute, maybe two, and Jacob frowned at me with uncertainty. Then he opened his eyes again. 'I was praying. Come. Let us go now.'

We set off along the road, away from the village. On either side of the road were fields of earth, but I could make out barely any details; there was no moon that night, and very few stars. The van rumbled along the road until Usman turned sharply onto a bumpier track which ran off along the fields. I could see the ground running by a couple of feet from the front of the van, and thoughts of scurrying creatures came into my mind. As if to validate the thought, I saw the shape of a grey animal, maybe a fox or a stray dog, dash into the grass.

When we had reached the end of this field, we turned right and followed the track along. Usman was singing now, rather than humming – an Islamic song which sounded like words to keep the wolves at bay – and with each judder of the van hitting a hole in the road, his voice raised up higher. Jacob was sitting with his knees up, and I thought for a second that he looked like a soldier being shipped out to Vietnam, with the look on his face and the way his clothes were so dirty. Suddenly Usman killed the van's engine, turned the lights down and told us to stay quiet.

'What? What's the matter?' I whispered.

He pointed to the hillside past the fields, and I could see some small light – torchlight, perhaps – moving along. It was so far away I could barely make anything out at all. I was impressed that Usman had managed to spot it.

'Police?' Jacob said.

'No. I don't think so. Just a farmer, maybe, looking for his lost goats. Let us wait a moment.'

All was quiet in the van for a moment. I saw the torch-light shine down at the floor, sweep around, and then carry on forward. 'Yes, look how he searches in the bushes there. We will go quietly now,' Usman said. He started the engine up and set off slowly, with the headlights still off. I thought he would roll us over or get a wheel stuck in a ditch at any moment, but he managed to keep it together.

We left the torchlight behind and reached a new road which led up the small hill that ran parallel to what I imagined to be the border. It felt as though we had driven for hours, but a glance at Usman's watch revealed it was only half past eleven. I felt tiredness kicking in, only offset by the small, niggling fear that Usman couldn't be trusted. I'd taken my knife out of my backpack, and I kept it in my pocket now, fidgeting the blade in and out of its wooden handle.

At the top of the hill, Usman pulled to a crawl and looked down. I could see no lights – I could see hardly anything at all, in fact – but I imagined the landscape to be a flat sort of desert stretched out in front. Usman shifted into third gear and we picked up speed along this stretch of road.

'How far is it until we reach the border?' I said.

'We are making good progress,' Usman replied. 'In a little while we will be safe. But we are already in Syria, my friend. We crossed the border a few minutes ago.'

I elbowed Jacob in the side, and he nodded to confirm he had heard correctly. For the first time, I felt as though there truly was no turning back. Everything before this had been an excursion, a little trip from which you could say you'd had a few experiences and so on, but something people would merely shrug about, something you'd mention as a footnote in the book of your life. Now I knew we were both doing something bigger.

We were silent for a while, the three of us, a lonely caravan in the night. I understood that Usman was as tired as we were, if not more so, and I wondered how many of these trips he had been on. I had no idea how far we were travelling, but I finally understood the need for what I had thought to be an exorbitant fee when we'd first met. Finally we passed a couple of houses and carried on to the left, onto a slightly larger road that ran through a small village. There was nobody around at this time of night, and no lights on in any of the windows.

As we had turned onto this road, Usman seemed to have cheered up, and once the village had disappeared behind us his mood was high again. He stopped the van to take off the headlight covers and put them back in the glove compartment. He explained to us that he was taking us to a place where we could sleep for the night and then we would continue on our journey in the morning.

'Are you sure?' I said. 'We're quite capable of finding our way from here. You've already done us a big service by bringing us across the border.'

He shook his head and smiled. 'Nonsense,' he said. 'I will not leave you here so close to the border. And also the police will want to see your stamps.' I guessed he meant the stamps in our passports. 'My brother can help you with that.'

'Thank you for all of your help, Usman,' Jacob said. It was the first time I had heard him thank somebody.

Usman drove us for another fifteen or twenty minutes past worn road signs written in Arabic which flashed up in the headlights and then disappeared again. We passed several more houses along the road, and then we came to the outskirts of another town. It was around midnight, I thought. The interior of the van was silent save for the grumbling of the engine, and none of us had the energy to go on making small talk. I looked through the windscreen at the buildings coming into view.

Just then the road lit up in front of us, and it was as though the night-time had turned to day. I shielded my eyes from the light, and Usman brought the van to a halt quickly. There was a commotion outside the van, and I had time to realise that we were caught in the glare of the headlights of at least two vehicles which had stopped on the road.

Jacob had already opened up the side door. He was about to speak to whoever had stopped us when a heavy hand reached in, grabbed him by the jacket and pulled him out. Somebody was shouting at us in Arabic, and Usman was shouting something back. I scarcely had time to wonder if this was some Syrian army patrol that he hadn't accounted for when the other side door opened and somebody was pulling me out of the car too. I pulled back for a moment until I saw the barrel of a gun being pointed in my face from the darkness.

My hands shot up purely out of instinct. 'Please, don't shoot,' I cried out.

Jacob had struggled with whoever had grabbed him out of the van, but now two men had hold of his arms and were attempting to get him onto the floor. None of their faces could be seen. Somebody seized me from behind. I allowed them to put my hands behind my back and then I too was forced face down onto the floor. I could hear the men discussing something with Usman for a while. I couldn't see Jacob on the other side of the van. I was acutely aware of the smell of the earth my cheek was being pressed into.

'Wait – we can explain,' I grunted, trying to turn my head to speak to whoever was holding me down.

There was no answer.

I had time to recognise the sound and movement of somebody about to put a cloth over my face. 'No!' I said, twisting away, but I was powerless to stop it.

The creeping blackness crept over my eyes and I started to breathe through the fabric in a panic. Then I was stood up and walked, tripping over myself, pushed up onto the floor of another van, and forced inside. I fell onto my side. It was only now that I realised my hands had been tied up.

There was some other shouting in the darkness, and then the engine started and we were away. The whole thing had probably taken less than five minutes.

27.

In all likelihood, a few hours had passed, but in truth I had no idea. My legs and backside were aching, either from being shoved to the floor or from sleeping in such an uncomfortable position, and my head ached so badly I wondered if I had been drugged the night before. My hands were still tied firmly at the wrists, and attempts to wriggle them free seemed futile.

I sat up with some difficulty. The room I was in was small, painted white, with a bare concrete floor and a large metal door blocking the way outside. I assumed the door was locked. There was a small window on the other side of the room, letting in light; I was surprised to see there were no bars on it, although it would certainly be a squeeze to climb out of, even if I could somehow haul myself up and through it.

You might not have forgiven me for sleeping, given the circumstances of our removal from Usman, but the truth was that tiredness had got the better of me somewhere in between there and the place in which I now found myself. Numbly I tried to recall the events of the night before. I remembered the flash of blinding light coming from the middle of the road. There had been a group of men with their faces covered, well organised, and I had seen at least one carrying an assault rifle.

I hadn't seen what had happened to Jacob or Usman during the commotion.

Had I travelled far since then? It must have been at least an hour's drive, I thought, recounting the time spent in the back of the vehicle they'd put me in, and I had the feeling that when I had arrived here and been pushed into the room, it had been sometime in the early hours of the morning. That put me at least fifty or sixty miles away from where I had last seen Jacob, and that meant at least a hundred miles from knowing where I was.

Pressing my back against the wall and pushing with my feet against the floor, I managed to stand up. I tried to get used to the feeling of my hands forced together, but the restriction still felt like mental agony. I longed to have them moving freely once again.

Two thoughts crossed my mind. The first was that crossing the border illegally into Syria was no doubt a serious offence; Jacob and I were British citizens, and were therefore quite likely to be accused of spying. I supposed the Syrians would not take kindly to finding two young males of any nationality sneaking across their border under cover of darkness. It was something the British embassy could clear up, but that was a process which might take weeks, even months. The second was that I felt extremely calm, given the circumstances. After everything I had been through, there seemed nothing unusual about being arrested for trying to enter Syria illegally; besides which, I knew that panicking about the situation wouldn't help me get out of it any quicker.

That being said, my backpack was gone, and with it my passport and mobile phone. Their loss would have been enough to make me nervous even in the best of circumstances, but now the sense of loss I felt was all-encompassing; I had spent the last few months living out of my backpack. Losing that, and Jacob, made me feel as though my whole life had been taken away from me in one go.

I looked around desperately and tried to hold myself together. Worse than the fact that I was here against my will was the fact that Jacob wasn't with me. I had no idea what they had done to him, or even who *they* were, for sure. I tried to prepare myself mentally by shedding any illusions of fair treatment or due process; I knew the real world was quite different to the one Jacob and I had been brought up to believe in.

Still, there was nobody I could blame except myself. I had been the one who had left home in the first place, and then left the country I was from – a country which, despite its many flaws, didn't *generally* torture people or let them starve to death or shoot them just for being in the wrong place at the wrong time. I had decided to go off in search of something more meaningful.

Except that wasn't really true, any more than it was a salmon's fault for swimming upstream into a grizzly bear's mouth. I heard Jacob's voice in my head for the first time: *Never mind thinking yourself to death about it. Try the window. Look around the room for something sharp.*

Crazily, I thought that Jacob might have a point. I walked over and looked out of the window. Outside I could see a small, nondescript hut, about a stone's throw away from this building, and beyond that there was a high stone wall which marked the boundary of what could only be described as the compound. The ground outside was dry, and there were broken stones and pieces of rubble near the building.

The window itself couldn't have been more than twelve inches square. Even if I could get my hands free, I couldn't imagine squeezing myself through it. I reached up and felt around the frame, looking for a piece of glass or a nail, but all I could feel was dry sand in the crevices of the concrete.

Suddenly there was a commotion outside, and I drew back and listened closely.

I heard the crunching footsteps of people approaching, and a couple of voices speaking in Arabic. They stopped outside for a moment, and I listened even more intently. The tone of the conversation was blunt and to the point, from what I gathered, and someone – the first speaker – definitely appeared to be in charge. The second speaker was asking questions, or perhaps making complaints, and the first speaker was quickly dismissing them and telling him what should be done. Then he said some final thing before walking off back in the direction he'd come in. I drew close to the door and was about to peer through the keyhole when the iron bolts came back with a slow, resolute clang. I drew back quickly. Light from outside flooded the room, and I held my hands up to my eyes.

The door swung open. A man was standing there, neatly dressed, with a well-trimmed beard and military-style boots underneath his khaki trousers. As far as I could see, there were no insignias or obvious markings on his uniform. He stepped inside, looked around at the interior of the room and then at me. I was dazed and my throat was too dry to let me speak at first. He knelt down, produced a bottle of water from a satchel and offered it to me. Uncomfortably, I leant forward and drank while he poured the bottle. I was close enough to pick up the faint smell of incense on his clothing.

'Who are you? Do you speak English?' I said in between gulps.

The man shook his head and then frowned at me with a certain understanding. It was a look which suggested he understood me perfectly well. I finished the last dregs of water, spilling some down my chin and onto the floor, but I felt better. The man stood up, tucked the empty bottle away and turned to leave the room.

'Wait, wait a second, please,' I said.

He hesitated, but before I could formulate a proper sentence he had stepped outside into the light and closed the door again with a bang.

An hour or two passed. I had never been detained before, and I suddenly became aware of what a torture that could be in itself – time spent alone with your thoughts, minutes turning into hours. For my captors, other things were probably going on, but for me captivity was the only thing happening, and the great unknowns about my situation were truly terrifying. I tried to pay attention to the sounds outside my cell, but they were vague and uninteresting, and I switched off after a while. I started to feel hungry, and tried in vain not to focus on the feeling.

A short time later I heard a car arrive outside and some more men talking outside the building. The door opened up, and in came Jacob, accompanied by another guard. He was more subdued than I would have expected, and there was a cut above his right eye. He was led into the cell, breathing slowly, his hands hanging loosely down by his sides.

'There you are,' he said. There was a strain in his voice.

'You. Yes, you,' said the man who had brought Jacob in. He had better pronunciation than I would have expected, the hint of an English accent – Oxford educated, perhaps. 'Are you hungry? Do you want something to eat?'

I nodded feebly. Jacob wasn't even looking at me. His eyes were firmly fixed on the small window at the side of the room.

'I will see what I can do,' the man sighed, as though it was an extreme inconvenience that prisoners needed to be fed.

I had not even considered yet where we were supposed to go to the toilet; the thought now crossed my mind briefly before he turned to leave again. 'Wait a second. Can you tell us what is going on? When do we get to speak to somebody?' I asked.

He turned and looked me in the eyes. There was a grim kindness there, but the smile which followed did not fill me with confidence. 'I am afraid I do not know myself,' he said. 'What I can tell you is that you will not be harmed, unless you try to escape. You are our guests here. You should tell your friend that some of the others are . . . reckless. If he continues to cause trouble . . .'

I nodded. The man left the room and closed the door shut.

Jacob took in a deep breath. There was a gap between us that I couldn't close right now.

'Are you alright? What's going on?' I said. He walked over to the other side of the room and kicked the wall – so suddenly it made me flinch – and then he started to cry.

28.

'I'm so sorry, Cam,' Jacob said, after he had got a hold of himself. 'It's all my fault. I should never have got you into this.' He turned to look at me for the first time proper. 'Jesus. Why are your hands tied?'

'I don't know. Do you know where we are? Have you spoken with anyone?'

Jacob inspected the rope around my wrists for a moment. He looked around the room for something and stopped to peer out of the small window, as I had done. Finally, he came back over to me. 'I wouldn't say spoken, exactly. They asked me a lot about who we were and where we were going. I didn't say much. Just told them we were tourists who had got into the wrong company. What about you? Have you found out anything?'

'Not really,' I said.

There were occasional sounds of traffic driving past, and I thought I heard a cockerel crying out maybe half a mile away. We were certainly somewhere remote. I had not heard the call of the muezzin since we had arrived here.

Jacob was silent for a few minutes. He nursed the cut over his eye and laughed. 'I managed to clock one of them,' he said, finally. 'You should have seen it. I haven't hit someone like that since school.'

'Did you see what happened to Usman?' I asked. I was hoping that by now he had come clean about our arrangement. Surely they would understand that we had been turned away from the border which we had tried to cross legally in the first place? It wasn't much of a mitigation, but at least it meant we weren't just trying to sneak into the country unnoticed; it meant we were foolish people who had broken the law, rather than proper criminals.

'They took him away, somewhere else,' Jacob said. He spoke glumly again now. 'I don't suppose we'll see him again. Cam, all of this is my fault. I should never have let you try to come with me. I should have never persuaded you here on this stupid, meaningless trip . . .'

'Calm down,' I said. I was worried, all of a sudden, that Jacob's mental fortitude was on the verge of cracking. 'I'm sure we can get this cleared up soon.'

His face changed, and he was about to speak again when the bolts were unlocked from the outside.

A soldier entered the room. He was of a different ilk to the previous man, the one who had offered me the water; he was young and ugly looking, dressed in dirty fatigues, and I suspected his might have been the voice I had heard admonishing the guard outside a few hours ago. The man had a Kalashnikov strapped around his shoulder and a radio on his waist. He looked at us both and then spoke as if reading from a script.

'My name is Amad,' he said. 'I hope you have not been injured or mistreated in your stay. You are being detained until further notice under the instructions of Commander Abu Ayyub al-Masri. There is no way of escaping, so please, do not try.'

Jacob said nothing. He was looking intently at this man, and I hoped to Christ he wouldn't try anything against a person holding a gun.

'Excuse me,' I said. 'If you look through our belongings, you'll see we are not spies. We made a mistake, that's all. We only wanted to travel through on our way to Egypt. If we could just speak with your commander, please, I'm sure we could clear it up?'

'I am afraid that will not be possible at the moment.' He threw a package wrapped in tinfoil towards us, which Jacob caught and opened up the corner of. Inside was a type of flatbread with a meat filling. 'Please, eat,' he said. 'I will return later, once your fates have been decided.' He seemed about to continue, but then stopped and turned away.

'Hey, wait a second!' I said, but Amad had already reached the door. He stepped outside as though the sound of my voice was completely inaudible to him, and I sensed, not for the first time since seeing him, that there was a deep cold inside him. I had felt this occasionally before in my life, particularly back on the streets in Manchester, but this was a trained, finely honed coldness that frightened me to my core.

Jacob quickly tore off half of the wrap and ate it greedily, offering me the rest. I took it in my bound hands and tried to eat as best I could.

'Well, at least the food's alright,' I said, after a minute.

Jacob scowled at me.

'What?'

'You don't get it, do you?' he said. 'Do you think there is anything remotely funny about our situation?'

'Well, there's no point in getting worked up.'

'*No point in getting worked up?*' Jacob was raising his voice now. I thought it was unwise given that the people outside could probably hear us, but he didn't care. 'Listen, I don't know if I can get through to that switched-off depressed brain of yours or not, but you'd better start waking up, Cameron. If you haven't realised what a heap of shit we're in yet, you're stupider than I thought.'

'What do you mean?'

'Alright then, let me spell it out for you. You asked me if I spoke with anyone before getting brought in here. Well I did gather a few points, in between getting my head kicked in. These people are not officials, OK? As a matter of fact, they're nothing to do with the Syrian or Turkish authorities, either, and that means we are *fucked*. Do you understand? Fucked. And it's my fault for dragging you into it all.'

'What are you trying to say?' I said, but already I had started to form the pieces together in my mind: a midnight carjacking, armed men with no uniforms, a disorganised kind of hierarchy more akin to a group of bandits than a military regiment. Unrest in the Middle East. And a couple of Brits in the wrong place at the wrong time who would make brilliant hostages for a ransom – either money or political concessions – fallen straight into their hands by pure chance. It was impossible, wasn't it? 'It doesn't make any sense. Syria isn't one of those places.' We were only a few miles from the Turkish border.

'Usman set us up,' Jacob said. 'All for a couple of hundred quid. That lousy bastard.'

266

'No, I don't believe that,' I said, and it was true. I had seen the look on Usman's face when the headlights blazed out of the darkness, and I didn't have any doubt that he was not involved in this at all. He was just a common, run-of-the-mill smuggler who had probably been betrayed himself. Jacob was always looking for somebody to blame. By now everything was dawning on me, and the weight of it was huge. Words were playing on my mind, words I had only previously read on the news, like *hostage* and *insurgency*.

Jacob looked out of the window and sighed heavily. He sat down with his head in his hands, and I desperately tried to think of something to say to him.

'There's something I should tell you. I was homeless, you know,' I said. 'Before you met me in Italy. I had been for about a year, and I had a dog and they put it down because it tried to bite someone. I didn't have anything after that. I had no idea where I was going when you ran into me. It always felt like a one-way trip. You don't need to apologise for anything.'

Jake nodded for a moment. 'No, I do. I got you into all this and I'm going to be the one to get you out of it, I promise. I'm going to get you home in one piece. I'm afraid there's no other option, mate.'

All of a sudden, he put his arm around me and hugged me tightly. A thought flashed into my brain, and I was about to tell him when I heard the sound of a vehicle outside; for a second, I believed we were about to be rescued. The doors slammed shut and then I could hear some people having a discussion again, outside the door.

'We may not have much time,' Jacob said. 'Whatever happens, when the time comes, don't stop running. Don't look back – and find somewhere to hide, away from the road, if you can.'

'Are you serious?' I said. 'Do you honestly think that's our only way out of here?'

'I didn't tell you because I didn't want to frighten you,' he said. 'In the room they took me into, there was blood on the wall. It looked as though they had tried to clean it up, but they hadn't done a good job of it. I think they mean to execute us, you know.'

I felt queasy. I was about to reply when footsteps quickly approached the door and the heavy bolts slid open.

29.

The men marched up to us and forced us out of the room and into the daylight. Blinded, I tried to register the shape of the fields and the buildings of the compound we were in, but with little success. We were hustled into the back of a van; the doors slammed, leaving us once again in complete darkness. This time, Jacob hadn't resisted or said anything to me as we were led across the dry courtyard. He was tense, like a cat ready to spring, though he did and said nothing.

I heard the sound of somebody getting into the van up front, and then the engine started and soon we set off. I looked around in the dark, jolted around by the movement of the vehicle. I couldn't make out the shape of Jacob, but in fact I didn't need to, because he kept bumping into me in the dark as we turned the corners. For a second, the image flashed into my head of a black Staffie dog with a white patch over one eye, barking in vain, pawing at unrelenting metal walls.

I listened carefully. The conversation emanating from the front of the van suggested there were at least two people sitting there; one of the voices sounded like Amad, the ugly-looking soldier from before, but I couldn't recognise the other. I imagined us passing police cars and towns where rescue was only a couple of feet away, and the thought was excruciating. I thought about kicking open the rear doors of the van, only to find ourselves in the middle of nowhere and shot in the back as we tried to run for it.

'Where do you think we're headed?' I whispered.

'I have an idea, but you're not going to like it,' Jacob said. 'You're right– Syria isn't a lawless country. Capturing us in the night was one thing, but keeping us there is another. If I were them, I would be taking us across the border, into Iraq.' Despite everything, I still thought Jacob sounded like he knew too much when he talked about this sort of thing. 'There, we'll be far out of reach of any security forces.'

'Then we don't have much time,' I said.

'Right. We need to get your wrists free, somehow.'

'That's it! That's what I was about to tell you before!' I exclaimed. 'My knife is still in my jacket pocket. They didn't even think to search me during the commotion.'

'Seriously?' Jacob laughed. He felt around my waist in the dark until he found the pocket, and pulled out the knife with a triumphant exhalation. 'You lucky bastard. Sit still. Wait a second while I cut you free.'

Trying to remain still was quite a challenge, but Jacob started sawing as best he could manage in the dark. At least once, the van jumped to one side and I thought he was going to end up sticking the knife in me by accident, but after a few minutes he had worked all but the last strand free. He finally cut it apart, and I brought my hands around to my chest, stretching them this way and that.

'Thank God,' I said. 'You wouldn't believe how painful that was. I felt like my circulation was cut off completely.'

'It's about time we had some good luck,' he said.

'Now what?'

'There's something I need to say to you, Cam. It won't take more than a minute or two, but it's important, OK?'

'Sure,' I said. 'What is it?'

The last kick sent the doors swinging open, and suddenly the speed at which the road was racing away was apparent. I barely had enough time to consider how hard we would hit the floor at that kind of speed. Jacob prepped himself against the side of the van, and I set my feet apart, picturing in my head how I would try to roll on impact to protect my body from the worst of the stones and gravel. The van braked harshly; the men in the front must have heard what was going on. I could see the gravelled ditch at the side of the road, and it was this that I decided to aim for in the few seconds before the van came to a stop.

'Go on, Cam! It's now or never, mate!' Jacob cried.

There was no time to process anything else. I jumped, hoping there was no traffic coming the other way.

The impact was immediate and absolute. I rolled as best I could to soak the energy out of the speed of the road, but gravity sent me crashing in a heap, limbs flying all over, the gravel tearing away chunks of my skin. I heard my arm go beneath me with a sickening crunch, and for a second I was sure I was dead. Then I realised I was alive, lying on the road in one piece. My head was reeling, and I tried to steady the horizon as I looked up the road.

The van had pulled to a stop a couple of hundred yards ahead. Around us was an expanse of flat, open fields, with no cover around for miles. The road itself was deserted, and the featureless horizon gave no hint of any salvation. Panic kicked in almost immediately. I pulled myself up, my whole body trembling and my brain screaming with too much adrenaline to compose myself, and I ran.

I could hear the men exiting the van and shouting at one another. Quickly I dived down the ditch at the side of the road and scrambled up the other side into the field. With hurried, frantic breaths, I staggered and tripped over the uneven ground. My arm was hanging loosely by my side and I had a good idea it was broken, though I couldn't feel the pain properly yet. I tried to turn my head. I couldn't see Jacob behind me.

I stumbled forward and then, like a sudden punch to the gut, I heard the fiery crack of a gunshot ring out. The noise was definitive, and terror came across me like a tsunami. I hit the floor, praying that some universal force would intervene, that this wasn't just it, that there was something more to life than being killed like a stray rabbit in a field. There was another loud gunshot, and though later on I would convince myself it probably hadn't happened like that, I would swear I heard a bullet whistle past me into the earth.

I crawled forward, replaying the short conversation I'd had with Jacob in the dark, swaying interior of the van.

'How long?' I asked.

'Twelve months, maybe eighteen,' he said. 'It doesn't really matter. The point is that it's coming, and there's no way of avoiding it.'

'But what about your family?' Suddenly, it started making

a lot more sense; Jacob's futile mission into the desert just like mine, really— a kick at the wind, in anger and frustration at the world more than anything else. The contents of a small, square biscuit tin which rattled around in his backpack. I felt sick, but I supposed there might never be another time to get it out. We were nowhere and it was now.

How long had Jacob been keeping all this pent up inside of him, the emotional toll of which I could barely begin to imagine?

'Don't,' Jacob said. 'I've been through all that already, and there's no point sitting at home, putting them through it all, watching me get sicker and sicker.' A renal cell carcinoma, he said, was attacking his kidneys but had started to spread. The five-year survival rate was very low. And that was with them filling you full of chemotherapy drugs and radiation.

I could not picture it at all. But now I knew the reason why Jacob didn't like to talk about his family much. 'I'm sorry,' I said.

'No, I should be the one who's sorry. Running into you wasn't part of the plan, Cam.'

'Forget it,' I said. 'Right now, we need to get out of here. I think the longer we wait, the less chance we'll have of escaping this nightmare.' Focusing on the present, I tried to ignore the thought of how it must have been for Jacob to have a death sentence, and to feel as though he had passed it on to me too.

I wished I had time for him to understand that when he found me, I was already dead. I wished I could explain to him that although he believed he had destroyed my life, really he had saved it. I knew that nobody out there in the world would know about it, if we were both killed, but the fact was that in the past months, travelling with Jacob had made me feel cured. And I think the only reason I wanted to try to escape with Jacob, rather than waiting the situation out, was that I had finally discovered that dying was not such a bad thing compared with living in misery.

'I know. I just wanted you to understand,' Jacob said. He helped me up to my feet, and I put one hand on the side of the van to steady myself. A sudden, strange flashback came into my head. It was of standing on the bus as a kid, holding onto those handles which hung from a pole at the top, trying to predict the braking and spacing your feet apart for the turns. Then, for some reason, I thought of Tony.

'Are you ready?' I said. There was a thin sliver of light where the doors joined. I thought I saw Jacob nod, though that was impossible in the darkness. I held onto his arm, and tried to steady myself.

'OK, this is it,' I said. 'One, two, *three!*' Together we threw ourselves forward, and I drove the heel of my shoe as hard as I could into the centre of the double doors.

30.

There was shouting coming from the direction of the road. I craned my neck to see, not wanting to raise my head and give away my position in the field. I thought it was just a matter of time until they found me lying here. I couldn't crawl properly with the arm, which fired up with pain every time I moved, and I had to control myself not to cry out.

'*Yalla, yalla!*'

I leant up and turned my head in time to see what was going on. There was fighting at the rear of the van. I could see one of the men struggling with someone, and then I realised it was Jacob with one of his hands on the barrel of his rifle and the other around the man's neck. Wrestling with each other, they slammed into the side of the van.

It was the one called Amad whom Jacob was holding onto for dear life. His accomplice, who must have been the driver, emerged from the side of the van, pointing a handgun frantically at the two of them and shouting something in Arabic. I saw Jacob swing his hand, hard, into Aman's fleshy upper arm. The gun went off. The glass in one of the van windows turned into tiny pieces and shattered. Then I noticed something sticking out of the insurgent's arm where Jacob had hit it; it was the handle of the knife I had given him. Fresh blood was pouring out of the wound onto the floor.

Jacob's voice fired into my head with astounding familiarity. *What the fuck are you staring at? Get yourself moving!* Though it was impossible, I could have sworn he had shouted it out loud. I crawled forward, away from the road, with searing pain shooting up my broken arm every time I moved. I kept my head forward and my fists together to keep from crying out.

Oh, why did you have to go and do that, Jake, you silly bastard!

I knew, deep down now, why Jacob had told me about his kidneys in the back of the van – and if I'd had the time to talk to him, to convince him of some other course of action, we could have escaped together. But there had been no time to think it through.

I was too sore, too afraid and too injured to cry. All of my remaining energy was placed into moving further away from the road.

The pain in my arm was starting to turn into a deep ache; there was blood running down it and mingling with the earth I still lay in. I desperately wanted to turn my head and see what was happening at the roadside.

BANG!

Another gunshot broke the silence. There was some more shouting, and then everything was quiet for a second. The quiet was worse than any of the shooting had been.

I heard the door of the van slam shut, and there was movement at the far end of the field I was in. I did not think it would take very long for the men to run up and finish me off with a shot to the head – or even worse, to drag me back to the van to be taken somewhere, held and forced to make videos, or have my neck cut in the dirt somewhere for an international audience. Several more minutes passed without any sound at all. There was no more movement near me at least, but I half expected at any moment a shadow to appear over me, or to hear the deathly click of a Kalashnikov being cocked a few feet away.

I was about to stand up when I realised, to my horror, that perhaps the reason everything was quiet was because the men were listening out for signs of my movement, scanning the rows of vegetables for a tuft of hair, or the coloration of a jacket. Like eagles, they were waiting until I ran out of patience and moved. I held still, breathing in the smell of the dirt and the sour natural odour of the foliage.

Coming up the road was the rumbling of an engine. It drew nearer, doing some speed, until it must have passed the van at the side of the road. I exhaled. The door of the van slammed again. Then the engine started. It lingered there for thirty seconds, and I held still even though my muscles were desperately cramped and crying for me to stand up. Then it moved off, and I heard the sound of the engine receding into the distance. I still dared not move for a few minutes, in case one of the men had waited behind exactly for this kind of trick.

All around me it was silent. A quiet breeze blew over the field, rustling the leaves and drying the sweat to my forehead, and then I could finally take it no longer. I stood up and looked around. The road ran away in both directions, and the view was unbroken until the line where the earth met the sky, suggesting some distance of great magnitude.

I scanned the road quickly. There was a pair of tyre tracks where we had come to a stop, a patch of dried blood and a few pieces of broken glass. That was the only evidence that anything had taken place here; the men in the van were long gone, and so too was Jacob, either dead or alive. I don't know how long I stayed sitting there, unable to move. It must have been at least fifteen minutes, and I was alone with the world, with what some people called God.

Everything within me found a chance to settle, like the sand after a big wave crashed, all falling to the bottom.

It was after midday. The sun, hanging dead centre in the middle of the pale blue sky, gave me no indication of direction. My arm was hanging down uselessly, and every time I tried to move it a shot of pain made me grit my teeth and scream out loud. I looked in the direction the van had driven off in, and a story played out in my head that I would somehow follow it all the way until I found Jacob and then I'd rescue him in the middle of the night, take one of the guards' guns and blast our way out of there. It was a silly fantasy, and it upset me that I had thought it.

Turning my back on him was the most painful decision of my entire life, but I knew I had to. Eventually, I started walking back the way we had come, with no way of knowing how far away the next town or settlement would be.

I had time to think about plenty of things as I walked. I thought about how I would find Jacob's family. I thought about all of my belongings, including my passport, and especially the notebook, my precious notebook in which I had written all about everything that had happened – things I would never get back. I thought about how Jacob had told me I was destined to get back home in one piece, about how much of a coward I'd been for letting him sacrifice himself like that. He seemed to answer me again, but I knew it was just my imagination.

He told me to stop being so melodramatic all my life, and to go and do whatever it was that I wanted to do.

'It isn't that easy, Jacob,' I said, but nothing answered me, save the wind and the dust blowing off the side of the road.

31.

Despite the 'advice' of the British Embassy, I didn't jump on the next flight home. Instead, I spent a couple of months in a youth hostel in Budapest, and then in the autumn I travelled through the Alps, staying with a French family in Champagne all winter. In exchange for a bed and a hot meal every night, I learned how to chop wood, sweep out the stables and take the dogs out for a walk. I earned my keep like everybody else; like the hunter-gatherers who spent their days looking for animal tracks and hunting deer in the old forests of the Earth.

I wish I could tell you that Jacob died trying to save me at the roadside, but I know now that it is not the case. I have even managed, using Google Maps, to find out exactly where it was that I last saw him alive: it was on the road between Al Hasakah and Al-Hawl, less than thirty miles from the Iraqi border.

Jacob was taken across the border, where he was held prisoner for almost a year. I don't know how he was treated there, or what went through his head in those final weeks. What I do know is that he was executed in retaliation for a drone strike on a Jihadist commander by the United States. The people who did it are probably dead by now, and I know that Jacob would have wanted me to forget about it and get on with my life.

So that's what I am trying to do. Of course, there are people who try to make it a political issue, or who try to blame his death on Islam. Nobody wants to talk about the hundreds of homeless people still living on the streets. Nobody wants to think about what goes through the heads of kids like me and Jacob to make them want to leave everything behind and head into a war zone thousands of miles away from home. All they want to talk about is what goes on in their own, revolving little worlds.

No one cares about the real story.

Seven months after that terrible ordeal, I walked along a quiet street, past the solitary shape of a graveyard on one side and terraces on the other, and followed the road up to the top of the hill. There was a woman hanging out washing on the line, who didn't notice me as I passed. Near the top of the road, a newspaper page fluttered past me in the morning breeze. I stooped over to pick it up. It was unremarkable, really: there was some sort of celebrity feud going on, Standard Chartered had been accused of money-laundering £50 billion which was being used to fund terrorism in Iran, Manchester United had beaten Hanover 4–3 in a friendly away.

The worst part had been the questioning. Not whether I recognised the men who had kidnapped me and Jacob, or what direction they had headed off in, but what were we doing in Syria in the first place – whether either of us had converted to Islam, whether, in fact, my story held up because I was, after all, the only person who knew of Jacob's last whereabouts. Had I run into any 'interesting people' during my time away? 'Yes,' I answered, 'Well, they were all a damned sight more interesting than you, anyway.' I had probably been marked down as some sort of potential threat for the future.

The second thing that frustrated me was that they told Jacob's parents. I would have wanted to be the one to tell them everything, but I suppose the authorities decided the less involvement I had in the matter, the better. I dread to think of how his family must have reacted to the news.

If I learned one thing during that time, it's that you can't change where you're from; there are no closed chapters, and everything we have we carry with us wherever we go. It is almost ten years to the day since I left home, and I think about it very rarely now, except if something happens to jog my memory – and occasionally when I think about Jacob – but my journey, though it ended a long time ago, is never really over.

At the top of the hill I stopped for a second and took in the view. The valley swept down from here, and the road snaked its way to the bottom and carried on until it reached the city. There it was, a huddled group of grey buildings straddling the plain, with the solitary tower of the Hilton Hotel recognisable above the skyline, its light blinking red above the city. I had not seen Manchester from this angle when I left, or ever before. I ran my fingers through the beginnings of a thick beard, humming quietly, and I thought about the future.

It wouldn't be easy, of course. I would start by going to see a couple of my old friends, and from there I would have to take each day as it came. I might even give Jenny a visit – not because I wanted to, but because she had something I needed: a place to stay, and a clean change of clothes. After that I would see about getting a job, and a place of my own to rent.

Everything seemed remarkably simple. And of course, through it all, you searched for things like happiness, and meaning, and true love. There was no guarantee of finding any of it. But you searched anyway. I would have no choice but to wait, like the homeless people huddled up in their sleeping bags, hoping that the sun would come up tomorrow.

A short while after, I stopped at the side of the road to have a drink of water. There were sheep quietly grazing in the field next to me, and behind them the rain clouds were easing off. It would be a cold night. I fastened up my backpack and was about to start walking when a car pulled up next to me at the side of the road. The driver wound down his window and called out to me.

'Where are you off to, mate? Do you fancy a lift?' he said. He was a young-looking bloke with short stubble and a cheerful smile. There was a girl with blonde hair sitting in the passenger seat. She was wearing a yellow jumper and she smiled at me as she flicked her cigarette ash out onto the road. There was plenty of room in the back.

'Yeah, that'd be super, thank you,' I said, giving her a wave as I got in.

'We've never picked up a hitch-hiker before. You're the first one we've had, isn't that right, Katie?'

'That's right. The first one,' she said. 'And you are?'

'Cameron. Nice to meet you both,' I said, shaking both of their hands as I slung my backpack onto the floor between my knees and fastened my seatbelt.

I didn't think it would be hard any more, in fact. We raced down the hill now, picking up speed, and the city grew larger and larger in front of us until I feared for a second it was going to swallow us all up, and then I laughed to myself as I realised I could just as easily walk out of it again in under an hour, if I wanted to, just by putting one foot in front of the other.

CPSIA information can be obtained
at www.ICGtesting.com
Printed in the USA
LVHW082347110322
713257LV00012B/525